To the

Original

Snow

Braver!

CHUTES, BEER, & BULLETS

NOT YOUR GRANDPA'S WAR STORY

Jesse C. Holder

authorHOUSE®

AuthorHouse™
1663 Liberty Drive
Bloomington, IN 47403
www.authorhouse.com
Phone: 1-800-839-8640

Published by AuthorHouse 6/1/2012

ISBN: 978-1-4685-7512-5 (sc)
ISBN: 978-1-4685-7511-8 (hc)
ISBN: 978-1-4685-7510-1 (e)

Library of Congress Control Number: 2012906202

ACKNOWLEDGEMENTS

I would like to express gratitude to everyone who played their role in this story. If I had never met Clark, Bruder, Archie, Bickford, Strandberg, and Lowell, my life would have been quite dull in Italy. I also would like to thank the 173rd ABCT, 1/503rd BN and Charlie Company, for giving my life structure and making me into the best paratrooper possible. A shout out to SFC Adams, Lt. Israel, and the other former members of 3rd PLT is also due. We had some good times and bad while we were together, this is our story guys; not just mine.

I would like to thank Dallas for editing, and for setting my path towards the tower. I also would like to acknowledge Mrs. Beals, Mrs. Guest, Mrs. Crawford, Mrs. Harrell, and Mrs. Wildes, plus all of the other teachers I had growing up in the Lowndes County School system. They always saw potential in me, and taught me to use my talents to the best of my abilities. Finally, I would like to thank my family and friends for supporting me on this venture; as well as God, and his Son Jesus Christ for granting me eternal life.

FOREWORD: BY DALLAS COWNE

Much like Ricky Bobby, Jesse Holder is not a thinker - he is a doer. He is a man of action. Those actions are oftentimes irrational, irreverent, or downright stupid, but they are actions of a man that is not afraid to live. He never fears the possibility or even inevitability of a future mistake. He sees possible mistakes as an adventure, but never the other way around. I don't think Jesse has ever met regret, but if he did, I like to think he'd kick its ass. Jesse Holder is a soldier, and he'd like to tell you a story.

If you are looking for a patriotic tribute to America and its armed forces, Chutes, Beer, and Bullets may not be your book. If you are looking for an emotion-filled, overly Romanticized, Nicholas Sparksesque telling of our struggles in Afghanistan in the early 21st century, you'd better stop reading now. However, if you are interested in a true account of young men struggling to understand their role in America's Army and its recent conflicts in the Middle East, then you will find this a compelling read. It is a story of men fiercely loyal to their country - some are drinkers and smokers, some are drug users and prostitute seekers. Although they are not your father's patriots, they are all real soldiers. America, this is your army.

PROLOGUE

Chutes, Beer and Bullets is the story of my life while serving in the 173rd Airborne Brigade Combat Team in Vicenza, Italy as well as deploying to Operation Enduring Freedom Eight for fifteen months of combat, fear, boredom, hilarities and many new experiences. It starts just as I am graduating Airborne School in Fort Benning, Georgia, and then follows me to Italy where my friends and I, the invincible men that we were of the 173rd, find ourselves in an array of foreign predicaments. This tale is un-cut and gives every detail of various situations, from Friday nights out with the boys to bloody scenes in a time of war. If reading about death, blood, sexual references, alcohol, drug usage, colorful language, and a tad bit of good humored racism disturbs you, then I'd say this isn't the book for you.

That being said this book is about more than just nights out on the town. It gives an in depth look at today's war and how it affects all soldiers. You get the experience of seeing how the airborne infantry soldier of today trains himself physically, mentally, and emotionally to take the fight to the enemy's doorstep. Follow me as a M240B machine gunner in 3rd Platoon, Charlie Company, 1/503rd Battalion, 173rd ABCT all around the world and back a again in this genuine, no-holds barred story. After all, this is not your Grandpa's war story.

This book is dedicated to Jacob Lowell and to the other paratroopers that made the ultimate sacrifice in OEF VIII. We miss you, Steak.

1ST BATTALION, 503RD INFANTRY REGIMENT

Sgt. Travon Johnson
1st Sgt. Michael Curry
Pfc. Jessy Rogers
Spc. Adam Davis
Pfc. Matthew Taylor
Pfc. Thomas Wilson
Cpl. Joshua Blaney
Staff Sgt. Michael Gabel
Pfc. Brian Gorham

2ND BATTALION, 503RD INFANTRY REGIMENT

Pfc. Timothy Vimoto
Spc. Christopher Honaker
Spc. Joseph Miracle
Pfc. Juan Restrepo
1st Lt. Benjamin Hall
Sgt. 1st Class Matthew Blaskowski
Staff Sgt. Larry Rougle
Spc. Hugo Mendoza
Sgt. Joshua Brennan
Capt. Matthew Ferrera
Cpl. Sean Langevin
Cpl. Lester Roque
Spc. Joseph Lancour
Sgt. Jeffery Mersman
Sgt. 1st Class Matthew Kahler
Cpl. Jason M. Bogar
Cpl. Jason D. Hovater
Spc. Sergio S. Abad
Cpl. Jonathan R. Ayers
Cpl. Pruitt A. Rainey
Cpl. Matthew B. Phillips
Cpl. Gunnar W. Zwilling
Sgt. Israel Garcia
1st Lt. Jonathan P. Brostrom

1ST SQUADRON, 91ST CAVALRY REGIMENT (AIRBORNE)

Maj. Thomas Bostick
Pfc. Christopher Pfeifer
Capt. David Boris
Sgt. Adrian Hike
Staff Sgt. William Fritsche

173RD SPECIAL TROOPS BATTALION (AIRBORNE)

Pfc. Andrew Shields
Spc. James Finley
Sgt. Ryan Connolly

CHAPTER ONE

NEW EXPERIENCES

The door of the C-130 Hercules flew upwards as the hot Georgia air poured into my nervous lungs. The continuous bump of the aircraft was not helping the situation...the sting of diesel nipping at my nostrils. The Black Hat[1] yelled, "Thirty-Seconds," holding up his index finger and thumb. We all replied "thirty-seconds" as was taught to us for the past three weeks. I could feel my right hand tighten around the yellow rip cord. The only thought circulating through my head since I hooked up was, *"Is the yellow cord really going to open this parachute that some nut packed?"* This was by all means a new experience.

"Standby!" the Black Hat barked, and the number one jumper turned to face the rustling Georgia Pines, pissing his pants as he did so...the Black Hat stepped back. I was the #4 jumper, or the fourth person that would jump from the plane. I was just close enough to the door to see the ground zipping by. The planes altitude hit 1,200ft and all I could think was, *"What in THE HELL am I doing here?"* "Green light go!" The Black Hat responds in a roar, and like ducks following a seemingly retarded mother, we all exited the aircraft.

What I confused for the wrath of God was actually the prop blast from our C-130, throwing my ragged body through the air much like your cat does with a cheap toy. I felt my T-10 Parachute opening, *"Praise the Lord!"* too bad Jesus didn't warn me of the opening shock on my gonads. The straps dug into my legs, and the risers were twisted behind my head. As I am bicycle kicking through the open air to untangle my straps, I see the

---

1 **Black Hat**—the name given to an instructor at United States Army Airborne School due to the black baseball cap which an instructor wears

Georgia clay approaching with terrifying speed. *Which way am I supposed to pull the risers again?*

As I am looking toward the horizon, I hear my 1st Lieutenant yell in agony accompanied by a sickening pop, which was his femur snapping. I try not to focus on the ground, staying as loose as possible. *Feet and knees together!* Then, as if the entire world is quiet except for the breeze though the pines...I hit like a ton of bricks thrown from the Empire State Building. Hey that was easy; only four more jumps, and I'm a paratrooper!

After one more jump that day, we run back up to the Airborne barracks at Fort Benning, Georgia. I'm in Delta Company 1/507th. Having just graduated Infantry School on good ole Sand Hill, I am with at least a platoon size of my buddies. One in particular, Clark, is a character from Seattle, Washington. The guy had nothing better to do than join the Army and see where that took him. In between serving time for high-speed chases across Washington State, and almost getting killed by his own dad for walking into the family business un-announced (AHEM...meth lab), he figured why not try something a little less dangerous.

Being from Georgia myself, I had my own vehicle there at Airborne School. A black 2002 Jeep Grand Cherokee named "darkie", my first ride. Clark and I often took it for a spin to my hometown on the weekend or around Columbus to see what kind of shit we could get in. Clark is notorious for getting to drunk and making outrageous claims about spaceships or how he can beat you in any event you think of. Plus, he likes to walk out on tabs...so usually Captain Shitstorm finds us.

That evening we decided to go to The Chop house in Columbus. Clark and I frequented this establishment. I heard the food was amazing, but we went for the beverages. The bartender, whose name has slipped my mind, was a hipster kind of guy. He wore a red goatee and one of those damn hemp necklaces, and he drove a 1979 Blue Chevy. Mr. Barkeep claimed he obtained a degree in bartending from one of the wacko colleges that specializes in such things. The steak house was small and sat in the corner of strip mall across from the fabulous Sheraton Hotel, where I had vomited many times in the past and even jumped in the hot tub with my clothes on, but that's a different story.

Clark and I sat there drinking a beer. He preferred German beer; I'm a Coors Light man myself. A shot was sitting in front of us, Jaeger-bombs no doubt; Clark would stroke the side of his shot glass like some perverted serial killer until it was time to drop the Black Death into Red Bull. I swear God smites a kitten every time one of those is drunk. Conversation in the establishment was entertaining as usual. Clark was trying to hit on a waitress who was way out of his league, hell out of his division; Clark wasn't much of looker back then, even less so now.

An unusual cat sat down beside us with jet-black hair slicked back and stripped polo on. He obviously knows the bartender as they exchange words, slaps, punches, and play grab ass a little longer. Meanwhile Clark is eyeing me, like "If you so much as slide a hand on me that's going to be it!" I have been known to throw a few lisps on my words to make the gayest man seem straight. Rex, the gelled-Guido grab asser, turns to us and says, "What are you soldier-boys havin?" Now I may have looked young, 19 at the time, but Clark was by no means a boy. Clark, in his usual forward manner, "Well...what are you buying?" I had another Coors, the grab-asser and Clark did shots of Johnny Walker...talk about a lush.

After some interesting conversation, we found out that Rex was a geologist for some institute that was going out of business, and I thought the business of being a rock whisperer was booming! Of course Clark in his infinite wisdom knew all there was to know about geology from volcanic ash to the sand in his vagina. Then as if Gabriel himself blew the golden trumpet, Rex and Mr. Barkeep looked at each other and wink. Rex turns to us, "Hey...do you guys play poker?" Now I am a hell of a rummy player, I use to beat one of my best buds every Sunday afternoon but I have never played poker; much less gambled for it. As I am sure you are imagining now, Clark once again in his most matter-a-factual tone, "Oh I'll murder ya...my knowledge of the game and the quickness of my hands...c'mon." I sat there pondering on the meaning of Clark's statement. It was too late though, the gauntlet had been thrown. "Well come on over, Mr. Barkeep will be joining us. I have ten beers and Kevin will be there too." Rex informs us.

I don't know who keeps the count of beers in their fridge, or who the hell Kevin is but before I could swipe my handy-dandy debit card, we were out the door, already at a BP gas station picking up a twenty-four pack of Bud Light; neither one of us keeping in mind that we have to do two maybe three more jumps tomorrow. No that never occurred to us. What a grave miscalculation.

Clark and I arrive at Rex's one-story brick suburban home. One of the older models you saw built in the 70' and 80's, a nice home for a Guido bachelor. The back door opened up into the outdated kitchen, a large wooden dining room table was in the dining room to my immediate right. The table should have given Rex plenty of room to count his beer on. Speaking of beer, low and behold, ten nicely arranged Bud Lights in the refrigerator. I'm no doctor, but I think someone had a touch of O.C.D. Only about five minutes had passed when Mr. Barkeep arrived. Rex had given Clark and me the grand tour of his lair, surprisingly not brandishing a plate of Fava beans and a nice bottle of Chianti.

Again, Rex mentioned this Kevin character as Mr. Barkeep was walking in, but he did so a little more excitedly now. Luckily the movie *Hostel* had not hit the market at this time, or I would have been out of there Clark or no Clark. We sat around the dining room table, fresh beers in hand (down to six now in the fridge oh no!) and Clark asks, "Well…are we waiting on Kevin and his playing partner?" "No my friend, Kevin is already here," Rex replies. By now the anthem for the movie *Halloween* was repeating in my mind, and I thought that either I have lost my mind or Rex has run off the reservation with his horse and all. Then…we see Kevin is not a person at all. Kevin is cocaine, ladies and gentlemen- a lot of cocaine.

Clark, being the former delinquent that he is, nearly bursts into tears of joy, along with the other two aficionados. Now, I'm no drug addict, hadn't even really smoked pot in high school, but I've never been a fan of wasting free blow either. After all this was a week of new experiences! The cards began to shuffle from one game to another, lines and straws were being passed quicker than offering plates in a Southern Baptist church. Next thing I know is its 3 a.m. and I am down $50, all the while remembering that we have to be in formation in an hour for our next jump. "CLARK" I yell. "We have got to go man, we have formation in an hour and it's a thirty minute drive, not counting I have no idea where we are!"

Clark replied, in his laid back manner as usual, "Well I guess it is about that time." I'd say we were so jacked though that jumping was the last thing on our minds. What about not *dying* of a heart-attack? We quickly thank our host as they have now taken about $75 of our money. But we inhaled at least $100 worth of cocaine so I guess it evens out. Jumping in my Jeep we are too high to remember which way is the way out. Naturally I find it without the help of Mr. Navigator beside me. "Oh my God…bro I am soooo jacked!" Clark exclaims and beats on the dash board, "Let's go jump out of a freakin plane!" I can't help but laugh at this. What were we thinking, not only do we have to be in formation in thirty minutes, but we have to run down to the hangar and learn how to rig up our parachutes. Then sit in a harness for God knows how long. I have found that "what the hell was I thinking" is not an uncommon question at the conclusion of an experience with cocaine.

The canopy of my T-10 parachute opens with as much fury as ever. Fifth jump…I am now a United States Army Paratrooper, now to land this thing! If you have ever jumped in Airborne school, then you know there is a long creek right smack dab in the middle of the drop zone. Pulling my risers to avoid the creek, and the inevitable slop that it entails, I lifted my legs to clear it…this did not make for a proper PLF[2]. My fall was over-shadowed by the curse which came from the creek about 100 meters from me. You guessed it, our trusty pal Clark covered in enough Georgia clay and mud to make an Indian Mound. Victory is mine!

In Airborne School you go through about one solid week of learning how to land properly (Week 1—Ground Week). In a perfect world the five points of contact should touch the ground in this order: balls of the feet, calf, thigh, buttocks, and the pull-up muscle (lateral muscle) but this is never the case. Usually it goes feet, ass, and head. In the case of my final jump my heels hit the side of the embankment which put me right on my head. No worries, I'm not the one the entire drop zone can hear can bitching about being drug through the creek! With Clark wet and whining like a cat two things were cast iron. One, Clark and I were United States Army Paratroopers. Two, the United States Army had just given us a free roundtrip ticket to the adventure of our lives; first stop…Italy.

---

2 **PLF**—Parachute Landing Fall, the proper technique of making a landing on solid ground, or water after exiting a military aircraft

CHAPTER TWO
XAVIER

Upon completing Airborne School, there is a pinning ceremony where you get your wings. Your wings are more or less an emblem you wear on the left side of your chest that say, "Why yes…I am a paratrooper…you're not?" You can pick who you would like to pin you, whether it be a Black Hat, friend, or family member. I picked my dad. He liked that I was doing what he wished he could have done. You can't pick what you're drafted into though; all of you draftees out there have my respect. Of course when my family came, being that we all live in Georgia, all of my family came including my some-what autistic, *One Flew over the Cuckoo's Nest* cousin… Xavier. Now I am going to back track here, to explain what is going on with Xavier. It will be worth every word…I promise.

Picture, if you will the two of us as young boys, walking through the newly logged Georgia woods. It's Thanksgiving, and the air is a cool 45 degrees. The sun is breaking through the trees and the spider webs have the brilliant dew glow. Both us boys are carrying BB guns and have just come onto a grey dirt road. I turn right to follow the dirt road away from the swamp to the left; apparently Xavier does not like this, which he, in no way, shape or form, let me know. So to break the silence, he shoots me. Oh, yeah…right in the left calf. Of course I don't know what the hell happen! I thought I had messed with a sleepy rattlesnakes slumber; maybe even knocked over his morning coffee and suffered his wrath!

As I turn on my right leg, hopping around like a fairy, I see Xavier's gun pointed towards my leg in all its smoking glory. Between the tears and shock, "Xavier did you just shoot me?!" Now I am thinking this cannot be! Both our dads and (I am sure yours as well) taught us that guns are not to be played with! Never ever do you point a gun at something you do not wish to kill…apparently Xavier was a slow learner. "Yeah I did" Xavier says calmly. To add onto that, "Hey do you want to shoot me back?" Do I what!?!? *Did he just ask me if I wanted to shoot him back?* Is it just me or is this guy suffering from dementia at eight years of age?

Regaining my composure from this shocking event, ceasing with my River dancing, I do what anyone else would, "Why the heck did you shoot me Xavier?" I think you'd agree that a normal reply should go something like this, "Jesse I'm so sorry…I tripped over this log, or stick, or rattle snake drinking his coffee, and it just went off…let's go back to the house and tell our parents, and I'll fess up to what I did." Oh no…not from this guy. Xavier turns to me, as if nothing ever happened, and says, "Ya know…I really didn't want to go that way. I kind of wanted to check out the swamp to see if there were any ducks down there."

You what?!?! Now I know that this guy, my cousin for Pete's sake, is off his rocker at this young age. Stepping back and being extra cautious, now that I am with the next "Son of Sam". "Hey, how about we head back." "Are you going to tell on me?" Xavier protests. Fearing my life, I say no. Two weeks later my left leg is swollen like a softball and infected with damn near Gangrene. The doctor pokes the swollenness to uncover a geyser of puss and greenness from the depths of hell itself. Surgery recovers our secret, a shining lead BB, squatting out in my leg for two weeks now. That was my last hunting trip with Xavier…but not his.

A few years later, Xavier is living in Roanoke, VA. My aunt, in her infinite wisdom decides to take Xavier off of his happy pills around the same time he is entering puberty. We all know puberty brings enough changes itself. At the moment I would say unleashing the beast is not the best idea in history. Hey, it wasn't my call. Xavier shoots to a good 6'4, 250lbs in the matter of a year. Now the beast not only is unstable…but he is an unstable bus.

Xavier decides to flip a switch again…this time locking himself in his house with a five-gallon can of gasoline. "Oh my", you say…oh it gets better. To talk him out of the house my uncle calls upon the expertise of his next door neighbor, a local Roanoke police officer. By this time the officer has called for backup, more officers arrive. They finally appease the mad man. The next day, Xavier decides to load up a couple of shot guns, steal my aunts car, and spin it out in the ditch in a nearby neighborhood; one of the kind police officer's neighborhood.

Xavier walks down the street, like one of *The Crazies*, shooting out lights on light posts, and taking out aggression on mail boxes. Can we say we're now getting Federal? Xavier walks up to the police officer's house (the kind neighbor that just helped him calm down) and takes aim. Xavier unloads on this benevolent gentleman's garage and house. I know you are thinking, "Where are the police to stop this lunatic?" They're on the way, and arrive just as Xavier unloads the last shell into one of the neighbor's cars.

My uncle is with the officers. Talking him down again, Xavier says he will go peacefully to the police station if…IF…he can ride with his father. This is a bad idea man, really bad idea. The officers agree. Squad car in front, squad car in back of my uncle's truck; the convoy starts toward the police station. Xavier flips a switch…deciding to tuck and roll out of the truck on the highway and sprint towards nearby brush. Now he's running from police officers. We've all seen *COPS*, they usually get you. Being 6'4 250lbs and in poor shape, you're not going to out run an officer, especially four of them.

This was before the time of the Tasers that shoot out at folks…thus the officers had their hands full. Wrestling down the behemoth, they lock him up, but he is still a minor, so he goes to a mental institute for minors. Now this is where it gets good. As the attendant is locking Xavier up (first night in his new home), he makes the comment that Xavier would not be able to escape this facility, so it was a waste of time trying. Why would you rattle the cage of a mental mammoth?

Morning comes, the sun breaks over the horizon and Mr. Smart Attendant checks on Xavier to give him his happy pills, but you got it already; Xavier is nowhere to be found. The alarm sounds, and the facility goes nuts. They search high and low eventually finding Xavier on the roof right by his room. "Xavier, what are you doing up here?" Mr. Smart Attendant asks. "Oh nothing just hanging out, told you I could get out of there." Xavier took apart his bed and used it to take the window out of its seal. Smart huh? But that's just escape numero uno.

This facility felt it could not contain Xavier any longer (surprise surprise), so the state had him moved to a "maximum security" facility. Now class what did we just learn from the previous experience? Let's all say it together; whoever is the loudest gets a treat I swear. YOU DO NOT… dangle meat in front of the beast! Oh yeah…they did exactly what Mr. Attendant #1 did. Mr. Attendant #2 told Xavier that this facility was "maximum security"…escape boys and girls would impossible. Come on, Nancy Pelosi knowing what she is talking about is impossible, escaping is certainly not!

Day three of Xavier's stay at the new and improved mental hospital chateau would be his last. Their last mistake was not learning from their previous blunders and placing the brute in a room with, yes, a window. This time fleeing the compound, Xavier makes a call to my uncle. After a lengthy conversation, my uncle (the Jedi that he is) talks Xavier into walking back to the facility; he would give him fifteen minutes before he called them. Xavier heeded his advice, but instead of going back through his window in hopes that no one missed him, Xavier walks right through the front door. That is escape numero dos.

Xavier stays at that facility; they have now realized their mistake and move him to a room with no window…FINALLY. He does well…until he is released on "good behavior." Now class, what happened when the lawyers asked Charles Manson what he would do if released? Good, he said he would do it again…obviously no one asked Xavier that question. Free to roam the world now, Xavier had lived with a bunch of hooligans who put God knows what in his head. There is no telling what his thought process was.

Xavier decides to pay a visit to the friendly police officer's house that he shot up not too long ago. What did this guy ever do to Xavier? No one's home, Xavier tries the door…locked. No real problem as Xavier just picks the lock. Xavier goes into an empty house, assuming everyone must be at work. Xavier decides to make himself a sandwich and a glass of milk. Sitting down at the kitchen table, but not remembering to shut the door all of the way, Xavier pulls out his father's Colt Single Action .45 and places it gently on the table.

Mr. Nice Police Officer comes home, thankfully before anyone else, and notices his backdoor is cracked. He draws his sidearm, you can't be too careful with all of these weirdoes around. Mr. N.P.O gently opens the door and sees Xavier sitting there with the gun beside him. Now I can't quite imagine what is going through Mr. N.P.O's head, but I know it has to be along the lines of, *why is this nut at my house again, eating my food, and why does he have a gun?*

Mr. N.P.O ask Xavier, "Well, Xavier…what are you doing here?" Xavier responds matter-o-factly, "I was hungry, and I'm here to kill you." Reaching for the gun, Xavier picks it up and fires a shot at the police officer. Now I know you are thinking, "Why didn't Mr. N.P.O end Xavier right then?" Well it could be the surprise of seeing him back at his house, this time in it, or he could have felt pity for Xavier. Who really knows these things? Mr. N.P.O backs out of the house as the revolver breaks the silence of the neighborhood, pulling the door with him; and calls for backup. They really need to have their own code for the beast.

9

Xavier empties three shots from the revolver into N.P.O's kitchen door, takes a long pull from the milk glass and throws it against the door. He turns to run out the front door, not remembering that a revolver only holds six bullets. He flings open the front door, firing at the squad car that had just driven up with its blue light special going. Feeling the click of the empty revolver, Xavier throws the weapon at Mr. N.P.O. who is now running around the house. Xavier unarmed and out of breath takes a knee...only to be tackled by Roanoke's finest. I'm sure Mr. N.P.O. never thought this would happen to him twice!

Alright, out of the mind of the maniac and back into the sun of that warm, May Georgia day, my dad has just pinned my airborne wings on my chest. Pictures are being taken, laughs are shared, and then I see him. Like you see a glass of water in mid-fall right before it hits the floor, I see him. Coming towards me, unarmed I hope, is Xavier. He shakes my hand and says something, something inaudible to me as the blood is evaporating from my very face. I glance at my father, who looks away! Whose idea was it to bring the beast to a military base? Class...have we not learned anything? Is this a good idea?

Being saved by my step-mother, we start walking towards our vehicles to go eat lunch. Olive Garden is picked, with all of its fine wines and breakables, Olive Garden is picked. The beast elects to ride with Clark (wise choice right?) and me...yikes. On the way, Xavier is talking about breaking into storage units and cars the previous night in Columbus. Of course Clark is looking at me like who is this cat? I give him an eye role that explains *I'll tell you everything later.*

Sitting at Olive Garden, and what a fabulous meal it was, Xavier decided to tell us how to make a bomb. Who let this guy out of the pen? Once again he was released on "good behavior." Some system we have. If you have ever been to a military town, then you will see a lot of active and retired military personnel....how about that! As Xavier is getting into the details of taking apart a microwave because you are lacking C4 (Composition 4, a moldable explosive) and not being too quiet about it, I feel all eyes on me. Since I am the only person at the table with a uniform on, I feel it is time to exit the premises and quickly hoping to put this pure evil behind me and avoid being picked up by CID (Criminal Investigation Division). It worked, luckily my family was on the same page as I was, and another Federal train wreck was avoided. Don't worry; Xavier's story does not end here. No, the President of the United States is not involved yet.

CHAPTER THREE
Italian Bound

Having avoided a monumental disaster in Olive Garden, Clark and I hit the road back to my home town of Valdosta, Georgia. Of course my parents were trailing us, but fathers do not always drive the fastest on country roads at least not mine. Clark's mother was living in Florida at the time, painting and sharing company with six or seven cats. Clark's biological parents have both been married and divorced seven times...to different people of course. Clark himself is engaged at least two or three times a year, and also to different people. What a world!

Clark was going to spend the weekend with me before heading down to Florida to spend the rest of his leave with his hippie mother. We had both received orders to the 173rd Airborne Brigade in Vicenza, Italy: the only self-sustaining combat brigade in the United States Army. Needless to say we were stoked-single, and in Europe? Now this was going to be a journey! So stoked in fact we decided to stop and pick up some booze...a pint of Mr. Barton's Vodka, a six-pack of Coors Light, and a Red Bull. That should be good for the two hour trip to V-town. We would make it just in time for happy hour!

Arriving in Valdosta and changing out of our uniforms, we hit Remerton, GA. Now Remerton is one of those little towns that have had a larger town grow around it, but refuses to be annexed. Valdosta, being a college town, understandably has a row of bars in it for the colts and fillies to get rowdy in; Remerton is precisely that, good times, drinks, bar food, and slack-ass cops. Back in 2006, there was a bar named Bungalow's in Remerton. An old wooden establishment with twin decks and a ramped walk way up the middle. Most of the time drunks forget they're walking down a ramp and fall everywhere. The bar sits right in the middle of the joint.

We usually sat on the deck, not for the beautiful weather, but for the 5 o'clock entertainment. Before I joined the Army, my friend Daniel and I happen to go to this bar for happy hour one day before a high school football game. There in the window is a family getting ready to go to the game. All of the adults are drinking, but there's one teenager, a down-syndrome girl who the cheerleading squad made an honorary cheerleader. Her parents would order her shots of Sprite with food-coloring or sometimes without and tell her that the drinks had alcohol in them. We would watch them sit there and cheer her on as she took these shots. This of course was high entertainment for a bunch of college drunks.

So we would sit out on the porch in front of this big glass window and enjoy ourselves…we called it "The T.V." Clark had to see this! A cheer leadered-out retarded girl taking shots of Sprite…c'mon! They were there, alas the cheer leader uniform must have been dirty, but it was still a good time. After drinking many beverages, Clark thought it would be a good idea to hit golf balls as the sun went down…what? I humored him though, I had the perfect spot. Outside of Valdosta, in Lowndes County, there is a pond on the back of some land, with no one around for miles. You can sit right on the spillway overlooking a peaceful tarn and sink balls to your heart's content.

Upon arriving at so, called pond, Clark decides he needs to relieve himself. Which meant basically taking a massive dump that he has been holding since our encounter with Kevin; which was three days ago! "Clark, we're in the middle of nowhere, now you decide that you need to drop a load? Why didn't you use a real live toilet at the bar?" Clark of course has no good excuse. Walking down the spill way, tan Army T-shirts in hand, Clark drops one of the foulest, smelling deuces I have even smelled. The flies immediately swarm our location, being as it is a nice 85 degrees outside, Clark was getting mauled by flies, dragon flies, and horse flies, and I was laughing like a crazed heretic!

Needless to say we had to move our location up the pond a bit to get out of the suction of the winged critters. Clark sank his balls, and I watched…now get your mind out of the gutter! Around eight o'clock the sun was on its last leg. Clark's drives had become horrible hooks, plus we were running out of Coors Light. I called up one of my best friends, Jay, to see if he would like to meet us at Loco's Deli and Pub for some dinner. Jay never can resist, he loves the lemon-pepper wings. What an idiot! Lemon pepper shouldn't be put on anything, its Satan's spice.

After a few Dixie Ice Teas, Clark was ready to take some shots, a Red Light, Green Light to be exact. As I mentioned earlier, Clark was notorious for walking out on tabs, and I can see that very thing happening soon… much sooner than I thought. Ever taken a Red Light, Green Light? I hadn't either, still haven't, but that night was the first time I had seen one. Its three different shots, the first are Green, then Yellow, and as you probably guessed it the last one is Red. I'm really not sure what's in them, but Clark would drink anything.

Successively ordering his shots, Clark decided to step out on the porch to try and spit game to a couple of housewives-yikes. Jay and I watched the plane takeoff then make a crash landing shortly after the landing gear was retracted. Clark came back in, un-shaken by his recent failure and showed that shot who was boss. Then, you guessed it, walked out on his tab! Angrily Jay paid for it, but we made a stop by an ATM before proceeding to the next watering hole.

Back in Remerton, we went to a bar named Bayou Bill's. A bat cave filled with cigarette smoke, and college drunks. Much like Bungalow's, Bayou's had one bar that is right in the middle of the place. Clark, the wasted character that he was, progressed to make a circle around said bar and buy everyone he came to a drink. It's easy to buy everyone shots when you have no intention of paying for them.

There was a band playing in the left corner of the bar, a dance floor in front of them. Clark was out there by himself with his beer over his head dancing like he was trying to make his hippie mother proud. It was truly hysterical sight. You ever had that buddy that would just go off by himself and dance, or try to get females to dance with him, but he is way too drunk to stand, much less dance? Yeah…that was Clark.

College drunk chicks will talk to about anybody, especially the ones who are already high as a kite off of the local Mary Jane, or jaw, jacking cocaine. Clark had found a sorority girl, who was probably on a combination of the elements I just listed. She was cute, too cute for him, but there is no telling what both of them were seeing. I lost track of Clark, as I said this was my home town, and I was having too great a time with my own friends to worry about him. Back in 2006 the bars stayed open until 3 a.m., a horrible idea for kids just getting away from mom and dad. The night progresses, and 2:45 a.m. rolls around.

The bartender asks me if that is my friend outside. Of course I say, "Which friend?" "The guy outside lying on that car's hood with one flip-flop on...is that your friend?" I go to the front door and look out through the window. There, in all of his glory, is Clark. He was lying on the hood of a car, with one flop on, yelling God knows what. My mind should have been blown. I turn back to the bar and display a cut off movement across my neck signaling to close our tabs. I walk outside to Clark who was now yelling, "He took her man! That frat mother fucker took my girl...the love of my life!" I am by now laughing my ass off, as is Jay.

It appears Little Miss Sorority Girl was spoken for, what did he expect? So Clark ends up throwing his flip-flop at Mr. Frat-Guy and then decided to rack out on this red Camaro. I leave Jay to tend to the bereaved as I walk back into collect our plastic. Walking out, Clark is still going on about this connection that he and Ms. Sorority had, that he would find her, that he would make her his, and they would move back to Seattle... this time he wouldn't go to jail. Too bad he wouldn't remember a lick of this in the morning.

To steal a line from Johnny Cash, we spent Sunday morning coming down. I went to church with my parents. That's right; a good ole Southern Baptist. Clark however was upstairs nursing his hang over. No doubt everyone I spoke to got drunk off of my breath and sweat. I'm a sweater, so when I start drinking best believe you can smell it. My step-mom throwing an Altoid case at me was a good indicator.

Arriving home, we had Sunday lunch, which is a big Southern tradition. Too bad my step-mother was from Pennsylvania and had to be taught these things after she married my dad. He only likes Southern food. Any other culture's cuisine would draw a response of, "That ain't food!" To my surprise I see a car trying to pull up next to our curb, but the driver is having very little success. I notice an Army of One magnet on the side. This throws me off a little bit. I look at my step-mother who can see out of the window from where she sits and she gives me a wink. Clark hasn't noticed anything.

A knock on the door...it opens...Clark turns, "What are you doing here!?" It was his hippie mother, who has driven up from St. Augustine, Florida. She was as hippie as Mountain Girl and Jerry Garcia dancing around a tie-dyed tree. She comes in wide-eyed as a deer, hugs Clark's neck (who does not get up from his seat), and asks how were all doing. She is originally from Seattle, and for some reason has a horrible mid-western accent...

yikes…I hate those type of accents! She has thinning out greyish-brown hair and basically looks like she did a bunch of drugs during the prime of her life.

Of course my step-mother, the kind, caring woman she is, offers Janice some lunch and a seat at the table. Clark turns to me and says he hates surprises but I didn't know she was coming either. As Janice is in the kitchen fixing her plate she says, "Yeah, ya know I just went by a recruiter station and stole that magnet right off of an Army car. I doubt they will even miss it, besides I have a son that is going to Italy soon don't cha know!" EH? I can hardly keep from laughing like a hyena at this scenario, her accent, and Clark's discontent. It made me extremely pleased.

Janice sits down with very little on her blue china plate. Clark had planned on renting a car and driving down to Florida, but now that he could see he was going to be forced to ride three hours with burned-out Janice, he was not pleased. Before anybody could say anything, like "How was the drive Janice?" she goes into another random rant. "Ya know I went by this gas station on the way up here don't cha know? I saw all these miniature American flags for sale in a basket by the cash register. I asked the cashier why they were selling American flags. They should just be giving them out. All Americans need at least one little American flag, don't cha agree?" We nod. I didn't really know where this was going. "So I bought all 100 of those American flags and handed them out to every person that came out of the station. I got a son going to Italy ya know I would tell em."

Clark looks up from his plate, "What are you even saying?" I can't take it any longer; this awkward dinner just became the highlight of my week! I look at my dad and he mouths to me, "Space-Cadet." This sends me over the edge, I am laughing hysterically now. Janice feels compelled to explain to Clark why this nutty act at the service station is a highly compassionate act of patriotism. It was a good rebuttal until Janice happens to mention that she has saved some flags for her cats. Feline patriotism is a major concern in this country.

Janice and Clark leave, but it won't be long before I see him in Italy. But seeing Janice again, on the other hand, could wait a few years. I have to say I was ready to travel abroad. Growing up, my dad would take us out west to go snow skiing at least once a year. Twice we went just to travel through the Mormon, infested states out there. Of course I had been all up and down the Eastern sea board, so traveling was nothing new to me. Trans-Atlantic though was something entirely new!

Passport in hand, I got on the Delta Connection flight out of Valdosta Regional Airport and was on my way to Atlanta. I like air travel, I like chilling in airports and watching people. People are so funny...just the way we are. Everyone is always in a hurry to get where they're going. At least, Americans are. I would learn that not all cultures operate the same.

CHAPTER FOUR
NO SIR, IT IS NOT
POSSIBLE

MY FIRST TRANS-ATLANTIC FLIGHT and I got stuck behind a family of Indians (Not scalpers, but dot Indians). It was Lufthansa; my and what gorgeous Aryans were to be our flight attendants! I happen to be seated by a couple other soldiers, also going to Vicenza. The Indians kept my attention most of the time. Their baby was straight out of *The Omen*, evil little thing.

Touching down in Venice, Marco Polo International, I was greeted by a family that was supposedly from Valdosta but I had never met these folks. The chatty Cathy of a wife just chatted my ear off like we were best friends. I had just flown for eight hours, I was jet-lagged, I'm in a new country, I just left my friends and family, and I got stuck with this gossip girl....GOOD GOD WOMAN! All I really wanted to do was find a bed somewhere. It was Sunday afternoon here, but my body said it was Sunday morning. Locating a bed was not an option though, Chatty wanted me to go back home to their house and have dinner. Half delusional and forgetting I wasn't in a country where the first language was English, I turn to an attractive Italian woman in baggage claim, "This chick is driving me crazy, do you mind if I go home with you?" Of course she looked at me like I had literally just stepped off a spaceship with E.T. and all of his friends.

Then with what I would learn was the Italian equivalent to "no" she said, "Sir it is not possible." No...it is possible...you just have to lead the way lady! My life preserver had sunk; I was going to dinner with these folks. Now don't get me wrong, Chatty's husband was easy going guy, short about 5'4, but in good spirits for being married to such a talker.

I would have pulled "Kurt Cobain" years ago. Her husband, Roy, ran the Commissary on Camp Ederle. It is always good to be friends with the food man.

Driving out of the airport, I could see Venice off in the distance. Italy's interstate operated much like ours as far as I could tell. Except of course there weren't massive bill-boards everywhere. Fields mostly lined the highway, old cottages dotting the land scape. Camp Ederle is in the Veneto region of Italy; it sits about forty-five minutes away from Venice, and four hours from Rome by train. I have to say, other than for the ridiculous amount of wordage coming from the front seat, my first ride in Italy was amazing.

Driving through the city of Vicenza, I could see I wasn't in Kansas anymore. The buildings sat an arm's reach or closer from each other. The streets were somewhat dirty, the cars were small, it's just not what you picture when you think of Italy. I think most of us still think of the Roman Empire, when Italy was at its finest. This is no longer the case. I would later realize it is probably the dirtiest country in the European Union. Most towns resemble American ghettos, except Rome obviously, it's a tourist trap.

Before I could attend dinner, I had to check in with the 173rd Brigade. The post is right next to a major highway, but so small that by the time I finished blinking my eyes we had past it. As I said, the 173rd is only one brigade, so Camp Ederle wasn't that big. The thing that got me was it was built right next to one of Italy's maximum security prisons-no doubt their finest were vacationing there! Driving though the main gate, I could see the Commissary (grocery store) on my left, a shoppette ahead of me, and the PX[3] to my right.

The buildings looked nice, with a reddish color and Spanish tile on the roofs. What I mistook for a main road was actually only about 200 meters long; we past a Burger King on the right. Farther down was a small, one screen movie theater. Making a left then an immediate right

we drove for about five seconds and we pulled up in front of Brigade (BDE)[4] Head Quarters. I got out, Chatty never missing a word, while a Staff Sergeant (SSG)[5] came out and handed me a sheet of paper. He told me to sign it, and then told me to report to 1st Battalion 503rd right across the street. Well that was easy, Chatty chatted him up while Roy and I walked

3 **PX**—Post Exchange, a merchandise store similar to Wal-Mart on United States Army Forts
4 **BDE**—Brigade, a unit size designator which is approximately 2,000 soldiers
5 **SSG**—Staff Sergeant, the rank after Sergeant

across the street. Walking in to the door of the more pinkish building, I was assigned to Charlie Company (C-Co) but would not have to report to in-processing tomorrow until 0800.

I was assigned a room; luckily the guy wasn't in there as they were on a four day pass, so he wouldn't be back until Monday hopefully. I strive to live by myself. Although this is rarely the case, sometimes I get lucky. Hopping back into the car with Chatty McChatster, Roy drove us to their home. It was getting late, but it was still daylight outside. Being that it was June, (June 11th, 2007), the sun would stay out until damn near 9:30 p.m. I was promptly informed that Italians do not eat dinner early like Americans; they usually eat around 9 p.m. At this moment I am sure this lady has certainly lost her marbles. The houses were mostly two-stories with a basement. Most families, like Roy's, had converted their basements into other rooms which also had spare kitchens.

Arriving at their house, Chatty gave me the grand tour, and went through great detail about every single item in the house. Chatty's enthusiasm was on par with Christopher Lowell's but I wasn't following a word of it. I was tired and DID NOT want to be here at the moment. I inserted a smile though where it was necessary, and gave half-hearted laughs where they were appropriate. The meal consisted of a popular Italian dish, Capresae (basically just a block of Mozzarella cheese with slices of tomatoes) then some Italian style pasta dish, which I'll be honest I never caught the name of. Authentic Italian food is different than American Italian, to you Olive Garden folks that think it's "authentic" this is hardly the case.

Italians cook their pasta for a shorter period of time, so it's thicker and harder. They use less sauce for dishes that require it, like spaghetti. Also their pizza is paper thin, which also has less cheese and sauce. They eat slowly, with a meal lasting two or three hours. Meals are for the whole family, time spent with the family, no one rushes. Of course that took some getting used to as well. After spending three hours with this family, I couldn't decide if I need a drink or therapy.

Finally finishing this dinner ordeal, Roy took me back to post. I walked in my room and was out like a light wondering why it was just getting dark at 10:00 p.m. The next day brought me some old friends. On the way to in-processing, I bumped into good ole Clark and a few other guys from basic training, AIT[6], and Airborne School. Needless to say we were well acquainted. So now it was Clark, Bruder, and me. Clark had gotten to Italy a week ahead of me and had been checking out the extra-curricular activity seen. What a lush.

Bruder was older as was Clark, well older than me, 24 I think at the time. He was a Chicago native, loved the Bears and Ditka. All three of us got along pretty well; they were assigned to Bravo Company. In-processing was supposed to last approximately two weeks. The first week was all of the briefs that the Army gave you, the last week was an introduction to Italy. It consisted of a class and also a field trip downtown to a popular restaurant which gave you a chance to see how Italians lived life.

The first week went by without a hitch. We would have brief after brief forced fed to us daily, and then we'd be free around 3 p.m. The act of letting young soldiers off so early in a new country, insured trouble was always around the corner! My roommate had returned from his pass. He was a bit of a weirdo, the *World of War Craft* gamer type. That's when I got my first taste of Infantry life. I told him I was going to check on my laundry, but I was leaving my key in the room, so if he goes somewhere in the next five minutes, please do not lock the door. What did he do? Just that-left and locked the door.

I was stuck. Walking over to Charlie Company (which I had not yet set foot in); to get the spare key was the only option. I crossed the street and went up the stairs. I was as nervous as needle sharer waiting on HIV test results. Taking a deep breath, I opened the door and walked in. There I was the new guy...without a combat patch; I immediately regretted that decision. I was doing push-ups for a good ten minutes, then mountain climbers, and then I had to talk to the 1st SGT, then more ridiculous exercises. An hour later, after dragging my smoked body out the company...I decided I DID NOT want to be a part of C-Co any longer. I had heard a new company was being started, Delta Company. I may try them out.

Finally on Friday in-processing was over. Bruder and I wanted to go check on Venice for the weekend. I told him I have to go report to my "new" company first, and then we would be on a train. Oh yea, I went to Delta Company. I fed their 1SG a line of bullshit. I told him that battalion had sent me to become his driver. Low and behold he bought it. I got a

---

6 **AIT**—Advanced Individual Training, the training soldiers go through to obtain a designated area of expertise in the armed forces.

sweet room BY MYSELF and was told to report back after in-processing, which lasted another week.

Boarding the train with Bruder, we set out for Venice. We had already been drinking. We didn't really know what we were doing or what to expect...we just knew were headed for Venice. It had to be a good time; it is the city of love! Stepping of the train and out of the station, you are right on the Grand Canal. What a sight it was! What a smell it was! I guess I have never thought streets made out of water could smell...well...like fish and ocean. First things first; we had to acquire a hotel room, some food, and most importantly more booze.

Walking in and out of every hotel we saw, still there was no room at the inn. Now I know how Mary and Joseph felt. Except, you know, without the Son of God in tow. Everything was booked. We made our way along the streets, and interestingly, everyone seemed to be carrying or walking some type of dog. Finally, we came across a liquor store. One of three down. We bought some Four Roses bourbon and a two liter of coke but they had no ice, which made the drinks horrible. The shopkeeper overheard us talking about rooms. "My friends, my friends, my friend has private rooms at good rates. I shall go get him." "Is that weirdo talking to us?" Bruder said, I only just stood there and nodded. *What did he mean private? Does he know Kevin?*

A few minutes later, a man appeared, who spoke broken English, and we got the picture that we needed to follow him. He led the way, post haste! As if the rooms would book themselves if we didn't get there in time. We walked down the street and over two bridges, then took a right down an alley that skirted the water. It was dark and you could hear the lap of water against the tied up boats and a fog horn off in the distance. It seemed like we had just trodden into a mystery movie. He led us into this dark house, except for the faint light of a television from the next room. We took an immediate left and up some stairs, one, two, three stories up. *Are we in an attic?*

Bruder looked at me as if this was going to be our last stand. I had the Four Roses bottle ready for any sudden movements that this creepy individual may make leading us around. He stopped, opened a door into a dark room, and flipped on the light. There were two twin beds with hot pink comforters on them. This guy was without a doubt touching and killing kids. He said in his broken English dialect, "Shower over there (another dark room behind him), you leave by 8 a.m......70 Euro okay." Everything was happening so fast. 70 Euro was about $85. Bruder and I

21

looked each other. I paid the man and he shut the door, we both let out a breath of relief.

Bruder was a bit conflicted about staying in our kiddie room it seemed as he said, "This guy is going to kill us man, and there is no way I'm staying here with this lunatic!" I was trying to mix hot bourbon and coke together in a two liter. We sat on the beds and stared at the floor. "You know...you're right. We are God knows where, back in this alley, three stories up in an attic. Let's get outta here," I replied. Leaving our faithful Four Roses bottle and some Coca-Cola Classic, we bolted for the door three levels down... grabbed the handle and got out of that house...no telling how much he was going to pimp us for!

Back on the main street and over the first bridge back towards the Grand Canal, we decided to stop for a drink or two. Bruder and I were laughing now, why did we even follow that guy to his "private" room is the question we kept asking ourselves. That is the second time in two months I have been invited into the home of a weirdo. What kind of people do I attract? Hearing my Southern accent, in Venice, a girl comes up to me... who also had a Georgian accent. "Hey, where y'all from?" I could not help but laugh at this! "Where are we from?" I replied back. "You have to be from the South."

The attractive blonde said in the cute, innocent Southern girl way, "Well as a matter of fact I'm from Atlanta and we're here on a trip with Georgia Tech. My name is Lindsey, what's yours?" This again took me by surprise, what a small world we live in with air travel. "My names Jesse, this is Todd (Bruder's first name), I'm from Georgia too, Valdosta. He's from Chicago. Were stationed here, about thirty minutes South, in Vicenza." Just then...I realized this girl was a loud drunk. She let one of those ten minute OH MY GODDDDs out and called the rest of her group over. Duct tape would be a must for this girl, should our encounter lead to bedroom adventures.

Lindsey proceeded to introduce the rest of the tour group. There were six including Lindsey. They were doing some type of summer study abroad/ tour thing all over Europe. I know if I had gone on a tour of Europe, in what little time I spent in college, I doubt I would have made it back. We sat there until midnight drinking and having a good time. When the bartender came out and conveyed last call, we were somewhat horror-struck. I asked the good man what time do all the bars close here and he said mid-night. Well shoot me in the foot. "Is it okay if we get some drinks to go?" I asked. Of course what answer did I get? "No sir…this is not possible."

A patron at the bar came over to us and said that he knew a place we could go that stayed open later, but we would have to follow him. What is up with people wanting me to follow them? Why can't you simply just tell me where it is? *Sir, it would not be possible.* I took this message back to my drunken group, who seemed to be down for anything that the night brought. Lindsey couldn't keep her hands off of me, she was quite loud though. Do I choose a girl or sanity? I went back to this character and said we were in-lead the way!

We went down the quiet streets of Venice somewhat noisily. Italians started to open their old World War Two shutters to throw ice at us…so that's where all the ice is! Our guide led us under a bridge and down a tunnel, "I swear I am going to get killed on this excursion" Bruder said to me. We came out of the tunnel and walked over a small wooden bridge, then took an immediate right into a courtyard. There was one door in the left hand corner. Our guide knocked four times and then rang the bell twice. *Oh what are we getting into?*

The door buzzed open and he stepped back and made a sweeping movement with his hand, "This is your destination friend, I must return home." I was somewhat confused by this statement, "Wait, you're not going in with us?" "No sir…it is not possible." *WHY does everyone keep saying that to me?!* We walked in and the door shuts behind us. All eyes were on the eight Americans. There were four guys in the bar wearing turbans, another five or six to my right on a couch…they looked like Black Panthers. There was a huge projector throwing a Blondie Live DVD on the wall…Debbie Harry was rocking. No wonder I had seen fanny packs for sale, Italy was still stuck in 1986. A pool table was in the back; that was our get away.

Bruder racked them up, and we played some serious pool. Just when I thought this Georgia Tech clan wasn't a bunch of book worms, they started complaining that they had class in the morning. "Well why didn't you say so three hours ago, it's almost four in the morning," I told Lindsey. By now the Black Panthers were looking at us, probably more at the three females in our ensemble. I thought it would be good to escape and we did, trying not to get lost in the maze of Venice. By now Lindsey had turned into a shit show. She was constantly going between loud and happy to sobbing and needy. Needless to say, I chose sanity that night.

I awoke on the floor of Lindsey's hotel room. *Where was Lindsey? Where was anybody?* Bruder stepped out of the bathroom, "Whoahhhh, look at you! Hey do you want to grab a Corona and steal some breakfast from the lobby?" Hey why not, it was only Saturday. Walking out of that hotel with enough croissants to feed an army, Bruder and I decided to get on a water bus to the island of Lido. I knew that the Cannes Film Festival was there, so it had to be a great island.

Docking on Lido, we took some shots from this crazy looking guy who was selling ice of all things, beverages, fresh fruit and booze. We had to get our minds back on a good plane of existence. There were dogs everywhere. We walked straight to the other side of the island, where we saw our first nude beach. Now I am sure there are some fine nude beaches in Europe... well our first sight was of a sagging 65, year, old strolling down by the water! Oh my gosh this cracked us up! Of course I tried to get Bruder to go talk to her, but he wasn't having it.

After drinking a few beers and scouting the beach for any other prime tail, we turned around. "Jesse...you know if I see one more damn dog I am going to lose my mind." I couldn't help but laugh at this. "OH MY GOD...JESSE LOOK!" I turned as Bruder said this and saw what he saw. There not twenty-feet away was our captor that tried to get us to stay in the "private" room. He was walking right towards us. "Bruder maybe he hasn't noticed us. Let's just keep walking." We did, Bruder bent down to pet one of the dogs he had grown to hate as the butcher walked by, leaving me out in the open...what a friend! "Jesse we have got to get out of here, that guy is following us!" I kind of thought Bruder may be right. Without wasting anytime, we caught the next train back to Vicenza. On the train I began to wonder if we should have stuck around, and in the best Italian accent I could muster, I said to myself, "No sir, it is not possible."

CHAPTER FIVE

TRAINING

HISTORY GOES TO SHOW that most people that attempted escape from the Nazis were eventually found. My case was no different. Charlie Company started calling around to the other companies to see if I was at one of them. Busted, I had to give up my badass room and go face my foes in C-Co. It had been a month since I had found my way to Delta; shit I thought I was home free. Getting my old room back with the weirdo gamer, I was back in Charlie Co. I simply told 1SG Collins, that some Specialist[7] at battalion told me to go over there. He bought it. Does no one question anything around this place?

I was now a part of 3rd Platoon[8] in 2nd Squad[9]. There were only three of us, since the unit was getting rebuilt after its last deployment. It was Staff Sergeant Carlson and Private Second Class Conales, a small Honduran guy, and then me. I was assigned a M249 machine gun, or a SAW[10]. Our PSG[11] was a douche bag named SFC[12] Parkins. He was one of those cats who had been in the Army for sixteen years but spent it all in TRADOC[13], so now he needed PSG time on the line to move up the chain. SSG Carlson didn't care for him too much, no one really did.

---

7 **Specialist**—a rank given to soldiers with at least eighteen months in United States Army
8 **Platoon**—a unit size designator of the armed forces which consists of approximately thirty soldiers
9 **Squad**—a unit size designator of armed forces which consist of six to eight soldiers
10 **SAW**—Squad Automatic Weapon, the M249 machine gun which is carried by at least one soldier in each infantry squad, excluding weapons squad
11 **PSG**—Platoon Sergeant, the Non-Commissioned Officer in charge of a platoon
12 **SFC**—Sergeant First Class, the rank that proceeds Staff Sergeant
13 **TRADOC**—Training and Doctrine Command

Our first training event was a company-sized affair, located in the worst place in all Italy-Fulcha Del Raino. The range was at a mosquito pit of an Italian base, right by the Adriatic Sea. It was humid, plus so damn hot the seagull droppings sizzled to a crisp before striking the ground. The fresh Lieutenants didn't think to plan on bringing any shade, Gatorade, or basically anything to get us out of the heat and keep our bodies hydrated. A lot of folks said their previous deployment to Afghanistan was better than this. Three days into this hot, bug-bitten hell, the leadership decided to go on a twelve mile road march…six miles in, there were nine people down. The medics were out of IVs and the road march had to be stopped due to paratroopers going to the hospital for exhaustion. Game over, C-Co had fallen to the elements. Elements-1, Lieutenants.-0.

The following week I was moved to 4th Squad, the Weapons Squad. I was now a part of one of the two M240B[14] teams, gun number one. We would be heading to Germany to attend a MGLC[15] in two weeks, in Weilflicken. I was stoked. Who wouldn't like to fire that machine gun?! Of course a new squad meant new people. My new Squad Leader was a big ole Samoan named Manuma. My team included a psychotic guy from Seattle, named Hampton, and our team leader, Anderson. Anderson and Manuma were with the 173rd on the previous deployment to Afghanistan. Manuma was in the 82nd Airborne for the invasion of Iraq. Needless to say, all of the leaders of Charlie Company had at least one deployment under their belt.

Naturally before we left for Germany, there was another weekend that had to be conquered. I didn't really hangout with the guys in C-Co. due to the fact that all of the people I started basic with and had become close to were in Bravo Company. Since being in Italy, Clark wanted to check out some of the local gentlemen's club. I had never been in a strip club being that I was only nineteen; curiosity was killing this cat.

We started drinking right after work, around 5 p.m. on Friday. Strandberg, another one of the guys who went through training with us, had arrived in Italy. He was from Boston and had that THICK Boston accent. He was a funny guy, always giving Clark hell about something. We all got along great. Around 9 p.m. Clark started talking about spaceships. He is getting lit. We headed downtown to the only American bar in all of

---

14 **M240B**—An air-cooled, open bolt operated, fully automatic machine gun that fires a 7.62mm NATO round
15 **MGLC**—Machine Gun Leaders Course, a course designed to teach soldiers about heavy automatic weapons

Vicenza, The Art Café. No one told us about the local taxi service, so we began to walk the two mile road that lead to downtown Vicenza, making pit stops along the way. One local establishment was this Asian bar that served Corona. Everyone in Italy seemed to like Corona, I don't know if they realized that it was a Mexican beer.

The Asian lady that owned the bar would literally grab your arm every time you walked by to tell you to come and have, "Corona Corona...wid de lime!" Soon we wised up and quit walking that way. After escaping the Asian POW camp, we proceeded downtown. I couldn't believe all of the Italian history, fountains, and art that were around. Vicenza is home to the first indoor theater, a remarkable building. Passing it there is a cobblestone road that takes you all the way through downtown and opens up into a huge square. Of course we had to explore this, being that it was our first time down here. Bruder found this Italian chick that spoke relatively good English, and he decided to sit down. Clark, Strandberg, and I continued to check out the bars around the square.

Bruder's roommate Humpries met up with us. This guy was hilarious. He was four hours short of graduating college and joined the Army. His new life ambition was to get out of the Army, work at the Burger King on post, and travel Europe...ahhh, the American Dream. Maybe I could set him up with Clark's hippie mom. Humpries knew just enough Italian to get himself in trouble. He walked over to Bruder, who was still talking to the Italian chick, and said, "She wants to know if you have a big dick." I don't think she said that, but it sent laughter throughout our group.

Humpries kept on with remarks like this and the chica finally got up and left. Bruder turns to look at us, "I have never been so cocked blocked in my entire life!" Oh my Lord this was too funny! The usually relatively quiet Bruder (except for when the Bears were on) was pissed! Victory was ours! Leaving the square, we finally walked the few blocks over to Art Café. It was packed with soldiers as you may imagine. It was two for one liquor drinks after 10 p.m. Jack pot! We all switched to liquor; they even had Captain Morgan which was very hard to find in Europe. God bless America and her bar's overseas!

Humpries ended up walking in to the cathedral next to us and passed out in a pew. The Father would find him the next morning, snoring. Clark, Bruder, Strandberg, and I were informed about the whole "taxi" business and got a ride with Johnny. He was an Irishman living in Italy for some reason. He became our regular driver. The taxis were not legitimately marked taxis, but private citizens trying to make a buck. Johnny took us to Kiss-Kiss, my first strip club.

Walking into this place was amazing. The flashing lights, the bass in your chest from the Techno music, the couches surrounding the stages, and the girls. Wow. Most strippers in Italy were from Eastern Europe, which included Romania, Bosnia, Czech Republic, etc. These were smoking hot girls. In Europe you don't sit up at the stage and throw money like you do in the States, instead the girls come to you. You can choose to buy them a drink and talk with them or, shoo them away. Unless you were after a particular female, or just plain loved the Johnson, there was no reason on earth to turn down such beauty, especially when it was there for the taking.

A trip to the private dance area, the "The Privea"[16], was their whole ploy. It was dangerous back there. Clark was known to disappear for hours and run up ridiculous tabs that he usually didn't have the money for. Sitting down on a couch, the main stage was set ablaze by this dancer doing a show. She set the whole thing on fire as she pulled the vibrator out of her mouth; there was no telling what was going on up there. As soon as the four of us sat down females came over to us, as did the waitress…I thought I was in heaven.

After a few drinks, Strandberg and Clark went behind the building to check out the other joint, Girls-Girls. Catchy name right? Bruder and I chose to stay right there. He had already disappeared to the "Privea." I was still thinking about it. It was about 50 euros per fifteen minutes back there, so about $65…pretty steep. Ah what the heck, it was my first time! A vixen with jet black hair led me back and threw me behind the curtain. I sat down on the couch, she straddle my lap and licked my ear…oh…my…God.

She kissed down my neck and I placed her top ties in between my fingers and tugged, revealing the most marvelous pair of breasts I had seen to that point. Her accent sounded sweet in my ear…like a Siren's lullaby. Her bottoms slid off her tan, long legs revealing her Turquoise Victoria Secret boy shorts, making my imagination go wild! She stood up as she playfully slid the shorts off and slid my hand between her legs. If this is what strip clubbing is all about, then what have I been missing? She again straddled me and rubbed her hand on my now throbbing wood. Just as soon as it seemed I hit the couch, it was over. The guy called for her and my time was up…victory was definitely NOT mine!

---

16 **Privea**—the private dance room in Italian gentlemen's clubs

It was worth it though to see her amazing body. Sadly, that was the only dance I got that night, Bruder was still in the Privea, Clark and Strandberg had yet to return, so I did a few shots with some guys from Charlie Co. I then decided to go run my tab which was 145 Euros or $200. Wow I wasn't planning on spending that much! This didn't sit well with me, so I told the cashier I was not paying yet and not to worry about it, that I was going to get another drink. What a silly bartender. I promptly left, flawlessly executing my best Clark impersonation.

I walked back into the Privea and past Bruder's room I hear, "Wasn't that your friend?" in an accented voice, then Bruder's reply "Couldn't be." Oh it was me, jail-breaking. I walked up to the fire exit and kicked that door off of the hinges! Shit was hitting the fan! Spot lights came on, alarms were going off, people were yelling, and instead of turning left into the alley (where I could have disappeared) I took a right and right into the parking lot-bad decision. Next thing I know there is an Italian midget running after me, his little feet pitter-pattering on the pavement. This shocked me, "Oh what the hell!" I bolted, trying to get away from the small monstrosity and ran right in to the arms of a massive bouncer. Damn it!

They escorted me back inside, and by now the Carbenari[17] had driven up. The bouncer took me to the cashier, who I assumed was the owner. He was yelling at me in Italian, but I couldn't make a word out of what he was saying. Bruder had come out, "Dude was that you?!" "Yeah man it was me, I didn't feel like paying this outrageous tab, so I decided to take matters in my own hands…hey have you seen a midget running around here?" I got off lucky, I only had to pay the whole punch card for trying to leave, which ended up being 200 euros. I guess it's better than getting raped in jail by Mussolini's long lost brother.

We loaded the buses Monday morning, preparing for the twelve hour drive up to Germany. We had to be police escorted in Italy when we had our weapons; and waiting for the police escort usually put us behind schedule. Italians are not known for their punctuality. We chartered buses whenever we went on training like this or when we would drive up to Aviano Air Force base to jump. Hell even the school kids rode on chartered buses…our tax dollars at work!

Hampton was trying to enlighten me on how he threw his sister's cat into the clothes dryer before he came over to Italy, "Yeah man I tossed that little bitch in and told my sister she still had some clothes drying like

---

17 **Carbenari**—The State Police assigned to the different regions in Italy

ten minutes later. There was blood everywhere!" I told you he was a nut; it takes a special breed to volunteer to jump out of perfectly good airplanes and sign up to be on the front lines. His mom was Israeli, maybe that's where the violence came from.

Finally the escort arrived, and we could get this show on the road. We piled on the buses and set off for Germany. The ride through Italy was amusing. There were plenty of old castles and Roman ruins left along the sides of the highways. The United States is only an infant compared to all that Italy has been through. Reaching the Austrian border, the police escort stopped, and we drove over the border. No police escort from the Austrians...they know the deal.

We stopped at a McDonald's in the Brenner Pass, near Innsbruck. It certainly wasn't American, but it would do. They sold some odd items such as, shrimp, cupcakes, and beer. That was the first time I had to pay for condiments, who the hell pays for condiments? Everyone pretty much spoke English, so that made conversing much simpler. After our fattening rest stop, we loaded back up on the buses and continued our journey. The huge Austrian Alps were astonishing. It's crazy to think how people in the dark ages use to climb up and down them when we can now drive around and through them.

Crossing the border into Germany, the rain began to fall in a drizzle. We exited the interstate and got on the back roads of Germany. The dark forests you would hear about in world history were at my very finger tips. If those trees could talk, what kind of journeys could they tell of ancient Germanic tribes and things that still go bump in the night? How many battles have they witnessed? How many times have they changed ownership due to land disputes or war?

Night was beginning to take us as we reached our final destination. Weilflicken was an old U.S. Army base that had been turned over to the Germans. The barracks we were staying in had at least been updated; two story bay rooms with heat/air. Everyone unloaded the buses, and the platoons were given their assigned bays. Each platoon has two gun teams, so a regular rifle company with three rifle platoons would have six gun teams. There were five companies' weapons squads present, Alpha Company through Easy Company. Approximately thirty gun teams were there, about 210 people all together.

The next morning we did some classroom-style instruction, about proper gun emplacement (emplacement is putting a gun in a fighting position), for platoon, company, battalion and brigade-size assaults. Our second gun crew, Gun 2, had some characters on it. Arruda from Boston was a loud mouth Portuguese fool; he always had an opinion about something and loved cars. Maddalone was from New York City and joined up because of the September 11th attacks. He wanted to show the Muslims some pay back. Maddalone loved frequenting the gentleman establishments.

Then there was Hafley. This guy was off the reservation. He had been a part of the previous deployment to Afghanistan but still didn't really seem to gather what was going on. Hafley believed in all types of conspiracy theories and wouldn't hesitate to share one if someone lent him an ear. For example, he believed that the Amtrak was the master mind of the next holocaust and proclaimed that he had seen the plans himself. He had even seen the train in which the people would be transported. What a nut.

After the classroom portion was over, we had some lunch. Bruder and I were smoking and joking when we met Lowell. He was new to B-Co., and was another native Chicagoan. There were a few people going down to the little Nazi convenience store for smokes and such. Lowell was tagging along as well, so Bruder and I asked him to get us a pack of smokes. His reply wasn't what I was expecting, "I don't buy cigarettes for people." I have to say I was confused since he was smoking himself, "But you're smoking a cigarette, I mean if it's your money your worried about, we got it right here." "No I just don't buy them for people, I don't agree with it. I don't feel I should contribute to a person killing themselves slowly over time." Lowell replied. Bruder and I looked at each other confused, "Do you realize that you could be shooting people in a year man. I mean…that's killing folks quickly. So what is the difference?" I replied to Lowell, who obviously had not thought about this situation. Lowell looked around, and looked back at us, "Nah I just don't believe in it man." *What is wrong with this guy?*

Bruder was a part of Lowell's gun team, Lowell would end up living with Clark when we returned to Vicenza and eventually we all would be best friends, as you have most likely gathered since I dedicated this book to him. Getting on a Nazi school bus after a lunch of MRE's[18], we made our way to the M240B range. It had begun to drizzle again, which didn't bother me; I love rainy days. I had always wanted to see the European rainy skies. We were going to shoot for the afternoon and establish positions on the gun team.

---

18 **MRE**—Meal Ready to Eat, a pre-packaged meal that is light weight and can be eaten without heating.

The range was 800 meters long and had different types of targets on it which included houses, pop-ups, stationary, etc. First though we had to zero the weapons at 10 meters. Hampton, who was supposed to be the gunner sucked at shooting the paper targets. You have to get three shots in each-they go vertically, horizontally, and diagonally on the paper. After his ridiculous display of marksmanship, I had to show him up. I had been shooting all my life, being from the country; machine guns have just a little more kick than your daddy's shotgun, but shooting is shooting. It's all about breathing and trigger pull, along with learning how the weapon responds. Hampton was from coffee break Seattle and hadn't shot much. He spent most of his time throwing cats in dryers.

Now that I had the gunner spot, most of the week I would be harnessing my craft. Today though was a familiarization day. After the zeroing, the different gun teams rotated through firing on the range. Of course every round that was shot ejected the brass casings. Cleanup was at the end of the day. The rain was falling with a continuous flow, the sun was dipping behind the trees, and it was still overcast. The ground was wet and starting to turn muddy with all the traffic going over hit.

SSG Manuma was taking a box of brass back when his legs came out from under him; his huge Samoan body hit the wet ground with a thud. We thought this was hilarious; he didn't. Hampton went to help him when his legs came out from under him and SSG Manuma then proceeded to drag Hampton through the mud, I was having the laugh of my life over there still picking up shells casings. Hampton's screams could be heard for miles.

Returning to the barracks, we cleaned our weapons and had chow. The cook would drive to Stugartt, and American base about 150 miles away, to pick up breakfast and dinner for us, a kind act because he was a chode from New Jersey and talked more than Chatty Cathy. Hampton and I decided to hit the Nazi showers before we hit the hay. The showers had two temperatures, scalding or iceberg. Hampton was going on about how he was at a party and threw two 32 oz. cups of booze all over the crowd and fell down the stairs when he was trying to make an exit breaking through the sheet rock at the bottom of the stairs. Disinterested I was trying not to burn my talley-wacker. Slapping Bruder's white ass, which was probably the most action he hadn't paid for in years, I headed back across the gravel road to the barracks. It was a cold, damp night. Tomorrow we were going to ruck march[19] about four miles to another range where we could practice drills, and live fire.

Two miles into the march our CSM[20] commented that this was a bad idea, being that the last two of the four miles was straight up. We all made it through. Gun 2 was having a little more difficulty than my team seeing as they were heavy smokers. I just smoked in the field; it gave me something to do. Plus it gave me a chance to work on my lung cancer. The drills went well; we all learned a lot as we developed our crew drill plans. A crew drill is the act of setting a gun team in place for battle. With our drills, the squad leader would decide where to place the guns, run a few paces in front of us, and point to where the two different guns would go. Then the Ammo Barer (AB)[21] would run up with the tri-pod and place it in the best spot for the gun. The Assistant Gunner (AG)[22] would be a few seconds behind the AB laying down to the right of the AB and left of the tri-pod. He would get the ammo he was carrying ready for the Gunner to put into the feed tray. Finally the Gunner would run up lastly and place the gun onto the tri-pod while the AG would hook the rest of the ammo up to the starter belt. A starter belt is 25-50 rounds of ammo the Gunner carries already loaded in case of an ambush.

When everything is running smoothly, this whole task can be completed relatively quickly, depending on how far the crew had to run to set up. My gun team was the fastest in the 1/503rd Battalion; we would eventually go on to win awards for fastest setup, and marksmanship. I was an artist with my gun, what could I say? Call me Leonardo Da Machine Gun if you want, I don't mind. Although this day, we were just figuring out how to make all of this work. Hampton was jacking it up. He was made AB, so when it was time for tripod installment, he would pick the worst instead of the best places for the gun emplacement.

It so happens that this time he placed it on a mud mound. After I had been firing, SSG Manuma called for a Dead Gunner Drill (DGD)[23]. A DGD is simulating that the gunner has been killed or wounded. The AG rolls the Gunner out of the way or the Squad Leader pulls him away.

19 **Ruck March**—the forced march of troops, usually in a type of formation, over an extend period of time.
20 **Command Sergeant Major**—the highest ranking Non-Commissioned Officer in a position of command
21 **AB**—Ammunition Barer, solider that carries ammunition for a M240B gun team
22 **AG**—Assistant Gunner, the backup gunner for a M240B gun team
23 **DGD**—Dead Gunner Drill, a drill used to simulate the gunner of a M240B machine gun team being killed in combat and the Assistant Gunner taking over the gun

Hafley (who switched from Gun 2 to Gun 1, Anderson going to Gun 2) rolled me out the way, and I ran around to the AB spot. Again Manuma called for a DGD, Hampton rolled Hafley out of the way, and I moved into the AG spot. Once again, DGD is called, although this time SSG Manuma pulls Hampton down the slope through the mud...victory is mine!

The rest of the week consisted of much of the same. We would drill and fire, working on muscle memory. We would also night fire with our Night Vision (NODs)[24] on. The last night Maddalone wound up shutting down the range. He kept firing outside of the range boundaries, since there was a Gestapo Headquarters below us, this was a no-go. Hopefully some of them got a few stray shots through their windows.

We stopped at the Austrian McDonald's in the Brenner Pass for some shrimp, cupcakes, and beer on the way back to Vicenza. I don't trust seafood from land locked countries, but I had to try McDonald's shrimp, which tasted like chicken. Bruder and I were discussing weekend plans. For the moment he and I were the only two out of our group that were on gun teams. Clark was a M249 gunner, Strandberg was in his squad as a rifleman. Lowell was yet to be inducted into the inner-circle. Upon entering the gates of Camp Ederle and after turning in all of the weapons, showering, and buying booze, I headed over to B-Company. I found Humpries making Spaghetti, which consisted of Top Ramen and Tomato Paste...yummy. "Humpries" I say, "you are in the land of pasta and you're making this college dorm business, what's wrong with you?"

"You know man...it's just so good, and filling too!" I could see I wouldn't win this battle. While Bruder was in the shower listening to Nelly Furtado's "Promiscuous Girl", and probably playing with himself, I went next door to see how Clark and his new roommate, Lowell, were doing. Jack Bauer was on the television, screaming at someone about another terrorist plot. Strandberg was also in here, talking about how his new roommate was just lying on the bed and had been doing so for a week. Strandberg's new roomie would also become a part of the group, and eventually Bruder's roommate, his name was Bickford. For now though he just wanted to lie on his bed and watch animal porn no doubt.

Clark was always "not going to drink tonight," but after one he couldn't stop. We started playing some kind of drinking game, Clark and Lowell versus Bruder and me. This ended badly for my team because I had never

---

24 **NODS**—Night Observation Device, lenses that are worn that allow the soldier to see during hours of darkness

really gotten into drinking games. After a few rotations of this we made our way downtown to an American restaurant named Papa Joe's. I'm pretty sure there are only two or three in the world, one being in Vicenza, the other two being in Florida. Either way, they had phenomenal fajitas plus wet drinks.

The rest of the night went much like last weekend. Downtown antics, then a strip club; but this time we went to a new one…Exstatia (X-sta-G-a). The place is much smaller than Kiss, with only one stage. The atmosphere is the same though. We arrived early this weekend. It was around 11:45 p.m. Rolling deep again, it was Bruder, Lowell, Clark, and myself. Clark immediately disappeared into the Privea of course. I was determined not to spend any money on females, only booze, now that I knew their tricks I was reserving all funds for my true love, alcohol.

The rest of us grabbed a booth in the left hand corner, right by the DJ booth. The night was going smoothly. We weren't even disturbed when Clark stumbled out of the Privea, eyes wide and hair a mess. He claims he was just raped by this gorgeous Eastern European broad, but we never put much stock in Clark's words. Bruder had been talking with this girl for a while now, Lowell and I decided to do another round of shots, and Clark was talking to a bouncer about something. They were getting along pretty well.

Clark comes over and explains to us that the bouncer knows his dad's side of the family from Herzegovina, Bosnia. That was the gist of the message, but he went on about several of his ex-step-moms and dads, being that there is seven of each. Then he drops the word Jolly Hotel. I had heard of this Jolly Hotel…it was run by the mob, and it was hooker central. Clark wanted to go check it out; of course I wouldn't leave him hanging. He said that his new-found friend, Bouncer Badass, would give us a ride since he was headed that way.

I ran this past Bruder really quickly, but he was lost in the eyes of that Romania she-devil; Lowell was smoking with a female in the smoking room, so off we went. As we paid our tabs (Clark actually had money for once). Clark turns to me and says Kevin was coming too. Kevin? Oh… KEVINNNN got ya. Well what a surprise! Clark and I followed Bouncer Badass downstairs and into his black Mercedes. Pulling out of the parking lot and taking the right back towards Vicenza, Bouncer opens his center console and pulls out a glass tray, Kevin has come to say hello. Once again, if you're going to place free blow in front of me, then by all means.

The ride back to Vicenza and then through to SS-11 (the street the Jolly was on) took about twenty minutes, which was more than enough time to get jacked. Bouncer pulled up to the Jolly and parked. We all got out, he pointed up and down the street saying where to find the best quality of street-walkers; apparently some street-walkers are better than others. I wasn't too interested in sticking my wang in something like that, but Clark didn't mind. We were on the hunt. Now this wasn't like a government run Red Light district, as you find in Germany or Belgium. Oh no, these girls were straight hookers. They were ready to give you a free ticket to the Syphilis show.

Italian, Moroccan, and many different nationalities were available, and then Clark spotted two guys he knew. One was laughing, the other seemed very distraught. We stopped and Clark of course asks, "What's going on?" The distraught guy looks at Clark, and then to me and says, "Get out of here while you can man, no one is what them seem." Then brushes past me, his friend thinks this is outrageously funny! "What's going on?" I say. The response I got was not what I was expecting. The cracked up paratrooper looks at us, barely able to compose himself says, "He (distraught guy) decided that he wants to bang this hooker. She was cute, a tad bit taller than him, but cute. He didn't want to go into the hotel, so he takes her behind a building into an alley. The hooker told him that she was ragging, but asked if it would be okay if he made love to her in the ass? Mr. Distraught said that would be fine and went about his business. After he was getting into it, he reached around the hooker to stimulate her from the front...and grabbed a dick!"

Clark and I looked at each other and almost had strokes as we were laughing so hard! "So did he finish?" Clark asked. "Nah he didn't, he freaked, pulled out, and kicked the 'dude' in the ass and ran off!" By now all three of us are laughing hysterically, no doubt sounding like a bunch of Hyenas to the native street-walkers. "This is too much, let's get out of here Holder." Clark says, while the laughing friend ran to catch up with the violated victim. By the next Monday, everyone knew what happened. Distraught victim #1 was meanwhile getting tested for HIV. Hey, dude looked like a lady.

Tuesday brought my first jump in Italy. We had to drive about two hours northwest to Aviano, Air Force Base. It wasn't really a bad drive; it just sucked getting up at 2 a.m. to do it. It was a warm August day, around 89 degrees, and the warm air was bringing in the smell of the Adriatic Sea. Aviano is a gorgeous airbase right at the foothills of the Italian Alps; its landscape is flat then all of a sudden goes straight up, a breath taking view if it's your first time there.

It was sunny skies, so the jump was a go. Our 1ˢᵗ Lieutenant, Lt. Kaffen, had the bright idea to eat some ice cream as we waited for the pilots to finish jerking each other. "If there's one thing I learned in college, it is when it's hot, eat ice cream." Yea sir, we'll see how that hot smell of diesel, the musty cabin of a C-130, plus the elements treat you with all of that dairy in your stomach.

We went through mock door training, and went over the rules of the air. Mock door training is when you sit in a fake plane on the ground and practice standing up, hooking up, and then exiting the aircraft. It's really not even a fake plane, more like two cement walls with a few benches inside, but it gets the job done. Now it was time to rig up. I was once again #4 four jumper, Lt. Kaffen was leading the way with #1 jumper, and another one of 3ʳᵈ PLT's squad leaders was behind me, SGT Matlock. Matlock was a big ole boy from Texas. He was a starter at Texas A&M but jacked his knee up, so he had to give up football.

We rigged up. I got inspected and now was just waiting. It would be a Hollywood Jump[25] so nothing too difficult. The aircraft was ready, so I assumed the USAF pilots had finished their orgy, and cleaned up the plane from the mess they most certainly made…fag fly boys. I was on the first load; luckily I wouldn't be in this harness for too long. Once we jumped we would get back on the buses and head back to Vicenza. The plane was running as we walked behind it, throwing the hot wind and exhaust in our faces. I love that smell.

We walked in and sat down. I have never really been a fan of C-130's, as they're way too cramped. As soon as we were seated, the ramp went up, and we were off. We taxied down the runway, made a U-turn, and now were getting some air. "TEN MINUTES!" the Jumpmaster[26] yelled and held up both of his hands all fingers extended. I undid my rip cord from my reserve chute, because I hate fooling with that thing when it's time to hook up. The aircraft banked, and we hit some turbulence, ole Lt. Kaffen wasn't looking to good over there. I nudged SGT Matlock and shook my head right towards the Lt. Kaffen. SGT Matlock responded with a throw-up gesture.

"STAND-UP!" We all rose to our feet, balancing ourselves from the rock of the aircraft, these pilots obviously were still drunk from their sex-a-pades.

---

25 **Hollywood Jump**—a jump out of an aircraft by paratroopers with no combat gear adorned

26 **Jumpmaster**—an expert Paratrooper qualified to teach, train, plus inspect the equipment worn by paratroopers. Jumpmasters also control Paratroopers exit out of an aircraft.

"HOOK-UP!" All of the paratroopers hooked their rip cords to the metallic static line, making sure it was on the outside of their right arm, so their arm wouldn't get snatched off when they jumped. I seized some slack near the top and grabbed on to it just below the weaving. "CHECK EQUIPMENT!" We all checked our helmets to make sure they were snapped tightly. No doubt someone would lose his.

We checked out reserve chutes to make sure nothing was tangled, then checked the jumper in front of us to make sure his static line was good, making sure nothing was tangled in his back. "SOUND OFF FOR EQUIPMENT CHECK!" Starting from the rear of the aircraft men of all shapes, sizes, and ages began slapping other men's asses, with a loud and thunderous "OK!" I have a feeling the pilots liked that part. I passed on my ass slap to the jumper in front of me as the plane dropped about twenty feet. Lt. Kaffen then threw his left arm in front of the Jumpmaster's face and yelled, "ALL OK JUMPMASTER!" The Jumpmaster slapped his hand; this meant that he heard him loud and clear.

The Jumpmaster was looking outside of the door, making sure no other aircraft were stealing our airspace. He came back in and shouted, "ONE MINTUE!" with one finger up. We all replied back like a black choir "ONE MINUTE!" The plane bumped again, Lt. Kaffen looked like he might possibly be sick. I had my fingers crossed, hoping for a show! "30 SECONDS...STANDBY!" The Jumpmaster took Lt. Kaffen's static line and turned him into the door. As soon as Lt. Kaffen turned to face out of said door, so did three scoops of Rocky Road... victory is mine.

Lt. Kaffen threw up the flow of chocolaty, marshmallow goodness as the light went green, and the Jumpmaster kicked him out, brown river flowing down his leg and all! I could barely hand off my static line I was laughing so hard. The Jumpmaster had a huge grin on his face as well. I exited the aircraft, once again murdered by the Prop Blast, chute snapping open. I heard Lt. Kaffen yelling as he was falling towards earth, "Oh My God! I'm covered in throw-up! Oh God it stinks!" Oh this was too much! Bicycle kicking to un-tangle my risers, and trying to slip away from this douche right on top of me, I land relatively near the buses. The green light to exit came on a bit early and some of the jumpers landed in a farmer's corn field.

I'm not really one for a corn stalk up my ass, but to each his own. SGT Matlock and I collected out chutes; we could hear Lt. Kaffen still bitching about his Rocky Road-covered clothes. One jumper managed to hit the only tree on the entire Drop Zone (DZ)[27]. It was a beautiful DZ, DZ Juliet, surrounded by farms on the three sides and the South end was marked by the mountains. Walking back to the buses, I put my chute and reserve into the Rigger's truck. Someone called out to Lt. Kaffen, "What the hell happen to you sir?" Before Lt. Kaffen had time to lift up his head from shame, I called back, "Hey when it's hot, eat ice cream!"

---

27 **DZ**—Drop Zone, an area designated to drop soldiers, equipment, weapons, or supplies into by parachute

CHAPTER SIX

24 DOWN

THE VINEYARDS BEGAN TO transition from a vibrant green to autumn's subtle orange. The Adriatic's warm inland breeze turned into a cooler wisp, bringing with it September rains that fell into October. October meant it was time for the whole brigade to make a trip up to Grafenwoer, Germany. This was a daunting task of moving equipment and personnel through three different countries; it was a deemed a "mock-deployment". It gave our logistics teams practice moving equipment, food, etc. around. Once up there it gave line units different scenarios that may be encountered on the battlefield.

1/503rd was busing up there, 2/503rd was going to jump into Grafenwoer, or Graf as we called it. I'm pretty glad we didn't jump in, as the DZ is a bitch filled with bunkers, holes, and post sticking up. I'll take the bus ride please and thank you! We started inventorying everything we were sending up there ahead of us, just as you would for a deployment. Layouts are the most tedious process in all of the U.S. Army. Everything from biggest weapon to the smallest bolt must be accounted for by serial number. Then one person must sign for all of the equipment on a hand-receipt. I have seen a hand-receipt that is over $100,000,000 worth of equipment. Would you want to be responsible for that? Yeah… me neither.

After everything was packed up in shipping containers, it was sent on flatbeds up to Graf. If everything went as planned, all of a company's items would be waiting for it when it got there. On October 15th 2006 we loaded up the buses, escorted of course, and our whole battalion set out for Graf. We could tell this was going to be a memorable three weeks. The companies were staggered in leaving Vicenza since we didn't want the Germans to think we were invading again. It also did not make us vulnerable to any terrorist mischief.

Stopping at the Brenner Pass once again, this was a usual thing when making the trip north, we took over McDonald's. The McDonald's staff was struggling at best to keep up with our large orders. A few grill employees slinging the 100% beef patties at each other proved their situation was getting chippy. You never know how good those fattening fries taste until you're out of the United States for a while. This time instead of heading straight up through Austria and into Germany, we swung right and stopped at the Eagle's Nest; Hitler's private mountain getaway. The Eagle's Nest sits right on the side of a huge mountain, and who would have thought it, but the man was scared of heights!

There's a bus that you can take to the top, or you can walk the three mile path that goes around, in, out, and up the mountain. Which way do you think the paratroopers reasoned to take? We just couldn't let the paratroopers that took the Eagle's Nest in 1945 be the only ones to climb that mountain, no sir! Charlie Company set out up the path, Guidon Barer with his flag, approximately 120 of us taking that mountain once again. It was a long three miles to say the least. Reaching the top, we were greeted by other veterans (who probably took the bus); they were clapping and shaking our hands. Hitler's house was now part restaurant, part museum. There's a huge cross atop the mountain overlooking a lake. Remnants of gun emplacements can still be seen, and the view is absolutely breath-taking. The sky was blue as far as the eye could see with colossal grey mountains surrounding the Eagle's Nest, which make for the perfect natural defense. I certainly recommend the visit if you're into World War Two history.

After looking around, photo ops, and munching on some of Hitler's food, we made our way back down the mountain, which was much easier than walking up it! Little did I know that this three mile trek was going to be put to shame within a year in Afghanistan. Loading back up on our mechanical steeds, we set out for Graf. Our new 1st Lt, 1st Lt. Israel, came over to me and said, "There ain't no mountains like that in Georgia, boy!" 1st Lt. Israel was from Alabama, a Roll-Tide fan through and through; no doubt he would bleed Crimson if I was to cut his left arm off. We hit it off from the start, and he would be the best Platoon Leader we would have.

Arriving that night in Graf, we got barracks (bay barracks) then unloaded the buses. Weapons Squad was already preparing for another MGLC, which would entail most of the same things we did last time we were here in Germany. The good thing about being in Weapons Squad was you were usually separated from your platoon to receive your own training. SFC Parkins (our PSG) didn't really care for this. He wanted to micromanage everything under the sun. Like I said he was a douche bag, but that is alright since he was about to get his.

We would end up road marching eighty plus miles in the next three weeks, but the first day we knocked out five miles to the first range. I don't mind ruck marching, but once you get down to a certain temperature (Germany was 34 degrees that morning) it becomes a pain once you stop. You're covered in sweat, and once the march is over, you start to freeze like a witch's tit. Bringing a fresh shirt and socks to change into is a must! This range wasn't for Weapons Squad, so why did we come you ask? Like I said, t'was the douche baggery. My squad watched for the next two days as the line squads qualified and did live fires. If you have ever been in the Armed Forces, then you know that sometimes, a lot of times, you do things that just do not make sense. You learn to accept it.

Picking up from this range, we went back to refit. Refitting is basically cleaning, fixing, or replacing gear/weapons, and washing clothes as well as yourself. My squad was finally going to get some training. The next morning we set off for range #314, re-sighted our weapons, and shot most of the day. It was a sunny day; the air was a cold and crisp, filled with smell of gun-powder and now Schnitzel. There is a guy on Graf that drives around a yellow van and grills Schnitzel, bakes pastries, and hands out your favorite cold drinks. It seemed that anything you ordered was $7... Nazi.

In the showers that night, with naked dudes all around, I decided to throw out my gayest voice possible. Some soldiers were looking at me in fear, others anger but when I slapped Maddalone's wet ass and caused a ruckus people began to leave...when you're surrounded by dudes and you're masquerading a homosexual, that's when shit begins to get real. SSG Manuma couldn't help himself, "Holder you're a fool." as he is dying laughing. I had to spice up this trip; it was just too dull around here. Hey, acting gay and actually grabbing cock on a she-male is two different things!

A day after another re-fit, weapons squad set out for the MGLC. There were barracks spread out all over Graf, so we didn't have to come back and forth every night. If there weren't any barracks, we would set up a small round tent that we called a circus tent, and we'd sleep there. Of course weapons guard was involved every night, so the shifts would be split up. The first day of the 2nd MGLC, we worked on crew drills. I now had a new AG, Specialist Snyder. He was a tall lanky Californian who liked to complain. We also had been issued new tri-pods. Instead of the old fixed tri-pods that we had previously used, the new ones were made of lighter Titanium, and they also were collapsible. Now the AG carried the tri-pod and extra rounds, and the AB only carried rounds. Naturally they both carried their own M4s as well. I still carried the M240, but now I carried about 200 rounds. We carried about 1,000 rds. altogether. A heavy load, 100 linked rounds of 7.62 weighs approximately sixteen pounds. The M240B weighs twenty-eight pounds, and the tri-pod with bag weighs twenty pounds. So once you add up the gun, 200rds, water, extra stuff in an assault pack, and my body armor and body weight; I was easily looking at carrying a 300-pound load! That was like carrying SSG Manuma on my back, the fruit eating Samoan! I would find out soon that it wasn't going to be too easy at 12,000ft in Afghanistan, but for now, it was a new experience.

The clouds came in low and slow. The temperature dropped to a freezing 20 degrees, the wind picked up; and it began to snow. The veterans that fought through Germany in WWII have my utmost respect for fighting in that kind of weather. I can't imagine taking up residence in fox hole with little or no winter clothing, just awaiting the next big push into Nazi-occupied territory. Once it started snowing, it didn't stop. The ranges were shut down and the playing cards came out. Soldiers who had nothing to shoot at started getting creative with their down time. We built a huge snow man, which was armed with an M-4 and a broom handle as a massive snowman erection.

Arduous snowball battles were fought throughout the cold, barren fields of Germany by our rivaling companies. Bloody noses, black eyes, and jammed fingers were beginning to pile up when the leadership cancelled the rest of the MGLC and bused us back to the main barracks. Good thing that happened when it did because I fear multiple barbarian tribes were about to clash with primitive weapons in hand!

Upon arriving early back to barracks, the rifle squads were still out in the field, no doubt holding each other close for warmth like the pole smokers they were. We would have the barracks to ourselves, or so we thought. I opened the door, and low and behold, who is trying to pull up his pants quickly; dropping the nudie magazine to the floor...SFC Parkins...our fearless Platoon Sergeant...BUSTED! "Wha...what...what are you doing here Weapons Squad?" his shaky voice not doing well to hide his naughtiness. "Well what are YOU doing SFC Parkins?" I said in return. This of course gets the rest of the squad laughing as they are coming in behind me.

The accused makes no attempt to push the magazine under the bed, which belonged to Maddalone, as he was sitting on Maddalone's bunk when we walked in...yikes. He picks it up, and walks out, no doubt going to fulfill his manly desires elsewhere. After we discussed what we just witnessed, we found out that SFC Parkins had been relieved of his PSG position, due to the 1SG getting tired of his douche baggery...victory is ours! After we racked out, worn out from the intense snowball wars, the douche bag attempts to slide the magazine back under Maddalone's things hidden by the cover of darkness. He thought he was sly.

The last week went by pretty quickly. Without a PSG, SSG Carlson stepped in and took over 3rd PLT. Everyone liked him; as I said before, he was an easy going guy and made decisions that made sense. We did one Platoon movement, which gave me a chance to let the rest of 3rd PLT in on what I had stumbled upon, and of course they found this to be quite humorous. Re-packing the containers and loading up the buses, we were on our way back to Italy. This time on the way back, we would make two stops. The first was the concentration camp of Dachau, and then the Hofbourgh House in Munich, as well as a tour of what Nazi Munich was like...the birth place of the National Socialist Party.

The day was cold and windy when pulled up to Dachau, I have always wanted to visit a camp, especially on this type of day, to try and see how it would have been. As expected, it could not compare without the soldiers, dogs, loud speakers, lack of food, and experiments; but it's the closest I could get. Hampton was part Jewish, so he wanted me to take pictures of him everywhere, "This is one Jew they didn't get!" he would say...I know he's warped. We spent a couple of hours there and were free to explore the site, which still housed the ovens, barracks, jail, and now a museum to see different artifacts uncovered once the camp was liberated. Visiting a concentration camp is another thing I would recommend to anyone.

Leaving Dachau, we made our way into Munich. The tour was very educational and hit on all of the major buildings and sites where Hitler or his counterparts started the Nazi party. After that is when things started to get wild. Our whole battalion (Approximately 720 Paratroopers) was now in Munich. All of us had been alcohol deprived for the past three weeks. We were let loose in this square where the famous Hofbourgh House sat; nearby was also a Hard Rock Café and multiple bars. The two beer limit was eclipsed giving that the beers at the Hofbourgh House were a liter each of 9% German brewed goodness!

I met up with my Bravo Co. crew, and we shared two of these beers and recanted tales of our different Graf experiences. Of course I had seen Bruder and Lowell quite a bit since they were now on the same gun crew. After we were finished with our sweet nectar, we made our way across the street, which was now filled with loud and drunken Americans, into the Hard Rock Café. It was time for shots all around. I asked the smoking hot Aryan bartender for ten Jagerbombs, and she looked at me like I just saluted Hitler.

"What is this Jaeger bomb?" she asked. Of course I thought this was some Nazi trickery she was trying sprinkle on me. "Are you kidding me, this is the home of Jaeger and you do not know what a Jaeger bomb is?" Clark was beside me already stroking an empty shot glass, no telling what demented thoughts were going through his head. "No, I do not know this Jaeger bomb, please tell me." She said in the hottest Nazi accent. Humoring our host, Clark and I explained the Jaeger bomb, which I knew then was another concoction of the Americans...do we make everything better or what?

Who turned around in his bar stool, alone, wanting to pick up the tab for the fresh shots we just ordered? Ole SFC Parkins...drunk, wanting to make amends for his constant four months of douche baggery. Of course I oblige him and allow his credit to be built upon by the buying of our shots; I gave him the "it's all good" speech and went along with my real friends. Things were beginning to get rowdy in the Hard Rock. Lt. Israel rolls over to my group with two beers in his hands and hands one to me. "Boy, don't you know you're under age?" He says with that good ole boy smile on his face. He sat there and talked with us for a while, and then we started getting into it over SEC football, which lead to the others getting into it over their preferred football conference, which lead to two SEC fans teaming up on them. It was a blast needless to say, but the blast was about to end.

Recalling everybody in the square was quite a task. The over indulgers were starting to throw up and fight with each other, or fight local Nazis. This mob of over 720 people could no doubt turn into a riot, which I thought it was headed that way for sure. Clark was getting me pumped up for a good street fight, as he and had been in multiple riots in Seattle. Unfortunately, the leadership had somewhat gotten us under control, and we had to walk about half a mile to the buses. What a poor choice to march a battalion of drunks, who had just finished getting jacked on three weeks of adrenaline, through Hitler's streets. Flashing blue lights began to appear, just to make sure the Americans didn't try to retake the city. We've been known to do that from time to time.

Windows were open with Nazis yelling at us, and of course we were yelling back. Scuffles between soldiers who were getting on each other's last nerves were frequent. Someone pushed Lt. Israel, and he turned into an Alabama country boy real quick. I had to piss on a wall; it's just something I do. People would stop off in bars along the way and take a few shots, by the time the end of the march caught up to you; you could just fall in the rear. It was glorious chaos!

Making it to the buses finally, with cops' cars everywhere, we loaded up and tried to get out of the city, but 720 people require a lot of transportation. One SSG in 3rd PLT got up from his seat, half asleep and drunk, whipped out his wang and started pissing on the paratroopers behind him! The guy he was pissing on slapped the offender's dick, and this brought the SSG to his knees and made him throw up as well. His throwing up sparked off chain reaction. With the smell and sounds of his vomit hitting the already hot, drunken air of the bus, people began grabbing trash bags and up chucking themselves. I thought this was hilarious! The buses stopped so people could get out and piss, while others ran to the nearby corn field and tossed up gallons of booze all over some poor farmer's crop…no doubt he lost a whole row of produce!

Making it through the gates of Camp Ederle, 3rd PLT met its new PSG, who I had actually come across when I in-processed in June. His name was SFC Adams. He was also a Georgia native who hailed from Dahlonega. He was a Ranger instructor at 2nd Ranger Training Battalion before coming here to Italy. It was about 3 a.m., so he introduced himself briefly, and we were out of there. Some went to get more booze, others went to be with be their families, but most went to go find a pair of loving arms at the Jolly Hotel. I, on the other hand, took my tired tail to bed.

It was now November, and Italy was going to get rained on for the next few days, which didn't bother me one bit. I love the rain, much better than dealing with snow. P.T. formation in the morning was brief due to the rain; who wants to run around in the dampness? The upcoming weekend was also going to be somewhat different. Bruder, Clark, and about 200 more paratroopers were going to run a marathon in Florence. Lowell and I were going to hold it down back in Vicenza; Bickford was now a part of our group. He finally decided to get off his bed and turn the DVD player off.

The shipping containers had yet to arrive from Germany. We spent most of the week cleaning weapons and gear that got messed up in Graf. Reset days are always the easiest. Thursday went by without a hitch, and since the marathon runners would be leaving Friday morning, they gave everyone Friday off. SFC Adams was adjusting well, or I should say we were trying to adjust to him! He was an in your face leader, who always paid attention to detail. Being from the 2nd Ranger Battalion, he didn't take shit from any man. He also didn't bring his family with him overseas, so he had no personal life.

A lot of times he would sleep in his office on a cot and shower there as well. Of course he did have a house off-post, but I guess he figured no one was there, so why should he be? Many a time we would stay late, say until around 8 p.m., simply because he had nothing to do. For now though, we were all getting to know the man, myth, and legend that would become SFC Adams.

The safety brief on Thursday afternoon couldn't come a minute to soon, which now included a lesson on checking to see if your hooker was actually indeed a woman! Since the runners of the group, were going to be leaving the next morning, and did not need to drink before a marathon; we took it easy that night. Friday it was on though! Lowell and I started drinking at noon that November day. He had a case of Bud Light, and I had one of Coors Light. The next weekend I would be out of commission due to getting a wisdom tooth removed, but not today.

We threw the football in the parking lot, and we frequently hit Bruder's car on "accident." He had bought a tan Mercedes for $500 from a friend and had already allowed it to get towed twice. It also had multiple dents in it and the left blinker would not go off once it was on. Needless to say it was a fine piece of Nazi engineering. We were hanging out, getting to know each other, and grilling out. Then we decided to take a walk over the bar on post. Club Veneto or Club V as the paratroopers had dubbed it. Club V had a pair of pool tables in it. Fights would spawn there nightly between fellow infantrymen. Clark and I would hustle many a man in there at a on the pool table.

It was around 5 p.m., which would be happy hour back in the states, but this wasn't exactly your hometown bar. It was slightly crowded due to the long weekend. Lowell and I went in and grabbed a liquor drink, Captain Morgan and Ginger Ale for me. No one we really knew was in there, but as we were leaving, a new guy in my company was talking to this Military Police (MP) officer who happened to be a 5'0ft female. She wasn't exactly on the top of my Privea list, but Clark would have gone home with her. I could see Grassell, who was in my platoon and was a recovering Heroin addict, was getting a little flustered by whatever it was he was getting talked to about at 5:30 in the afternoon by this MP.

No one likes an MP, much less a female MP, and you could clearly see that Grassell had no intention of standing here for much longer. As he was starting to walk away, little Miss MP grabbed his arm and spun him around. This did not go down to well. "Bitch get your hands off me! Don't think you won't get slapped!" Grassell yelled as he was turning. MP chica responded in her best police woman's voice, "Soldier I'm not going to ask you again to stand here peaceably. I do not want to draw my sidearm on you!"

Lowell and I turned and looked at each other, watching this priceless entertainment unfold before our eyes. Good thing we were smoking a pork loin and it had a few more minutes! "Draw that shit then bitch!" Grassell said in return. With that Ms. MP drew her 9mm side arm, what she failed to realize is that Grassell was quicker than her and had been training with this very weapon for the past three weeks in Graf. Before Ms. MP could have the weapon raised, Grassell had taken it out of her hands, dropped the magazine, ejected the loaded round, and slipped off the slide which housed the barrel and everything needed to allow the weapon to work. I thought I had just taken the pill and was inside of the Matrix.

"What you got now bitch!" Grassell yelled with laughter as he threw the gun pieces in the bushes and took off. Lowell and I looked at each other again, this time dying with laughter! The antics we had just witnessed were too much and it wasn't even dark yet! Ms. MP called for backup on her radio, and Grassell would not get very far. As I said before Camp Ederle wasn't a huge place; it could fit in most mall parking lots. The priceless look on her face though was worth every bit of it Grassell would later say Although he got his rank taken away, she would not be working the bar any longer.

Walking back the 100m to Lowell's room, we took the meat off the grill and made some fresh pork loin sandwiches as we talked out what we had just seen. The other guys were not going to believe this! We were now about twelve into our twenty-four packs, plus the few liquor drinks we had before the recent hilarity ensued. Lowell had broken out the camera and was leaving Clark a message as he sat naked on Clark's bed. Clark had found this stuffed animal somewhere; we called it Gertrude, and Lowell naturally was making a porno with this poor stuffed animal, so Clark could witness the heinous acts when he returned on Sunday. Yep, it was just a typical Saturday night for us.

After a few hours had gone by, we had finished about eighteen out of our twenty-four packs; Lowell decided to jump in the shower. Actually it was more like lay in the shower. After a certain amount of alcohol, Lowell would lay with his feet upon the wall in his stand up shower and sing whatever song was on the radio with all of his might. It was his time of refreshment. Afterwards he would get up as if nothing ever happened. At first this came across to me as pretty strange, but by then it was just Lowell; who also took the name Steak after a certain amount of booze.

When the stroke of midnight hit, we had finished our twenty-four packs...a case down! That was the first time I had drunk a case of beer in my life. What a milestone, one that would kill some people. We were still fresh however, and it was time to head out to paint the town! After I jumped in the shower, standing up like most people, we called our faithful cab driver Johnny up. We decided on Blue, another strip joint, but this one happened to be two stories. Blue had a nice basement bar, which was usually less crowded, although still full of half-naked European harlots... yummy.

Walking up the stairs, you could already smell the smoke from fog machines, as well as heavenly perfume. The beat rose in your chest as you opened the door, a firework display of colors shattering your vision. Since the club had just opened, all of the girls were on the stage, kind of like meat for sell. Lowell and I headed straight for the shiny glass bar. Upon entry you always got one free drink. The big drink in Europe was Peach Vodka and Red Bull, but I usually switched to the Four Roses Bourbon. Tonight it was going to be Tanqueray Gin and Tonic, in honor of Snoop Dogg.

We took a seat to the right of the stage, which was adjacent to the DJ booth. Lowell was already requesting Bob Sinclair's "World Hold On", while I was checking out the scenery...and making sure I didn't see a Johnson under any of the G-strings. Now you could point out a girl if you desired to have her for the evening or if you just wanted a taste; otherwise they would come to you. If you bought them a drink they would stay, if you didn't then they would leave. It was a pretty simple game really. Sometimes you just could not say no to some of the stunning women that would sit in front of you. At least 75% of them could easily be Maxim material.

A Pamela Anderson look-a-like had come and snuggled up next to Lowell, and my, was he digging her. I wasn't trying to have just anyone

49

come and sit beside me, so I met the eyes of Mila Kunis's identical twin on stage and called her over. We all four talked like we had known each other for years. Drinks. Shots. More drinks. More shots. After I entered the Privea with "Mila," I got her to let me take a line of blow off her amazing ass, which was way better than having weirdo Rex staring at me! Yes, ladies and gentlemen, I had just reached rock star status. Lowell had also made a move and was downstairs with his "Pamela" and for some reason he was yelling my name. I ignored him. Now I know what you're thinking, once again I have mentioned doing cocaine. Aren't you in the Army? Weren't you afraid of getting caught? The truth is no, we weren't. We felt untouchable, like we were living a rock star's life without any of the work. Being single in Europe was no joke. You were surrounded by different countries, which contained different food, beer, and girls. We had no bills, and travel was easy. To add to that, we were all young and dumb; consequently, tomorrow didn't matter. Today was what counted.

"Mila" and I had a great time. She loved my Southern accent, and I was digging her Eastern European dialect. She wanted to give me a sexy show, but all I wanted was to enjoy the company of this bombshell. Most of the strippers spoke decent English, but her vernacular was broken at best. I didn't mind it though because it left room for the imagination. Unlike the other club Kiss, no one came and got you when your time was up, instead a little blue light would flicker on the wall which was synced to the beat of the music. Either you paid for more private time, or you went your separate ways. I had bought thirty minutes, so I figured Lowell was either already dead or had found his was to their shower to lie down in. You best believe I got another fresh line off her tight tan tummy before exiting the compartment.

After collecting myself and stopping by the restroom to make sure I hadn't wasted any white residue on the outside of my nose, I went over to the bar downstairs and found Lowell talking to another girl; it was now 2:30 a.m., which would be late in the States, but most of the clubs here did not close until 6 a.m. or later. Lowell had not partaken in a pick-me-up like I had but was adding to the twenty-four pack foundation with more drinks and shots. I made the call to get us out of there due to the fact Lowell was again talking about naked time in the shower. I didn't want him to give off the impression we were the kind of guys who, you know, Didn't Ask and Didn't Tell.

The week before Thanksgiving of 2006, I had elected to have one of my wisdom teeth removed. The Army Dentist assured me that this was a must, "although the tooth has yet to break the skin and would not for a year or so, it's best to take it out now, son." So like a good soldier, I heeded Mr. Tooth Cracker's advice. Walking into the dental office that cold November morning, I laid back in the chair; waiting for someone to knock me out for the procedure…no such luck. One of the hygienists waltzes in humming some ridiculous tune, like a serial killer trying to fuck with me. "I'm going to be put to sleep for this tooth excavation right?" I ask, in a matter a fact way. "Oh, no you are mistaken." The somewhat disconcertingly cheery creature responds, "We're just going to numb ya up a bit." Then she flails out of the room, blue dental shirt in tow. *NUMB ME UP A BIT!?* These folks are about to go dumpster diving in my mouth, just to see if that tooth even exists, and they're just going to numb me up a bit!? Her last sentence is still reverberating throughout my mind as the doctor walks in, grabs the first injection, and says, "Open wide, you may feel a pinch." Yeah no shit Sherlock, a shot in the roof of your mouth is more than a pinch!

He finishes with three shots, and lets me know that it will start to work soon. I let him know that those three will not be enough. He says we'll see. *Oh we'll see alright.* Coming back in the Doc gets all of his teeth-cracking tools ready and picks up some gruesomely sharp object while making the comment, "I'm going to make an incision over the site; let me know if you can feel it." *Oh my Lord I'm going to die right here in this chair.* He cuts, and I grasp his arm, "Yes sir I can feel that, I told you that three wouldn't be enough." I can feel and taste my blood, both bitter and metallic. Finally he loads up two more syringes, "This should be enough you horse." he says laughing.

I can no longer feel my face (*now this is more like it*) the procedure begins again. I can still hear and smell, and the stench of burning tooth from the drill is pretty overwhelming. The hygienist's sucker thing keeps slurping up my blood and saliva. The Doc stops drilling, "I think we're going to have to remove a little piece of your jaw; don't worry it will grow back." *Excuse me?* Before I can protest he has some alien apparatus in my mouth, and the pressure I felt is hard to describe even now. Place both your hands on your head, one on either side, squeeze, there you go.

"Ok I can see the tooth, I'm going to grab it with this whatchamacallit and get it out of there. You may feel a crack." Unable to make the slightest protest through all the fluid, he grabs, twists, and my blood covers the lamp above my face with a deep crack. "Wow is that supposed to happen!?" I try to say, while the sucker is having a hay day! "Okay let me stich that up and you can be on your way." *Just like that huh, you use me for some grotesque experiment and then kick me to the curb?* Now I know how the strippers feel.

With the terrible tooth trial complete, I was out of commission for a week, which coincided with Thanksgiving, my favorite holiday. I had little pain considering the removal of half my jaw, just stiffness, along with and the fact I could barely open my mouth. This kept me from the turkey, but not from a straw in a beer. No matter, Christmas was right around the corner and we all were taking fifteen days of leave. I would be headed back to Georgia to see my family and friends. The rest of my group would be headed to their various homes; Clark's mother had now moved to Valdosta, which promised some entertainment. Sadly, Kevin and hookers were not readily available at my parent's house…sir, it just wasn't possible.

CHAPTER SEVEN
POKER, TEQUILA, AND
THINGS THAT GO BOOM

RETURNING FROM MY UNEVENTFUL trip home, I touched down once again at Marco Polo International and was delighted not to see Chatty Cathy waiting for me. I did run in to Bickford and Archie leaving the baggage claim. Archie was the newest member of my Italian group of friends; he was also in Bravo Co. (surprise, surprise) and hailed from Las Vegas. We talked about how our different leaves went while we waited on the bus that made the trip to Camp Ederle. Since it was Saturday, I still had two days to get used to the time difference and detox my liver.

We all reported to formation that Monday morning. Everyone that went to the states was dragging their tired bodies. Our Captain, Capt. McCrystal, thought it would be a great idea to go on a company run around the post. Of course we all protested in jest, but it was one of those things to remind you that you are still in the Airborne. After the four mile run, I got news that I would be participating in an Emergency Medical Technician class; oh and by the way if you fail you have to pay the Army back the tuition money. So they're going to make me take a class, which I did not sign up for, and if I fail I have to pay? Does that make sense to anyone?

I went and did the necessary paperwork to take part in the course; Bickford would also be joining me. It was going to be two weeks long, getting me out of foolish details for a full fourteen days, and I would be a certified EMT once I was complete, good stuff. It was starting the following Tuesday, so that meant there was going to be a three day weekend in store for us. The week went relatively quick. Plans were starting to be made about the train up that would take us into the upcoming deployment. Also, ideas were being made about when the Weapons Squads could do another MGLC, this time including heavy weapons, such as the Mark 19 Automatic Grenade Launcher,[28] and the 50.Cal Machine gun[29]. I was looking forward to that next MGLC because I loved firing the MK-19. It made me feel like an artist with deadly tools. Of course before I could do that, I had to finish the EMT course and before that could commence I had to make in through another three day weekend, what a life.

Friday night I was re-introduced to poker. I had not played since Clark and I hung out with Rex and Kevin, and then I was so jacked out of my mind I didn't really recall the object of the game. Clark, Bickford, Bruder, Archie, Lowell, Strandberg, myself, and this talkative son of a bitch named Rotundi, who really never knew what he was talking about, dealt out cards on a pool table. Clark really didn't care for Rotundi and the drunker Clark got the more he and Rotundi would get into it. Rotundi was raised by his single-parent mother, and joined the Army to show her a thing or two. He was a punk basically.

The cards were turning as smoothly as the booze was going down. I was picking up on it some but had to rely on Clark occasionally to tell me what kind of hand I was holding. I praised God when I was out and could simply mix a drink and pick the music. We got on the topic of drugs; all of us except for Rotundi were social drug users, that guy could hardly take a Tylenol. Rotundi makes the comment, trying to fit in, "Hey guys…lets go do some weed." This sets Clark off, who was already losing his money pretty quickly, "You DON"T DO weed man…you SMOKE it. If you hadn't been sucking on your mom's tits until you were eighteen, you would know a thing or two about Ganja."

This sent us into an uproar. Rotundi didn't have anything to say back as he usually didn't when one of us knew his chosen topic better than he did. With that Clark was out of cash, so he and I strolled over to Club V to hustle someone in pool real quick to get some club change. Our strategy was pretty simple. We would find someone playing doubles. Clark would size them up. We would then play beside them; of course they would be watching us play. Clark was more skilled in pool than I was, so I would play as usual, and he would play unenthusiastically when he knew the targets would be inspecting us. We would then ask the other team if they

---

28 **MK-19**—Mark-19, a belt fed, fully automatic grenade launcher
29 **.50 Cal**—.50 Caliber fully automatic machine gun

wanted to put some cash down for a round, say twenty bucks a round. I'd lead, make what I could make; then Clark would come in behind me and make the rest. Easy business, the funny thing was no one ever caught on to or scheme…drunken paratroopers. That night we played four rounds and ended up making about $50. That would cover a round trip cab ride easy.

Walking back to Clark's room, we found Lowell upside down in the shower as usual. He was "preparing his mind for an evening of entertainment." This time we broke out the camera and caught this ritual on film, much to Lowell's chagrin. While everyone was showering and getting ready, I was playing DJ as I did most of the time. Lowell decided it was time to sing O.A.R.'s "Revolution" word for word. Bickford also captured this on film. Saturday was going to be a recovery day due to the fact the NFL showed late on Sunday (since Italy is six hours ahead of Eastern time the games are shown around 2a.m. Monday mornings), so that would be the next drinking night. Tonight it was on.

Route 66 was first on the list; this was a sort of cowboy bar right next to Exstatia. Italians may not like us being in their country, but they loved the American West and Hip Hop cultures. We got a few drinks in there, as Clark failed (as usual) at singing Karaoke. His rancid display of "Thunder Struck" sent most of us over to Exstatia. He soon would be on his knees begging the girls please. The music was booming, and the girls were happy to see the regulars. Bruder always got this girl named Gulia, pronounced Julia, but she liked the G for some reason. We took the big circular maroon booth by the DJ.

It was around 1 a.m. when we hit the booth; Rotundi was out cold as soon as he sat down. He would pass out early, or he would get some kind of reaction to booze making his face red, then the Benadryl would pass him out. What a fucking light-weight. Lowell was in rare form, buying shots and talking to every person in the joint. Bickford and Archie were in the smoking room with their women of choice; I was having a good time just chilling and watching the stage show. They had this show were the chick would come out and dance slow then speed it up, while she literally lit the stage on fire. She was then joined by a friend and they participated in questionable actions and lesbian adventures.

I decided to walk back into the Privea. This was strictly forbidden unless you paid, but there was no guard at the front. What were they going to do? Throw me out? I stumbled on to Clark's chamber; he saw me and yelled at me to pull him out because she was draining all of his money.

"You're a big boy Clark, get out of there yourself." I replied. He was still yelling my name as I ducked into Bruder's cubicle and held Julia with a G's mouth so she would not cause a ruckus until the attendant passed. Boy she DID NOT like that, but Bruder thought it was hilarious. "Do you like causing a stir at these places?" he asked. "It's just something I do," I replied as I slipped out, and she went off in her native tongue.

Archie, Bickford, and Lowell were at the bar where they had a shot waiting for me; Rotundi was still catching flies in the booth. We slammed the shots, and Lowell turned to me and said, "Let's get up there and strip!" I followed him as we slid under the railing, without really thinking about it. We got up and started moving our bodies to the beating house music with the kaleidoscope lights flashing in our faces. He swung around on the pole and I caught his hands, dragging his heavy ass body up to me. Now the owners seemed not to like this, but all of the other soldiers in there were going nuts. Camera flashes add into the mix of already blinding lights. Our shirts came off, now we looked like two Chippendale dancers. Lowell took another swing on the pole and it broke out of the ceiling. Whoops, time to go! The Romans made buildings that are still standing today, but these guys couldn't make a simple pole?

We re-shirted, leaving Rotundi and Clark to their own devices and did not bother to pay our tabs. Bruder was stumbling out and saw what had happened. Lowell, Archie, Bickford, Bruder, and I all went down the stairs like we were exiting an aircraft. For reasons unknown to man, Clark had already slipped downstairs, and I saw his boney fist connect with an Italian's face...oh yes! The Italian fell backward opening the door with him, we all jumped over his body. Only five people could fit into Johnny's cab, so I started running. The way home was well- known since we rucked marched out here sometimes; it just happened to be six miles away. Guess we can't go back in Exstatia anytime soon!

Bickford and I walked down to the small school house together than cold Tuesday morning. I didn't know much about emergency medicine, I really didn't even know why I was in this class; but I was going to make the best of it. We walked into the class room and saw that our instructor was a happy Hindu. Luckily, he was not complete with a crying baby. The Indian man looked at the room full of paratroopers and said, "Today, we will start with CPR." The Indian man was the EMT instructor, a short brown thing; whose accent was unbearable. He wore round silver spectacles and continuously used his hands to talk. This is something my dad does as well, and for me is comparable to nails on a chalk board. Can you just sit still…PLEASE!? The CPR certification was the first two days of class, so we alternately made out with dummies and crushed their sternums. The Indian man was always saying, "Make sure you secure the seal when giving mouth-to-mouth. All air is precious!" As he was right there in your face like a football coach in your face mask. I found myself constantly asking if I could please save this dummy without his curry spit going everywhere.

Since the EMT course started a day behind schedule, we were going to have a test on Saturday. Um…yea…about that. We informed the instructor that most of us would not end up making it. This upset the Indian man a great deal. "How do you expect to save a life, if you cannot pass the test?" he said in all of his gas station sounding glory. A lot of us did end up skipping that test, but were still allowed to take the practical examination and pass the class.

The ending of EMT class took us into February 2007 and the upcoming MGLC. It was going to be a little south of Vicenza in the small town of Monte Carpenga. I was going on ADVON[30] to help set up, while all other weapons squads would follow in two days. Naturally we were escorted by the Italian Police in their wussy squad cars. It took about three hours to get there, due to the winding in and out of the Italian hills and finding detours because some of our mammoth Army trucks could not make some of the sharp turns. The wussy Italian car escorts felt we were ruining their life with these detours, since there elevator size automobiles could turn on a dime.

As we were arriving in the small Italian army base, the wind had picked up, and to the surprise of the senior leaders in charge of the range the weather was going to be bad all week. As the leaders were trying to figure out who didn't plan for the weather and if they were going to push back the range for another week we stopped unloading and piled back on the buses. The leaders meanwhile walked off to call back to Vicenza to find out what course of action they should take, I mean while got off the bus to look for some water.

The fearless leaders returned and decreed that the range would continue because we were paratroopers damn it! On a side note, we also didn't bring any water or food, as it was coming with the main body. We did bring a cook-just nothing for him to cook. He was fat and obnoxious so I voted we should eat him! Sadly, the others disagreed, and we went hungry. We

---

30 **ADVON**—Advanced Party, personnel that arrive on site of a base ahead of other members of their unit to insure everything is in working properly.

all unloaded in the wind and drizzle then began to unfold the tents. Then we stopped and realized that these tents were new, and no one had put one up before. What could possibly happen next? We did figure it out; pole to hole isn't that hard of a calculation…even for straight guys.

The next day we drove the twenty minutes up to the range. The range was a mountain top more or less, which put everyone right into the elements. It was also the scene of some intense fighting back in WWII. A massive sign that read "live ordnance" was right in front of it. Oh this was going to be a blast. A back-hoe had come and dug up some pits, so we could place these massive pop-up targets into them. First they had to be cleared out, and my…were there a lot of old Nazi and American shells everywhere. To my dismay a young Asian PFC[31] jumps in, grabs an UXO[32] and throws it out of the pit. One of the SSGs yells "Everybody down!" dropping to the earth I followed and some people played copycat but others looked around like mouth-droolers.

The shell hit, and we were still alive. That SSG jumped and grabbed PFC Atomic Bomb and drug him down to the ENORMOUS sign that read "UXO's Present ENTER AT YOUR OWN RISK!" Obviously they didn't teach English in shipping containers. I didn't see PFC Atomic Bomb after that. We did get the job done. The targets were in, and the range boundaries were set up. I figure that the leadership either didn't know we would be firing on an unstable field when they planned this excursion, or they didn't care since we were shooting explosive projectiles ourselves. After all, what's the harm in a few secondary explosions?

The rest of the Weapons Squads descended upon the small Italian base like locusts the next morning. Thank God they remembered to bring food and water. It had cleared up somewhat, and the breeze was bringing in the smell of morning pastries that were baking in the Italian village down in the valley. I was stuck with an MRE, oh yeah! We wasted no time that day. After the other companies had settled into their tents, the ranges commenced. The concussive boom of grenades and the tak-tak-tak of 50. Cal's reverberated off the mountain top, no doubt throwing the villagers into flashbacks of World War Two fighting. I personally like the MK-19 better than the 50.Cal. I never miss with that thing. It is great listening to

31 **PFC**—Private First Class, the rank given to soldiers after at least one year in the United States Army
32 **UXO**—Unexploded Ordinance, projectiles or mines that have been fired but did not detonate

the ding, ding, ding and then watching your rounds fly out, only to see your target disintegrate under six or seven grenades. What a blast!

After a day of firing, learning how to take apart, and putting together the heavy weapons, we called it quits. The rain had rolled back in and everyone was more than enthusiastic to get off of the wind-raped mountain top. My black sleeping bag was deliciously warm! The next day Maddalone, Arruda, and I had to help the cooks in the kitchen. We reported around 4 a.m. and helped the cooks get ready for breakfast. Powdered eggs and frozen breakfast business isn't that difficult to make believe it or not. Why they needed our help I still do not know. The paratroopers came through, bitched as usual about the breakfast, and of course gave us shit because we were on kitchen duty. The joke was on them as it was now pouring outside and we would be in the warmth all day.

There was going to be a dinner served as well so we cleaned up after breakfast and helped the cooks separate various food groups. After that I got my hands wet with some dishes, then tried to cut open a box with a sharp Michael Myers knife, but I made the mistake of bringing the blade towards myself. Yea, yea I know: never cut towards you. Well, I know now. The knife slipped through the cardboard and right into my left index finger's knuckle, where it came to rest.

I pulled the knife from my split knuckle, which was starting to look like something from the scene of a Helter-skelter type massacre. I walked out of the dish room and took a right into the dining room where the hot bar lay. The head fat ass cook saw the trail of blood I was leaving and freaked out, "Oh my God have you been stabbed!" "Well not really, I just kind of sliced myself." I said, trying to stuff something into my knuckle. He grabbed a rag, which after I had wrapped it around my hand realized was not sanitary, so there's no telling what kind of food or cleaner I put into my body. I walked over the Aid Station and showed the medic my wound and he laughed; finally, someone who doesn't mind a little blood, or a lot.

He made the obvious comment that I would need some stiches, which were my first. Yeah I didn't get any when Xavier almost murdered me, as they just packed some gauze in that long ago wound. The Doc filled my knuckle with some type of cleaner than fizzed up like a science project and then neglected to tell me his next move was some straight alcohol…shit that stung! After that he used a quick clot solution to stop the bleeding. He shot up the knuckle with an anesthetic and slid the first needle through then all of a sudden, he apparently forgot how to stitch someone up and looked up at me asking, "What am I doing again?" "Mmmm…why are you asking me man? You're the medic" I replied, not really trusting this guy any longer. Obviously this guy had been participating in the same extra-curricular activities as I had, which is something doctors shouldn't do if they want to recall the BASICS of medicine.

As if God reached down and smacked the vacant mind, the Doc all of sudden began his work. He worked his thread like a veteran seamstress, interweaving seven stitches in my swollen knuckle. I can still see the one inch scar today, one flat knuckle out of nine. After I was mended, I returned to the chow hall where Arruda and Maddalone were helping the McFatsters with dinner. It was going to be a night of canned corn, canned green beans, pre-packaged salad, bread loaves, plus pre-made teriyaki chicken stir-fry. Much like Paula Dean I spiced everything up with butter, maybe a few stitches to here and there.

The next day was much like the first day of the range. We ended up running out of ammunition for both weapon systems, so we cleaned upped and made our way back to camp to clean all of the weapons. All of us smoked and joked until chow time and ate like kings to get rid of all of the extra food. Even the Italians joined us that night; not that we could understand half of them. The next morning, Friday, we packed up, cleaned up, and hit the road towards Vicenza. Another range down, Graf coming up in March…but before all of that…another weekend was upon us for the taking.

Chapter Eight
Final Preparations

I SHIT MYSELF. I walked out of Club V before Lowell did and decided to take a leak behind a dumpster, before we exited post for the night. I unzipped my fly, like any other time, whipped out the Johnson, and forced a little too hard. My jeans instantaneously fill with a massive steaming pile of shit! It started running down the inside my legs before I could finish my piss. I stood there, evaluating if this indeed just happened before making the executive decision to shower and change. I did my best to waddle to my room, trying not to give myself diaper rash. Luckily my roommate was not home to witness the aftermath of my feeble sphincter

I met the guys at the gate and explained what had happened. This of course brought howls of laughter and I was laughing too. This was a good start to a good night that would be one of the last we all had together. With Graf coming up, which would be a little over a month, plus predeployment leave after that, weekends in Italy would soon be a thing of the past. This Friday night we didn't make it to any clubs. Instead we hung out downtown with the natives. There was a bar that was going out of business after the weekend. Although we called it The Luxury Bar, we didn't have a clue as to its real name. Since most of the booze was half price we started to drink them out of house and home.

Another guy had joined our ranks, Gordon. He was a part of Delta Co. and in one of their Weapons Squads, and so we all knew him pretty well. Now our group had gone from four since arriving in Italy to eight, Bruder, Lowell, Clark, Archie, Bickford, Strandberg, Gordon, Rotundi, and I. Things were good. We were all single except for Strandberg, and we all had similar outlooks on life. That's if you call illegal activities and spanking strippers an outlook.

61

The night went well. There were drinks, laughs, failed attempts at taming the natives, and of course, more booze. Then the rain began to fall. I was down stairs in The Luxury Bar taking a piss (and trying not to shit myself again) when I heard the thunder. I went upstairs expecting to find everyone waiting on a cab, but instead I found no one. HA, they had left me. Sluts. I have to say I was pretty drunk, and it was about 2 a.m. Furthermore it was now raining. Well, I went into the stairs of this apartment building and was going to pass out right there. It was warm, and was out of the rain; I would walk back to post when the rain slacked up or in the morning. No biggee.

The entry door opened and a waitress from The Luxury Bar walked in, looked at me and smiled. "Cold?" she said, with her best English. "Yeah I am. I'm going to chill here until the rain stops." As I pointed out and made the universal rain sign with my finger and arm coming down. She got the drift, grabbed my arm and brought me to her place. Now my mind was full of ideas. The door opened and I was hit by a wave of Hash smoke. The room was full of people, hash, blow, booze, and a crazy looking Tabby cat in the corner eyeing me down. Well now this could be promising. The thought of trying Hash crossed my mind, but if that wasn't going to happen, I was certainly going to toss that cat out of a window if it kept eyeing me.

The waitress vanishes, as a Beck's beer is placed in my hand and I am seated by the door at a table where at least half a brick of cocaine is piled up in the middle. Kevin, oh how I've missed you! The three Italians at the end of the table are passing some Hash back and forth; the guy to my immediate left sitting against the wall had the dumbest grin on his face I had ever seen. "Welcome my friend, excuse me I am so drunk, I do not remember your name. All is for you, take what you want," The grinning idiot said. "Well I don't think we have met. I'm Jesse...and do you mind if I steal a line?"

I sat there for a good hour, participating in the fun. The loft apartment had even more people in it now, its brick walls trapping in the heat of the crowd like an Italian pizza oven. The grinning village idiot kept talking to me about Communism, and then offered me a room at his apartment upstairs. This I thought would not be possible. I told the Grinner that I had to call someone and would be back. I slipped out of the apartment, jacked as ever, walked down the stairs, and into the rain.

I saw a few bicycles parked on the sides of the buildings...locked... locked...found one. So I stole a bike. I was living in a video game of my creation-Grand Theft Bicycle, complete with cocaine and the occasional whore. I pedaled back to the gates of Camp Ederle and who do I see GETTING OUT OF CAB when I arrive? Clark and Bruder...dry as the desert sand. I stood up on the bike and swung my right leg over to the left side and jump onto Clark as I rode by! He never saw it coming. Bruder leapt back and realized it was me and took off into the gate, leaving Clark yelling for his help!

As we were walking back to our barracks, Bruder tells me of a fight near Art Café that night. It was two Weapon Squad SGTs from my Charlie Co. versus eight Moroccans. Moroccans were flooding Italy because of the free health care. The Moroccans had a few weapons which included a Samurai sword, bat, and some numb-chucks. I didn't realize Moroccans were skilled in the order of the ninja. The two paratroopers put five of the eight in the hospital, despite sustaining wounds from being sliced by a sword and hit with a bat. I think that shows American military superiority, at least against Moroccan ninjas.

The following night started much like the previous. We all went down town to The Luxury Bar to get cheap booze. I was first to walk in, and who's sitting at the counter? The Grinner, he watched me stroll in with a crew tonight. "Oh Jesse, you forgot to say bye last night." Everyone is looking at me now with a "what the hell is this about" kind of look. I guess it slipped my mind to tell them of my own adventure. So I tell them while we were sipping the first round of beverages, and then Gordon and I get up to go see what the Grinner was up to.

The Grinner's mood has changed now. He turns to us, "You mustn't be seen with me, Jesse. It will be trouble for you...both of you, for I am a Communist Spy." Gordon and I look at each other. Did he really just say that? "You're a what? There aren't any Communist countries in Europe anymore," I said, Gordon confirming with a nod of the head. "You should go Jesse, you should say bye now." "Hey man what you do in your own time is fine. We're just trying to buy you a drink tonight." Gordon says in a matter-a-fact tone, I can't but help laugh at this conversation that's actually going on.

The Grinner, turning in his bar stool to face the bar, takes a drink of his Vodka on the rocks, and says with finality, "Spy." Gordon and I just walked back towards our table, making sure we heard the same things. I have to say, I didn't know spies gave their cover away like that, no wonder Russia is no longer a super power. Everyone took a vote to move this party to the dreaded Exstatia. It had changed owners, so we figured we would be good, they wouldn't know about the pole breaking or the unpaid tabs or the mass exodus…hopefully.

Just six of us strolled in since we left Rotundi downtown, and Strandberg was fighting with his wife on the phone back on post as usual. Guns from under the bar didn't come out as we took our usual seat by the DJ booth, so everything must be good. It was almost midnight. The stage would be lit on fire soon by one show or another. The waitress came to take our drink order, and Bruder fell in love instantly. Stripper turned waitress, he could deal with that. As she came back he spoke to her. Surprisingly her English was pretty good, and that only deepened his desire. He found his project for the night. Since Julia with a G no longer worked in Exstatia.

Clark had disappeared into the Privea so I walked into the foggy smoke room, stole one of Bickford's Camels, and talked with one of the guys from my C-Co. His name was Swinehart, he was in my platoon, and Maddalone was also here with him. I was informed that these two had been coming here every night for a week. Maddalone was a man whore, while Swinehart just liked staying drunk. I walked out and took a right towards the Privea to see if I could sneak my way back there. Oh yea…no lady taking the Privea cash. I slipped to the back and walked into Clark's usual stall, where I got an eye full of his cock being worked on by this stripper, who happened to be named "Georgia."

Clark begins his introductions, "Holder, this is Georgia. Holder is actually from Georgia in the States. See we all have something in common. Holder would you like Georgia to service you next? I think I'm going to take her back to the barracks tonight." I respond "Nah, I'm good man; I just wanted to check out the scenery. Does she have any Kevin?" Clark said, "I will let you know when she as finished her duties," as I slipped out. Little did I know Georgia was going to be a mess…literally. I moved back up front, the time was about 2:30 a.m., and everyone was getting pretty drunk. Gordon said he had run up a significantly large tab and didn't feel like paying for it. We all decided to go get some Kebabs and call it a night, or so I thought.

While Bickford, Archie, and Bruder were paying, Gordon and I went to use the pisser. Gordon claimed the real toilet, so I was stuck with the hole in the ground with porcelain over it. Damn it! I had to take a massive dump since the cigarettes had loosened up my bowels. I hunched over the hole and hear Swinehart come in and try the door. "I'm in here man, Gordon is almost done though." I called out. Come to think of it, why wasn't Gordon pissing? I hear an "OH FUCK!" followed by a crash and me being startled as my legs began slipping out from under me; which sends my head back onto the porcelain nearly into fecal matter. I then hear a bottle hit against the mirror in front of the sinks. What THE HELL just happened!?

I yank up my pants and open the door. Gordon is getting up, and I look into the stall. The roof is gone and half of the toilet is broken. "I was trying to climb out man; I didn't want to pay my tab." Gordon says laughing. Swinehart is standing there with glass all around him laughing as well. "Why'd you break the mirror crazy?" I said, laughing now; thinking about the monkey butt I'm going to get if I don't get home soon, and how the hell we were going to get out of here. "Shoot I don't know why I did that. I heard a ruckus so jumped back and added to it I guess." This would only make sense to a drunk.

"Okay," I said, "Here's what we're going to do. There is a door in the stripper's locker room, but we have to run through the Privea to get to it. Once we start we can't stop, every man for himself. Bruder has our cab Gordon. Swinehart you're on your own. Ready?" Just then the door flew open and the owner saw the mess and went off in his terrible Italian tongue. "GO!" I yelled, as Swinehart threw the owner into a huge fountain by the Privea cashier. We went through the Privea and into the locker room. For good measure I smacked a stripper's ass while she was bending over, causing her to rise up and turn around.

This started a commotion, but I was already out of the door. I could hear the security behind us now, almost catching up to Swinehart. He threw the girl around into the guard, and they tumbled over a wooden bench. We all made it out of the door and to the cab, where Gordon and I squeezed in and Swinehart leaped into the trunk that Johnny had opened while he was re-arranging something. This seemed to surprise Johnny, "GO JOHNNY, GO" I yelled, while everyone wandered what was going on. And oh my God, there was Georgia up front with Clark. "GO!" Johnny hit the gas; I could hear Swinehart yelling in the trunk. What a way to break in some new owners!

We made it to post, Gordon and I explained the bathroom ordeal to Bruder and Clark as we were walking to the barracks; Georgia was still in tow. Clark had scored us a gram of Kevin from Georgia's employer. We took it back to his room where we all hit a line, and Clark took Georgia into the bathroom. After a second I hear, "Oh fuck no! Clean that shit up bitch!" The door opened and Georgia stood their naked with a priceless look of embarrassment on her face while Clark was yelling at her from the shower. Turns out that after Clark was done banging Georgia, he pulled out and she shit everywhere. God it stunk. Bathrooms had some weird shit happen in them that night.

We arrived in Graf with snow still on the ground. It was March 3rd 2007, and it was promised to snow some more before we left in early April. The bus ride was long as usual-this time only 1st Battalion came, since 2nd Battalion was deploying a little later then we were. The shipping containers had already arrived, and equipment would be unloaded tomorrow. We would stay two weeks here in Graf, then move a few miles North to Hoenfels training center. Hoenfels is where we would do a mock deployment near a mock Muslim town.

While here in Graf, we would go through another MGLC, platoon live fire, and a company live fire. It was going to be like the last time pretty much, except it was a lot colder in March. I had a new team leader, SGT Rodney; he had come from Alpha Co. Also the companies were being nicked named for the upcoming deployment to Afghanistan. Alpha was Attack, Bravo was Legion, Charlie (my company) was March or Die (M.O.D), Delta was Havoc, and Echo was E.Z.

The first week at Graf was going to be the MGLC, or Machine Gun Leaders Course. It was the usual business, crew drills and emplacements. We did target practice with moving targets and stationary. We did all this at night. It was cold but at least it didn't snow thank God! The next week we started with the platoon live fire. Of course the first day it was a dry run, all three platoons participated so it was an all-day event. This is where we started incorporating Humvees into the training. To start the exercise each platoon would have to drive down a road that was "occupied" by an enemy. Of course they may or may not attack us, and we had to stop at least once to check out a suspicious looking object that could be considered an IED[33].

The rifle squads would dismount from the Humvees and do a 5 &25 around the area; this where you check for anything that could be dangerous, like an IED, within 5ft and up to 25ft away. The rifle squads would then mount the Humvees, and we would drive to an open field with a mock enemy village skirting the side of the field. Weapons squads would dis-mount their M240B's and set up a Support by Fire[34] over watching the

---

33 **IED**—Improvised Explosive Device, a homemade explosive device used to disrupt or destroy property, commerce, an human life

34 **Support by Fire**—A fighting position occupied by heavier weapons to support a unit advancing on a target

field, while the rifle squads went in from behind the village. Also there was a mortar team accompanying the weapons squads with 81mm mortars.

Sounds easy, right? Yeah but when the Battalion Commander (BC)[35] and Command Sergeant Major (CSM) are out there watching everything, people tend to lose it a little. We ran through the dry drills a good bit. One of the other platoons was short an AG so my AG, Snyder, got the job. He ran the drill twice as much. He was a complainer in any case, so it was good for him. We also ran the drills at night, because you must certify at night and day. I was under the impression that once you were trained to fight, you just trained and then well—you went to fight someone. I was severely misguided. All units go to places like Graf and have people watch them to make sure they are doing everything correctly. Who would have thought?

The next day was live fire, so once you completed you were done. The live fire was bogged down because our CSM didn't like how 1st platoon was assaulting the village. 2nd and 3rd platoon (my platoon) went through without a hitch. Of course we had to wait for it to get dark before the night training could be completed. We smoked and joked, cleaned weapons, and ate some MREs. The good news is that the company live fire was cancelled due to a snow storm coming in, but we had to get over to Hoenfels before the snow stranded us at Graf.

My gun team was the fastest during all of the training and my platoon did the best overall. My team could set our gun in position in nine seconds at night, and both guns burned through 1200 rounds each in a few minutes. Between our tracers and the mortars exploding with a magnificent fury you could pretty much see everything. That was my first big fire fight; only that one was fake and an open field and empty village doesn't shoot back!

With pre-deployment training winding down, my unit returned to Vicenza and prepared for the upcoming deployment. A lot had to be done. Containers had to be packed, bags, personal stuff, etc. It was the end of April and we would be leaving in early May. A few people had already departed. ADVON would be leaving next week. Afghanistan here we come!

Before you could leave Italy, you had to go through all the checks and double checks. Dental, shots, mental health, hearing, and so on; the out-processing took a week to complete. The military was very expedient in the

---

35 **BC**—Battalion Commander, a Lieutenant Colonel that is placed in charge of a battalion

process. One minute you would have multiple needles going in your arm, the next you would be laid back in a dental chair. Some of the strongest men turn into babies when someone starts rooting around in their mouth. We did get off at mid-day, to maximize time with our families. Of course my crew had no family here so we mostly drank.

Lowell and I would go to this café that had opened up on post and get lunch plus some Jack Daniels to get the day started off right. The lady kept an open tab for us since we frequented the establishment. I don't think this Italian chick realized we were leaving for another continent in a week; we certainly never closed that tab. We made the most out of cooking out and going out. Bruder decided to get rid of his car. No he didn't sell it or anything like that. We drove it down town one evening to go to dinner, and we left it there; keys in the ignition. He only paid $500 for it, so that was easier than having the Army store it for the whole deployment. That's just one more thing that you have to worry about. He never got the car registered so there's no telling who it actually belonged to on paper.

The April weather was nice. Each person did the things they felt they needed to do before going to war. Lowell and I went to church, Clark messed with strippers, Strandberg flew his wife out, and we all got ready in our own way. None of us knew if we would come back from this adventure. None of us knew what the future held, or if we would all would be together when we got back. It's a very surreal feeling, knowing you're about to walk into the Valley of the Shadow Death—hopefully fearing no evil. Our group went out to dinner one last time and split on Rotundi so he would be stuck with the bill...it was Clark's idea.

The buses for Aviano showed up about 8 a.m. on May 6th, 2007. Families gathered outside of our company to say their last goodbyes. Tears and laughter flowed as we tried to make the lightest of the situation. One more shot was injected into our arms as we got onto the buses, no telling what that one was for. Families waved goodbye as the buses exited the safe gates of Camp Ederle, police escorted in tow.

We had departed post just like this countless times, but this time it felt different. There would be no coming back in a week or two. No weekend to put the rough training behind us. This time we were driving out into the unknown. This time some of us would not be coming back. This time... it was for real.

CHAPTER NINE
MAY: BERMEL

I HAD FLOWN ON numerous flights with American pilots. The minute I get on board a jet with an Italian pilot, shit goes all wrong. The Italian countryside was becoming a thing of the past as we flew over the Adriatic. I looked out the window and saw a white-looking smoke coming from the wing. I got the attention of Arruda and asked if he saw the same thing, just then the pilot came on and said there was a problem with the tail fin, and we would be turning around. How does a tail fin just up and break?

The white smoke wasn't smoke; in fact it was fuel they were dumping. To land we had to dump most of the fuel, because of weight, and the fact that the plane couldn't steer properly, and we might come down in a ball of flames. We all cheered and started singing "Gory, gory what a hell-of-a-way to die!" It was an original paratrooper cadence. You may have heard it on *Band of Brothers*. If there were any boats or sunbathers under the plane, that was now dumping all of its fuel, they were about to be in for a rude awakening! The plane came in heavy and bounced around, the roughest landing I had been a part of. It seemed we would get one more night in Italy. Although we would not be headed back to Vicenza, Aviano was just fine with us. The USAF[36] bases are way nicer than Army posts, and the females are something more to look at.

The next morning another World Airways plane came in; hopefully this one would do the job. As we were walking up the stairs to the plane a couple of F-16 fighter pilots saluted us while they were taxiing by in their aircraft. They too were on their way to make a run over Afghanistan;

---

36 **USAF**—United States Air Force

no doubt they would get there a little faster. Having had watched the ridiculous safety video on the plane, which didn't include what to do if the tail fin breaks over the ocean, we were back in the air, and on our way to Asia. The plane made it over the Adriatic; farther than the last one did, so it seemed we might make the four hour trip. A pit stop was made in Turkey for some fuel, and then we landed in Mannas, Kyrgyzstan about 7 p.m. Mannas was the gate-way to the Afghan theater, much like Kuwait is for the Iraq Theater.

We stayed·there until May 11th and then headed towards Bagram, Afghanistan. Touching down in Bagram, we were escorted to massive brown tents by the flight line. Bagram is extremely noisy with planes always coming and going, helicopters hovering around, and the sounds of machinery, but you get used to it. They issued us ammo in Bagram, I didn't get any obviously for my M240B since it takes belts, but I did get some for the 9mm I was carrying as a sidearm.

We stayed in Bagram for two days and then moved out to COB[37] Salerno. This was the last stop before taking a helicopter out to Bermel, the FOB[38] where we would be stationed. Salerno had a small gravel airfield, and I remember it was my first combat landing. The plane started diving and banking, and of course all of the people who had never done this before started freaking out; now I know it was just to throw the enemy off. Salerno was headquarters to the 82nd Airborne Division's Task Force Fury. The 173rd was now attached to them, but both of our units fell under Joint Task Force-82. Salerno was significantly smaller than Bagram, but was green and had trees. I liked it.

The Chinooks touched down in Bermel on May 16th, 2007. This would be my home until June 28th, 2008. Bermel was a very small FOB at about 7,500ft above sea level. It had a Hesco[39] perimeter and four guard towers. Hesco is basically chicken wire with a burlap lining that comes in various sizes. You fill up the inside with dirt and it makes a pretty reliable wall. Charlie Co. would be taking over Bermel, along with a company of 173rd Calvary Scouts, which was Anvil Co. from 1/91 Calvary. Roughly there would be 240 paratroopers sharing this small space.

---

37 **COB**—Contingency Operating Base, a base that is larger than a forward operating base and usually has an landing strip, helicopter pad, and hospital.

38 **FOB**—Forward Operating Base, a base that is smaller than a Contingency Operating Base and larger than a Combat Outpost which houses approximately 200-500 soldiers

39 **Hesco**—a durable wall developed to cut down on construction time that is little more than burlap placed over wire, which is then filled with dirt

Bermel itself was the village beside our FOB; we borrowed the name. The FOB itself sat six kilometers away from the base of the Hindu Kush, the mountains we would end up patrolling all over. The FOB was in the middle of nowhere. The only quick way in was helicopter because any drive would take considerable time. Supplies were brought in by helicopter and kicked out of the back of planes with a parachute on them…that was always an interesting mission to go on.

Walking through the make-shift gate, there was one small chow hall with only the lowly Army cooks. Places like Bagram have their food service provided by KBR[40] a private company that gives you everything from ice-cream to pasta at every meal. We, however, would have the same weekly menu for the next fifteen months. That's why God made hot sauce! The building itself was no larger than your average McDonalds. Good thing I am a fan of shelf milk and cafeteria food.

There was one MWR[41] which had six computers and two phones. A small mechanic's bay was on the other side of that to fix broken vehicles and other machinery. There were two small TOCs[42] one for MOD and the other for Anvil. Ours had a spot for the FDC.[43] These were the guys that controlled the two 105mm Howitzers on the FOB. Our barracks were called "bee huts". They were kind of like shotgun houses. Plywood walls divided the concrete building into rooms for two, bunk beds of course. The building itself was made of a shitty mixture of Muslim concrete and iron bars. It was supposed to withstand a 107mm rocket, but there's no way that was going to happen; so we put Hesco all around them.

The laundry room and shower room were two in one. There were five sinks. However, you were supposed to use bottled water to brush your teeth, but I never had a problem using the water they trucked it. Its chlorine content was so high you could smell it; some people would get rashes as a result. There were four dryers and washing machines. There was also a Muslim worker that you could turn your laundry into if you wanted to but I didn't trust his scandalous ass.

Along with our two companies we had some Afghan local nationals living on the FOB. Once they started working for us, they had to stay

---

40 **KBR**—Kellogg, Browning, and Root, a contracted company the military uses
41 **MWR**—Moral, Wellness, and Recreation, a facility designed for soldiers to relief stress, utilize a phone or computer, and play sports
42 **TOC**—Tactical Operations Center, a facility where combat operations can be ran
43 **FDC**—Fire Direction Control, the center that controls and directs artillery fire as well as some aircraft

with us. If they walked home every day, they were sure to get picked up by the ACM;[44] so they lived on their own section of the FOB, behind the chow hall. They did all of the manual labor around the FOB mostly like pumping our fuel or burning the shit buckets some helped cook, and some were learning mechanics from our Army mechanics. Basically, if there was a job they did it. Our interpreters (Terps) also lived with them. Terps would go with us out on missions to help us talk to the local population. Some were good and could speak perfect English, but others needed to be interpreted themselves!

Part of the FOB, separated by a gate and Hesco wall, was inhabited by the Afghan National Army (ANA). The complex housed roughly 200 ANA soldiers and a dozen or so Afghan National Police (ANP). They were a wild bunch to say the least. They constantly played soccer, and on occasion we would venture over and play with them. Their Muslim prayer music would be the first and last thing you heard at night. Some were corrupt, such as taking bribes, murdering higher ranking officers, and giving the ACM information about our technology, but most of them wanted to fight for their country. They were so passionate in this cause that they would beat and eventually kill prisoners when we captured them. We would hear the one shot after a prisoner we had captured was released to the ANA. Ultimately we quit handing prisoners over to them.

Bermel was small as I said, but it was going to be home for the next fifteen months. When moving into a new home, there always seems to be the annoying neighbors. Our neighbors were about 6-8k away, and they were constantly pissing on our lawn, so to speak. The first 107mm rocket (which is about two feet long) came in with the low hum of an organ, another one in tow. The rockets landed only about 50m outside of our perimeter. This we found out from 10th Mountain (the Infantry unit we were replacing) was going to be an almost daily occurrence, and the ACM were becoming better shots. Oh, well that's just out-fucking-standing! A few 107s were going to be the least of my worries.

On May 26th, 10th Mountain was getting ready to transfer the reigns to the 173rd. We had one more mission to go on with them before they flew out. They had been there almost fifteen months, so it goes without saying that they all were ready to get the hell outta there! The mission was up to the northern tip of our battle space (an assigned area to a company,

---

44 **ACM**—Anti Coalition Militia, remnants of the Taliban government, mercenaries, and local fighters that fought against ISAF forces

battalion, or brigade); as far as you could go on the road we dubbed Volkswagen. All roads have street names of course; this makes it easier to plan a mission. All of ours happen to be vehicle models.

We stopped at a few key villages on the way, so we could show the village elders that someone new would be taking over Bermel. These were meet and greets essentially. As we were coming up to the last village, I noticed the dirt kicking up around the vehicle. Of course I was on my trusty M240B in the turret so I could see what was going on. Then I heard the machine guns echo throughout the canyon. A truck, which was a few back from me, opened up on the top of this cliff that was right above the village and laid waste to it with MK-19 and 50.Cal fire.

SFC Adams, who I would gun for the whole deployment, asked me if I saw anything. "Well I saw the rounds kicking up, but whatever was up there is gone now." Our Captain thought we were making the whole ordeal up, and that we just wanted to massacre a village, due to the fact he sat a couple trucks behind the contact. Depending on how many vehicles are in a convoy, they can be extremely long, from 500m to almost a mile long. If you're in the rear, then you may never know anything went down.

Lt. Israel got out of the vehicles and took a platoon into the village. No more shots were fired; either we killed the shooters or they were blending in with the rest of the village. Lt. Israel would try to find them though. He took teams all around the village and up to the cliff, plus beyond; he certainly was thorough. The problem with fighting the ACM is they look the same as everyone else. No uniforms are worn, no special insignia that says "Hey, here I am, I'm a Muslim douchebag!" Nah, none of that, so it was often difficult to pin something on someone. We had to rely on Human Intelligence (HUMINT)[45] for the most part. HUMINT is basically your buddy telling on you. Informants would get paid by us for information, just like in the drug game. I missed Kevin.

Returning to the FOB we performed maintenance on the Humvees; each platoon had six. Before every mission we would perform inspections, and after the mission we would tighten everything that could come lose on the rugged terrain of Afghanistan. Daily we would clean the windows, tighten the lugnuts on the wheels, and check oil, brake fluid, washer fluid, shocks, brakes, and the tires. After that basically anything else that could be damaged. If a soldier had no vehicle to complete a mission, then someone would be left to carry his weight. The vehicles were as important as feeding

---

45 **HUMINT**—Human Intelligence, intelligence obtained from a human source

ourselves. Some people, (cough...Anvil Company...cough, cough) didn't seem to get that and were constantly breaking their Humvees.

10th Mountain left a few days after the final mission. Now the FOB was completely ours. The rocket attacks had been stepped up a bit. They were usually in the morning, but they had begun to take place during mid-day as well. The mid-day attacks were most likely rockets on water timers, sitting on a crude metal launch platform. When the water would evaporate, the detonator's wires would touch, hence launching the rocket. Of course they had nothing to aim with, and from 6-8k away it's a wonder they came as close as they did. It was part of daily life, the low whine and the explosion afterward.

With 10th Mountain gone our battalion commander, Eagle 6, was ready to stretch his legs and look for a site where we could place another COP.[46] We had one to the north, Margah COP, but he wanted one in the mountains east of FOB Bermel. A site survey meant a mission; a mission meant we were going to be hiking up the mountains. Who wouldn't want to hike up to 9,000ft with all that gear on, in 100 degree weather, just to look at the ground? MOD would carry out the mission. Anvil said they were Cavalry scouts and didn't walk, but they would be kind enough to drop us off though. We inserted at 2030 Zulu[47] (1:30a.m. local). MOD was spread out, each platoon inserted into different areas. Our scouts were already out in the mountains, hopefully providing diligent over-watch.

My platoon crossed the small creek and climbed out of the dried river bed. It was pitch black except for the glow of fluorescent glow sticks in our helmets. Our night vision was okay, but it works better with more ambient light. My gun team was in the rear of our column with MOD 3-5(Call sign for SFC Adams) while the other gun team was in the front with 3-6 (Lt. Israel). Up we went, about 1k, right up the side of this mountain. This is no easy accomplishment during the day with all of your gear on, but at night it's a whole new beast. Needlessly to say we were not quiet.

We were now at about 8,000ft above sea level, carrying all of our gear, sucking air, searching anywhere for the next breath to fill our flat lungs. I don't think anyone expected it to be this difficult. No one really thought about us being nearly two miles up and having not really conditioned for this type of mission. Yet, there we were. I slowly moved in front of Snyder who moaned like a slut every step of the way. Lt. Israel had stopped us

---

46 **COP**—Combat Outpost, a position that is closer to the combat front than a Forward Operating Base and is usually fortified with towers, walls, and holds thirty to sixty troops
47 **Zulu**—Greenwich Mean Time

on a ridge to wait for day break. Although that meant a short respite, it also meant my sweat would cool and freeze me to death. I mounted my trusty 240 on a rock and clipped on the 400rds Snyder was carrying for good measure. I can hear the vulture-sized crickets and grass-hoppers flying about, taking part in their own sweet symphony. As the sun rose it began to cast a purple and pink aura over the sky, which was really quite amazing. Afghanistan would be a great place for outdoor activities. Hiking and such in the summer, snow skiing in the winter; alas, it's filled with Muslim fucks.

The smoke from cooking fires in the nearby villages was starting to take hold in the air. It has a very distinct smell since they use their own feces to cook with. I kind of think it smelled good to be honest, like some kind of meat. There is no telling what they did with their urine. The wind blew through the pines, but my silent moment was interrupted by ACM rockets being launched somewhere nearby. The loud organ sound cascaded over the mountains, as everyone got ready for an ambush. The rockets were being fired at Bermel, and as soon as they hit, I heard the sound of our on Howitzers fire. The whine of friendly artillery soared over our heads, landing with a deafening report. A few more rockets went off. *Were we really having an artillery battle with all of us scattered over these mountains?* I couldn't help but think that the FDC didn't have our current position, and they were going to drop a shake and bake right on us! A shake and bake is three or more rounds of explosive 105mm followed by White Phosphorus[48]. WP is no joke; it sucks the oxygen out of the air, consequently sucking it out of the enemy's lungs. You might remember the Marines getting in trouble for using it on the city of Fallujah, Iraq.

Our counter fire slammed into the mountains again, accompanied by a mortar team on top of the mountain, Hilltop 2474. All of this is extremely loud, but a pleasure to the senses nonetheless. The heart starts racing as the body prepares for fight or flight. You can feel the adrenaline making your hearing and vision sharper. It's an addicting feeling. The next volley of rockets were never fired, either the assailants were massacred by exploded shells or ran out of ammunition. Either way, we were on the move again. Up, up, up!

Now that it was light, moving up this rugged rock was a tad bit easier; still the air eluded our tired bodies as we crested the top of the mountain. MOD-6 and 7 (MOD-6 was code for Capt. McCrystal and MOD-7 was

---

48 **WP/Willy Pete**—White Phosphorus, a chemical used in artillery shells to displace oxygen

code for 1ˢᵗ SGT Collins) were up here with the company mortar team and 2ⁿᵈ PLT. 1ˢᵗ PLT was across one of the valleys about 3k away, while our Scout team was God knows where. I set up overlooking a dried river bed, or wadi⁴⁹, that was frequented by log trucks. Bermel was one of Afghanistan's hubs for the wood business. Massive piles were scattered throughout the town, and the trucks were always trudging their way in. Jingle trucks is what we called them. Americans spiff up their rides with rims, spinners, custom paint jobs, etc. Afghani's put a bunch my metal chains and bells on theirs, hence the "jingle."

The wadi had a small stream moving down the middle of it. I could only see down it about 400m, and then it made a sharp left curve into Route Shadow. SSG Manuma came up and sat down beside me, wiping a big black ant off his assault pack. This cracked me up for some reason, and he started laughing at my laughing. "Well, we should have spent more time climbing the mountains of Germany than blowing up shit with MK-19s." I said, and the big Samoan took a long pull from his Camelbak before answering, "Yeah…no shit."

The sun was beginning to get hot. I was constantly trying to move my gun into the shade, but I was running out of it fast. Our sweat soaked shirts were starting to give us prickly heat rashes. This is where the moisture from clothes, skin, or anything against your body can't dry, so it lays against your skin. In turn causing the skin to itch and turn red. It's pretty uncomfortable. Next time we would take turns changing shirts and wiping down our backs with baby wipes. We were always living and learning.

We would sit on top of hill 2474 for another night and then withdraw back to FOB Bermel. The survey team had some of the information they needed on where exactly to build our new COP, but another mission was going to be a must. For now we were returning to showers and a fresh meal. Our first month in this wasteland had come and gone quickly, after a day of reset, 3ʳᵈ PLT would be heading out to Margah COP for a week, and shit was going to be getting real…really quick.

---

49 **Wadi**—the Arabic term referring to a dry riverbed that contains water only during times of heavy rain or simply an intermittent stream

Chapter Ten

June: Shit Gets Real...

Real Quick

I WAS CLEANING MY turret windows and getting harassed by SFC Adams (as usual) before 3rd PLT pulled out of Bermel to head towards Margah COP. We had everything we needed for a week's stay, and we would be taking our own food (real food, not MRE's). I wound up being made the platoon cook. Before we mounted up, MOD-7 called a company formation. Of course we all bitched like kids, but we formed up nonetheless.

1SG Collins came out, and we all fell in on him in a horseshoe formation. He wanted to give us an update on how things were going with different companies throughout the battle space, since most of us had a lot of friends in different companies. I had heard from Lowell only once after leaving Vicenza, and, no one else. Legion was stationed farther North than us in Naray. The news I was about to receive was not what I was expecting:

Near the vicinity of Gowardesh, Lowell checked his M240B before mounting up in his Humvee. Bickford was smoking with Clark and Bruder, and Archie came walking up to bum a smoke. Legion was setting out on a HA[50] mission to make contact with a village a few clicks (One Click = 1 Kilometer) away. They had arrived in Naray to find it was a desolate FOB high in the mountains, where tents would be the only shelter from the war outside. Rotundi strolled up talking his usual garbage as Clark walked away to get into the back

---

50 **HA**—Humanitarian Assistance, assistance given to humans that in need, which may include water, food, shelter, clothing or all four basic needs

*of his Humvee. With the convoy ready to SP[51], Lowell, Rotundi, Archie and
Bruder jumped into their turrets. Bickford would be staying behind, to give
others a chance to "go outside the wire" (leave the FOB). The convoy rolled up
the hill outside of the FOB, Humvees straining to make it. The armor they put
on those things was a constant strain on the engines.*

*Bruder was scanning the high cliffs for enemy activity; the sharp drop off to
his right was somewhat disconcerting. Rotundi moved the .50 Cal shell in his
butter-fly trigger as the bumpy road was loosening it. The wind coming through
the river valley was cool against Lowell's face as he cast an eye over his sector,
the blue sky reminding him of days past when he and friends would throw
bean bags all day. His thoughts were interrupted by the sound of an RPG[52]
slamming into the cliff face beside him. "Contact!" he yelled and opened up
on the ridge in front him. He was trying to get low enough so he would have
adequate cover. The cliffs were high, giving the ACM a distinct advantage.*

*Bruder spotted ACM and opened up with his M240, spitting out the
sounds of a fresh battle. Radio chatter inside of the Humvees was marked with
directions and numbers, attempting to locate the enemy and push out of this
kill-zone. Rotundi burned through his can of .50 Cal rounds and bent down
to get another from inside of the Humvee as AK-47 bullets slammed into the
bulletproof glass behind him, sending a fresh shot of adrenaline through his
veins.*

*Lowell felt an AP[53] round rip through his left thigh, grabbing it as
he faltered down into the Humvee. He gained his composure, and then he
proceeded to stand back up on his trusty 240, and lay down fire once again on
the enemy. Clark cocked his M-249 in case he had to dismount his Humvee,
but a RPG erupted into the front of its hood, shattering the bulletproof wind-
shield, throwing glass into the body-armor and faces of the driver and TC.[54]
Another one came through the back hatch of Clark's Humvee, killing an
Afghan interpreter and gnarling Clark's left leg.*

*The driver and TC were shouting to get out of the Humvee as flames
engulfed the engine. Lowell threw accurate fire above Clark's truck to cover
their extraction. An additional ACM bullet reverberated through Lowell's left*

---

51 **SP**—Start Patrol, the starting point of tactical movement by soldiers

52 **RPG**—Rocket Propelled Grenade, a shoulder fired grenade designed to destroy vehicles
and troop positions

53 **AP**—Armor Piercing, a type of ammunition designed to go through heavily armored
vehicles

54 **TC**—Truck Commander, the soldier that sits on the passenger side of a Humvee and
directs it where to go

color bone, right above his body armor. "Oh God" Lowell softly said, as he exhaled his last breath and fell limp into the Humvee. Not feeling the pain of his left leg, Clark tossed the door of the Humvee open and placed it out first. Turning to run back to the Humvee behind him, his left heel twisted almost completely off. Letting out a painful yell, Clark began to hop on his right leg out into the open road, struggling to get to the Humvee nearest him. A medic ran up to give him support, getting both of them to decent cover.

The valley was awash in the echoes of a battle, deafening the closest voice to your ear. Archie leveled the cliff with MK-19 rds., as he watched the gunner in front of him go down as the gunner's right hand's fingers were shot off; Bruder was behind Archie, following up the grenade's explosions with 240 fire. The medic looked at Clark's mangled leg and decided to wrap a tourniquet around it, telling Clark to hold on and not to end up like Lowell. Clark took a swing at the Doc, because the tourniquet's tightness sent a renewed jolt of pain through his broken body. Then he then asked for a cigarette; bullets still thrusting up dirt all around him.

A-10 Thunderbolts[55] checked onto Legion's battle-space—their low rumble was a cause to rejoice for us in the midst of any fire fight, but a source of panic in our enemy's hearts. As the ACM broke contact and tried to flee from their high positions, they became easy targets for the might of the United States Air Force. The unmistakable sound of a 30mm cannon opened up on the ridge, the ground kicked up into a furious dust storm, and a 500lb JDAM[56] found its final resting place across the river upon the other ACM position. Radios inside Clark's PSG's Humvee were crackling about the incoming MEDEVAC[57], "1 U.S. KIA,[58] 1 Local National KIA, 5 WIA[59]...HLZ[60] will be marked with red smoke."

Clark was carried down the road a few hundred meters on his litter. The other four followed with a cover from the A-10s. They were headed to a field just large enough for a Blackhawk to land. Other paratroopers carried Lowell's

---

55 **A-10 Thunderbolt**—an American single-seat, twin-engine, straight-wing jet aircraft developed by Fairchild-Republic in the early 1970s. The A-10 was designed for a United States Air Force requirement to provide close air support for ground forces

56 **JDAM**—Joint Direct Attack Munitions, is a guidance kit that converts unguided bombs, or "dumb bombs" into all-weather "smart" munitions

57 **MEDEVAC**—Medical Evacuation, efficient movement and en route care provided by medical personnel to the wounded being evacuated from the battlefield by aircraft or ambulance

58 **KIA**—Killed In Action, when a solider is killed in combat

59 **WIA**—Wounded In Action, when a soldier is wounded during combat operations

60 **HLZ**—Helicopter Landing Zone, a designated space large enough for a helicopter to land

and interpreter's bodies on litters as the first Blackhawk touched down, and the WIA boarded. The two A-10s were still letting their presence be known, as they flew close to the cliffs in case the ACM were regrouping for another assault. The first Blackhawk lifted off and the second landed right behind to pick up Lowell and the interpreter. A five minute fire-fight had turned into on hell of a bloody day.

MOD-7's words drifted off into oblivion as he began to talk about another company. I felt like I could hardly breathe, and my head was filling with many questions. There was no way he was talking about my friends, the ones I had been with since basic training, the ones I had so many good times with in Italy...not my friends. I looked around and saw that all of the WPNS Squads were looking at the ground as I was. All of them had known Lowell pretty well, due to the fact that we had been through all of the same training, but none of them had known him like I had.

As the formation began to scatter, SFC Adams put his hand on my shoulder and asked me if I was okay, but before I could speak he said, "Don't you worry about Legion's firefight. It's over, and there is nothing you can do about it now. I need you here, I need your mind here on this mission were about to go on, you savvy that?" "Roger that, I'm your man." I replied, and jumped into my turret to get ready to travel to Margah COP; trying to clear my head...the war had become personal.

The entire week in Margah I couldn't help but think of Lowell and what his family must be feeling. There was no communication at Margah. No phone to call home and no mouse to click. I was stuck with my inquiries for a week, nearly driving myself insane as I thought about Lowell's last moments. I wondered if Clark was alright, I wondered if more of my friends were injured than 1SG Collins had reported. All of the post-deployment plans Lowell and I had made were now shattered. All of my friends were far away, and I truly was feeling alone, in some backward country I didn't give a damn about.

We returned from Margah COP on June 6th. It was a pretty uneventful stay. I was made PLT cook, and one of my uniforms was completely ruined from the soot of an open fire. Considering that I had never had to cook for 30 grown men, I did pretty well. Not to mention I had to cook over an open fire like a savage Muslim. Anvil Company would be trading battle-space with us; therefore, they would start manning Margah. Anvil claimed that they were a Calvary company and that they did not climb mountains, well, la-fucking-da...bitches. So 1/91 would patrol our old battle space with Humvees, while we got the privilege of climbing the mountains of their old battle-space. What a treat! Now you can see why MOD (March-Or-Die, my company's call sign), didn't really care for Anvil, this event started the animosity. A free lower body workout while mountain climbing would save a shit ton in monthly gym membership fees at the ROIDS-R-US.

Since the battle-space had been flip-flopped, we began to go around to each of our new villages, conducting leader engagements with the village elders. Of course we provided HA after every laborious chat. Interpreters were our only source of communication with the locals, so these meetings sometimes took hours. Not that I had anything else to do. I would stand up in my turret and day-dream my ass off, enjoying my amazing mansions in my head, or perhaps creating my alter-ego as a super hero. He became pretty powerful after 15 months of practice. He also didn't have to pay for strippers and Kevin was one of his best friends.

This went on for most of the month of June. The three platoons would rotate on a schedule, two days on mission and one day on Force Protection, or guard duty essentially. That was another job Anvil just couldn't do, since they just didn't have the "man power" to supply a few guards for the four towers we had on the FOB. Their company was the same size as ours. But, oh my, what were they to do…have some of their people up in a tower, to look out into the vacant wasteland of Afghanistan? They thought not! Sluts. No matter that the rockets, still an everyday occurrence, were starting to land closer to their side of the FOB…to MOD's delight.

Lowell was buried on June 18th. My parents sent me the article that his local newspaper wrote up. The streets of his city, New Lenox IL, were lined with citizens bidding him farewell. Clark had also been MEDEVACED to Landstuhl Hospital in Germany. Landstuhl is the largest U.S. hospital in Europe. Clark was trying to save his left leg, but the doctors were not hopeful. I was still having difficulty believing that Lowell had been killed, and that Clark was now facing one of the biggest decisions of his life. But on the battlefield, you can't let such thoughts drive you insane.

The day after Lowell was buried we set out on a mission to investigate POO[61] sites. POO sites are where the rockets are launched from, POI[62] sites are where the hit. The day was getting us nowhere in the search of who was firing rockets at us. One village elder gave a good analogy of how he felt. He said that Afghanistan was caught in between the way of two Rams

---

61 **POO**—Point of Origin, the sight where ordinance is fired from
62 **POI**—Point of Impact, the sight where ordinance impacts the earth or fortified position

banging heads. Of course he meant the United States vs. the ACM. He couldn't figure out which side was better for his village. The locals didn't talk much, but some had some decent information. Most of our Intel came from HUMINT, paying the locals to spy for us.

The day was drawing to a close when MOD-6 (Captain McCrystal's Call Sign), decided to check out one more of the villages that sat up Route Ram. The village of Gangrekhyel (Gang-RA-kel) stood up a terrible wadi that we had yet to explore; eventually it would be the site of our new COP. 3ʳᵈ PLT led the way, but my truck was not the last truck—as usual due to MOD-6 and 7 having their Humvees, 2ⁿᵈ PLT was behind them. MOD had twelve Humvees in all up this rugged terrain, not knowing what lie ahead.

I saw the first RPG slam into Lt. Israel's spare tire on the back of his Humvee. The seconds seem to freeze. All at once the wadi is engulfed in ACM machine gun, RPG, and AK-47 fire. They had a distinct advantage over us as the wadi embankments are approximately 20ft higher than our Humvees. I yelled, "Contact, contact, contact!" as my hands worked by themselves to chamber my rounds, and pull the pin that holds my gun in place. A sniper's round spider webbed the left side of Arruda's turret, then the glass on the back of it, despite the fact he was pounding the hill side with MK-19rds.

I heard MOD-7 on the company net calling in artillery fire from Bermel. I put my shoulder on the butt stock of my trusty M240 and pulled the trigger as an RPG hissed past my head and explodes on the embankment behind me; my neck is on fire while I am blown back on the rear ballistic glass of my turret. Then my left hand goes numb as a ricocheting ACM bullet bounces off my gun in through my left wrist and off my bone. "I think I'm hit, SGT Adams!" I say as I place my right hand on my neck and feel the blood pouring over my body.

"Oh shit." I think to myself, this is it. My neck is blown out and any second I am done. SFC Adams yells up, "Well get the fuck down here then!" I dropped inside and am thrown into the empty seat as one of our tires was blown out from an RPG landing directly behind our truck. Usually one of our Forward Observers[63] rides with us, but he was not on the mission that day…thank God. I looked over at 3ʳᵈ PLT's medic (who also rides with SFC Adams and me every mission, praise the Lord again) and he is just

---

63 **FO**—Forward Observer, the soldier on the front line that communicates with the Fire Direction Control and aircraft as to where ordinance should be dropped

staring at me. I yelled, "What the fuck do you want me to do medic?!" I saw the passenger side mirror shatter from bullet fire and think to myself that *I had just replaced that mirror damn it!*

Medic Plantiko finally comes to and starts trying to find entrance and exit wounds on my neck. I thought I was done and said a quick prayer to God while the radio screamed of a possible disabled truck and to stop the convoy. *Great now we're caught in this crossfire for good.* SFC Adams yelled at the medic to check my left arm to as he could see the blood pouring out of my rolled up sleeves. Plantiko didn't think the RPG shrapnel hit anything major in my neck and started to pack it with gauze. Right on top of my Adams Apple was the largest wound which extended over the trachea about two inches to the left. Shrapnel also went in multiple places up the right side of my neck reaching to my ear.

I got my body armor off to make sure I hadn't been hit anywhere else. The convoy was moving again, trying to push up the wadi before the artillery came crashing in. The top of the Humvee sounded like a tin roof in a rain storm from all the gun fire that was being bounced off of it. SFC Adams was calling up my injuries, trying to raise a MEDEVAC. We thought my left arm was broken as the mangled flesh hung from it. Plantiko gave me a splint to hold on to as he wrapped it tight. At this point I haven't seen God yet, so I think I am going live, but the adrenaline is pumping into my veins, so it may be the only thing keeping me alive.

A bullet hit right above of our driver's wind-shield from an ACM fighter hiding on ground level, the crazy Muslim got blasted by the 50. Cal behind us. The convoy pushed into an opening and came to halt. We were out of the 400m long kill zone, and the artillery turned the death trap behind us into violent earth-moving attack of our on. The ground trembled from being so close to the impacting 105mm shells. A MEDEVAC was in-route from FOB Salerno. Turns out I am the only lucky person out of 60 people to get hit! Anyone can obviously see this was an assassination attempt on my life, which was most likely initiated by some outraged stripper.

SPC Morris ran over and hopped in my turret to make sure we had a gunner, in case the ACM regrouped and attacked again, now that we were stationary. He said, "Hey man, there's a shit ton of blood up here, are you okay?" I yelled up that there's a muffin up there if he wants it, not to worry about the blood on the wrapper. Two Apaches checked on station and rolled out past hill top 2474 then lit up the exit route of the ACM. MOD-6 said we have to go back down Route Ram to get to the MEDEVAC as this area is too hostile. We'll let's jump back on that roller coaster!

The trucks turn around, most have two or more flat tires, and others are leaking fluids and may not make it back to the FOB. I put my bloody bulletproof vest around me as much as possible, which wasn't much since I am now a gauze and bandage monster. 2nd PLT lead us down the route... silence. You could hear the trucks creaking over the rocks and a radio calling out grid coordinates for more fire missions. The wadi that was awash with flames only a few moments ago now appears to be the most tranquil place in Afghanistan. The route is littered with expended casings from U.S. and ACM weapons. There were drag trails where the ACM drug off their wounded and dead before we could get to them and capture the fighters for questioning. The Apaches overhead were certainly moral lifters.

Our broken convoy came out of the wadi by the village of Malekshay as the MEDEVAC touched down. MOD-6 ran over to me and tells me that they may have taken us by surprise today, but it won't happen again. I tell Lt. Israel that I will be back to watch the Georgia vs. Alabama football game and hop into the MEDEVAC Blackhawk, SFC Adams flicked me off while we circle overhead.

The flight medic asked me if I was in any pain, I told her that my arm was broken as she turned the IV on. My head went to cloud nine all at once, and I started to serenade her with "Champagne Supernova". Too bad she didn't have a lighter to hold up. Seeing the ground from the air is an experience when you're high on Fentanyl. The bird flew through the mountains with ease on that summer evening and touched down at FOB Salerno. By now the medicine had worn off, and all of my injuries were starting to swell; breathing was also becoming difficult as it turns out the shrapnel was actually in my trachea the surgeon would later tell me.

I was whisked into a room, and the next thing I knew my uniform was being sheared off of me as my boots were being un-tied and removed. A cow hide was placed over my naked body while ten different people were asking me all sorts of questions. An X-RAY Tech was messing with my arm and chest, a guy with a clipboard kept asking me about my body armor; another guy was slamming morphine into my veins while he asked me if I was allergic to anything. He then told me my chest was about to get hot. Obviously Mr. Clipboard paid attention in medical school, or he was sneaking drugs for himself. The Morphine hit my heart like a bucket of hot water, but my head didn't mind. Kevin would be pissed if he knew I was cheating.

One female nurse asked me what my favorite type of music was. "What does that have to do with anything? Are yall fixing me or getting me ready for my funeral?" I replied, she laughed as I then complied and told her The Dave Matthews Band. Her friend was asking me about my unit and the ambush, what I remembered from it, as if she was compiling data for her own novel. A surgeon came in to tell me my arm was in fact not broken, but there was plenty of shrapnel in there that needed to come out. They would also work on my neck. They rolled me into a make-shift Operating Room made from a shipping container and to my high delight turned on some Dave Matthews.

Morphine Monster hit me with another cocktail, and I was half out of it. I remember hearing the DMB song "Drive In, Drive Out" and seeing a surgeon over me sewing my neck up, but a blue divider was between me and my arm. Then darkness…I was out in my own dark world for what felt like an eternity. Shadows of men in dark clothes seemed to come into view, and then I awoke with a gasp as the nightshift nurses were putting the breathing tube back in my nose. Turns out the Morphine Monster threw too much juice into my veins, making my heart rate drop too far; also these nurses were wearing all black, and I thought I was crazy.

After they had their fun, playing with all the hoses coming out of me and trying to keep me awake long enough to get a good read on my heart chart, I was out of it once again. Awaking a day later, I found an Afghan man standing at the end my bed, speaking to me in his foreign dialect. An interpreter was nearby and told me the man said that he was sorry this happened to me, and that he felt personally responsible for it, being that it was his country. The Afghan man was there because one of his sons had hit an IED. No doubt intended for an ISAF[64] convoy. I told the Afghan man, through an interpreter, that we would beat this ACM disease together. Their zealotries were now affecting their own people. It had to be stopped.

While I was being forced to pee in a bottle for the all black nurse ninjas, 3rd PLT rolled out to Gonjaikhel (GON-ji-kel) and was ambushed while trying to provide HA to the elders. *The first round landed by SSG Manuma as he was smoking a cigarette, telling Maddalone to scan the tops of the hills for movement. The ICOM[65], which is the type of radio used by the ACM and one we used to listen to them, had been going off about hitting the Americans since the convoy arrived. The dirt kicked up around his feet, and the Samoan returned fire into the wood line then dove behind the open*

---

64 **ISAF**—International Security Assistance Force, the multinational force in Afghanistan that is rebuilding and securing the nation
65 **ICOM**—a type of radio developed by the ICOM company

Humvee door. Maddalone opened up with his MK-19 on the muzzle flashes to silence them forever.

Meanwhile, the platoon was half mounted and half dismounted. MOD 3-6 (Lt. Israel) is in the village with 1st and 2nd Squads, while MOD 3-5 (SFC Adams) is at the trucks with the gunners and drivers, as well as the big Samoan target getting shot at. Another ACM group opened up on the stationary Humvees from the other side of the wadi. 3-6 consolidated in the village as another attack may come from inside there as well. He called back to Bermel on the radio to see if CAS[66] or CCA[67] was in the area.

Arruda turned his .50 Cal on the other side of the wadi and hammered the area of the muzzle flashes. Maddalone started to hit the top of the hills as he could see movement coming down them. The rifle squads in the village started taking fire as MOD-6 tells MOD 3-6 that there is one B-1 bomber[68] checking on to their battle space. MOD 3-6 gave the grid that he wanted leveled to the pilot and the mountainside erupted with a violent tremble. Not only did the blast silence the shooters but it also liquefied some goat bystanders. Or maybe the goats were martyrs for the cause.

I was released from the hospital after 48hrs and set up in a tent. I had to stay in Salerno another four days, so the medical staff could monitor the healing of my wounds. As I mentioned I had no uniform or anything else. Luckily, The Wounded Warrior Project had delivered care packages to the FOB just days before I arrived. I had a blanket and a pair of shorts, plus a t-shirt to bum around in until I could get a new uniform. I have to say I felt somewhat out of place in combat boots, a t-shirt, and some gym shorts.

After a week of sitting around and trying to talk to some Polish cats, I got a flight back to Bermel. I still had a considerable amount of stiches in my arm and neck, but other than that I felt like a million bucks (after taxes of course). I was met on the main drag of downtown FOB Bermel (all 50yds of it) by MOD-7. He led me into our little chow hall where SFC Adams and MOD-6 were eating. They were also surprised my arm wasn't broken since they saw the way it looked when I got on the MEDEVAC bird. There I sat, almost as good as new, with SFC Adams shoving ice cream at me like Forrest Gump.

---

66 **CAS**—Close Air Support, support given by aircraft to ground troops during a battle
67 **CCA**—Close Combat Aircraft, support given by helicopters to ground troops during a battle
68**B-1 Bomber**—The Rockwell B-1 Lancer is a four-engine variable-sweep wing strategic bomber used by the United States Air Force

MOD-6 and 7 said I would be off mission-ready status for ten days, until I got my stitches out. Also, they felt that it was important for the other soldiers to see that when someone gets injured that they do comeback. The morale in 3rd PLT was certainly lifted, as they thought I would be in Germany right now getting something amputated. It was good to be back in my own bed and among familiar faces.

With my being off for ten days, things started to get ridiculous. First I was dared to get sprayed in the eye with Listerine. Which sounded like a great idea, but I did not take into account the 21% of alcohol that makes up mouthwash. My, what an unpleasant experience, it was probably the worst pain of my life. Next, I was dared to eat a Pringle suspended between the butt cheeks of one of our squad leaders. Of course I delivered. I put a gay sweat ban around my head and a Hooters t-shirt on that had been sent via mail. SSG Daniel, bent over, saying not to get his face in the camera, the tiny room crowded with paratroopers and filling with roars of laughter. I slid over to him like a seal and took the Pringle from his clenched ass cheeks, then swallowed it! That really sent the laughter to the heavens! Hey, you'd get bored out in the middle of nowhere! Since I could not pull my weight on mission, the least I could do was provide some entertainment, and test out new Pringle recipes.

Chapter Eleven

July: "What's that Medic? You're a butt Pirate?"

THE BRIGHT AFGHAN SUN made me squint my eyes as I carried my M240B out of our barracks and jumped atop my turret. It was July 11th, and my convalescent time was up. We'd be rolling out today with 1st PLT plus MOD-6/7 to check out one of the sites where our battalion commander intended to build a new COP in August. SFC Adams threw a Gatorade at me as if he was trying to stone me and yelled a welcome back. He was ready for me to be back on the gun instead of SPC Hafley. Hafley wasn't the sharpest tool in the shed.

We all got inline and turned on our CREW Duke Systems.[69] Dukes are a part of the Army's attempt to combat wireless IEDs, so you never left the FOB without it on. The back gate was opened while our Humvees creaked over the road, turning right to go around the FOB and onto Route Chrysler towards the mountains. It was nice being back on a mission. I liked the wind in my face and looking out into nothing. It also beat sitting around seeing everyone else roll out.

Where we were intending to go that day really had not been explored since our dismounted mission back in May, so there was no telling what we were going find...or what may find us. We pulled up to the bottom of the mountains and a few squads dismounted as MOD-6 and

---

69 **CREW**—Counter-Radio Controlled Improvised Explosive Device Electronic Warfare, a system designed to intervene in radio controlled explosives

7 debated on which way to take up. SFC Adams, a master at figuring out how to get Humvees up hills and pushing them to their limits, found an old log truck path that we could fit up. 3rd PLT led the way naturally, and we strained the heavy trucks up the road that would eventually become the real road that led to our new COP, after much construction of course.

Going as far as we could, everyone dismounted the trucks to walk up the supposed site for the COP. Drivers and gunners always stayed with the Humvees. SFC Adams felt he could push our Humvee a little farther. While dipping and eating some type of Greek creation, a leaf with meat in it, he thought he could get our truck all the way to the top. That way MOD-6 and 7 would have at least one heavy weapon for support. "Well Adams, if you think you can do it without rolling the truck then go ahead. But it's your ass when you slip off the mountain," MOD-6 said as SFC Adams started to guide our driver SGT Adams (that's right, riding with two people with the same name gets confusing) through pine trees. I was constantly battling the limbs and bugs, interrupting their mid-day slumber when I broke a limb that was coming for my head. Grasshoppers the size of softballs had started their own jihad against me.

Luckily, we made it, and had just enough room to turn around in. I provided over-watch over Route Ram. This was the first glance I had of it since June 19th; it looked a lot different from overhead. The village of Gangrekhyel on the route appeared to be vacant, its residence most likely leaving after that ground-shaking encounter.

Captain McCrystal (MOD-6), got his fill of observing the site, and we started to head back down the hill. The dismounted squads scooted around a different way than they had come up—you've always got to keep the enemy guessing. Coincidentally, that day it worked out well for everyone. As the line squads were getting into their Humvees, I heard the sound of what sounded like someone firing blanks from an M-16. Then the first RPG flew past my turret and took out several trees with a fiery fury. Here we go again, "Contact, right…100meters!" I yelled as Medic Plantiko stared up at me from behind the spare tire.

"Get the fuck in the truck medic!" SFC Adams yelled as I turned to lay down fire. "Where are they at Holder?" He then said, as I was still trying to find some muzzle flashes. The MK-19s and 50. Cals had already opened up on the hill to our right, so it was hard to distinguish between one of the grenades blowing up and ACM muzzle fire. Another RPG flew in between my truck and the Humvee in front us. "There's one guy behind us!" I yelled as I turned my turret to get a shot, but the ACM fighter was down the hill leaving only a rag behind before I could fire.

Most ACM fighters are horrible shots, and are hit and run specialists. My left leg felt as if it had no life as I knelt down for a fresh belt of ammo. I was somewhat skittish about getting hit again. "I know your nervous being back in the saddle Holder, but you got it!" SFC Adams yelled, but I couldn't hear much with all of the gun fire. "Yeah, you got it Holder!" Plantiko yelled, "What's that medic? You're a butt Pirate?" SFC Adams said which sent me into uncontrollable laughter as I re-loaded my belt and heard the whistle of an additional RPG flying past us. "Oh my God, those RPGs make my ass tighter than the Virgin Mary," SGT Adams yelled.

Just like that, it was silent. MOD-7 came over the radio to make sure no one had been injured, and the squads dismounted to pursue the ACM fighters. The hill to the right was completely destroyed from MK-19 and 50. Cal fire. It resembled hamburger meat. "Either we killed them or they are already running for Pakistan, and we can't let the latter happen!" MOD-6 yelled over the net right before he called in a shake and bake on the border. A few squads flanked out left and headed back up to the COP site, while others headed towards the hill we just massacred. A few moments later the guns in Bermel went off, annihilating the Afghan/Pakistan border with explosives and Willy Pete, the white smoke rising in triumph.

After we had scouted the hills and found various weapons but no bodies, MOD-6 decided to RTB.[70] We fueled up the trucks in anticipation for tomorrow's mission. 3rd PLT would go atop another hill, right beside the one from today, to scout out another trail that could be used for access to the COP, while 1st PLT would kick out to the next valley on Route Espree to see if we could trap the ACM if they attacked again. We were determined to drive them out of our battle space. The higher frequency of rocket attacks on the FOB showed that they were also determined to drive us out of their battle space. It was kind of like East coast rap versus West coast rap, minus the drive by shootings.

That night we received news that three paratroopers from Delta Co. had been killed by an IED. It was two I knew from attending MGLC's: SPC Davis and SGT Johnson. Delta Co.'s 1SG had also been killed in the truck, along with his interpreter. Their truck rolled over an Anti-tank mine so powerful it ripped the Humvee in half. Most likely the four passengers were killed from the blast before they burned alive like the gunner that

---

70 **RTB**—Return To Base

was still strapped in. The gunner had 3rd Degree burns on over 85% of his body, and would later succumb to his wounds at Fort Sam Houston. An Alpha soldier was also killed that day by a sniper up at FOB Tillman, which was named after the NFL player Pat Tillman who died nearly in the same spot. Those deaths brought the KIA total to ten and it was only July, eleven more months to go.

As the news past between the squads every one dealt with it their own way. Usually it consisted of a lot of us walking outside and smoking a few cigarettes. We would talk about the paratroopers that had died and each of us would usually tell our own story about them; whether it was something funny that happened out on the town in Italy, or a memorable event that took place during training. You could see that everyone now knew we were in some serious shit. But, we couldn't fear the reaper.

Rolling up the hill the next day, we sat overlooking the hilltop where our little skirmish took place the previous day. Two of our trucks followed the ridge over to the left and were just at my 11 o'clock. 1st PLT was moving up the route in the next valley over, their dust tail being seen by more than friendlies no doubt. SGT Matlock got out and walked over to a tree, observing the COP site. Our mortars squad had brought out its hand-held 60mm, and SFC Adams wanted to proceed with a Recon-By-Fire. This is when you shoot in an area, really just to see if someone will shoot back at you, much like bothering a bee hive and sometimes just as dangerous.

The first mortar flew out of the tube and almost in tandem with its report; SGT Matlock's tree was getting fired on. "Contact from the hill we were on yesterday!" I yelled. I could see the white smoke of an RPG headed our way, but it missed by a long shot. My current position was about 500m from where the ACM were. However, SGT Matlock and SSG Daniel's trucks were much closer and taking most of the fire. SSG Daniel was pinned down as was SGT Matlock behind lone trees while SPC Snyder fired on the ACM with his M240B, the bullet proof glass around him spider webbing from the impact of a round.

MOD 3-6 was already on the radio talking to 1st PLT and MOD-6 back at the FOB about our next course of action, seeing as we had two squads cut off and were too close to use artillery or CAS. The mortar squad was getting close to the ACM occupied hill since we were starting to receive fire, but nothing was effective. SFC Adams climbed up on my turret to see what he could gather about the ACM hill and if there were more fighters moving around us. "I'm beginning to think you're bad luck

Holder, you know that?" He commented while the stray bullets were zipping past us.

A few rockets went off to our left and shot towards the FOB, one impacting in the back of the chow hall as the border was being lit up by a shake and bake. The object here was to try and trap these bastards, especially since they just took out our kitchen! If it was up to me, I would have made the slimy bastards rebuild, then thrown them on potato peeling duty until Jesus came back. SGT Matlock made it back to his door just as his front right tire was flatted from an ACM round. We could see the 50.Cal and MK-19 rounds impacting all over the ACM hill—there was no way anyone was living through this again. A B-1 bomber flew past us, dropping a 1,000pd JDAM on the supposed POO site on the other side of Route Ram. Then, as if God himself spoke stillness into the world, the ACM went quiet. A few more of Snyder rounds echoed off of the mountains then all was silent on the Eastern Front.

With the B-1 still flying pretty close to our position, SSG Daniel and SGT Matlock's trucks limped back over to re-join ours. They certainly needed to RTB so that they could get fixed. MOD-6 and 7 were already out with 2nd PLT. Captain McCrystal and 1SG Collins would be joining us, as 2nd PLT drove up Route Ram to cast a sort of net all of the way to the border, or as close as they could get without inhaling the Willy Pete. MOD-6 and 7 took SSG Daniel's and SGT Matlock's spots, as they were sent back to get their business repaired.

MOD-6 was calling in all sorts of fire missions to try and make all routes to Pakistan impassable. We rolled off of that war torn hill and started to go up route Ram. I have to say I was pretty tense while going up it. Looking up at the steep river bank I could only think about June 19th and how this now seemingly peaceful dried up river would turn into a hellish inferno at any moment. I came to when I felt my heart was going to leap out of my chest and SFC Adams slapping me on the leg with a bottle of water, plus a pack of grape Gatorade Propel…his favorite. "Holder there are some good drink mixes out there, ya know don't get me wrong. But grape Propel just takes em all and fucks them hard, ya know what I'm saying?" He would say, in a number of different ways a few times a month.

We made it up Ram unscathed to check out where the JDAM had impacted. Once again, there were no bodies but there were weapons. This was starting to frustrate all of us. 1st PLT's Lieutenant came over the net and said he saw locals walking up the hill that we were just attacked on. MOD-6 asked him several times if they saw anything in their hands, like weapons, trying to get the 1ˢᵗ PLT PL[71] to say yes. Who else would walk up a hill that there was just a battle on, other than ACM fighters going back to get the gear they had left and to move bodies before sundown.

The 1ˢᵗ PLT PL Leader just wasn't getting the hint. Finally, he saw a fighter pick up a machine gun and replied. The B-1 that was previously in our air space had checked off to go re-fuel, to the dismay of MOD-6. "The shit ends today!" He said over the net and called in a high explosive artillery strike on the ACM hilltop, COP site, and all surrounding hills. Our trucks moved back down Route Ram and up past Malekshay around to where all of this had started while the artillery barrage was taking place.

3ʳᵈ PLT drove back up the hill where we came into contact earlier, which was littered with weapons and unfired RPGs. Alas, no bodies were to be found. The ACM most likely had heard the guns from Bermel fire and ran back to their cover. We gathered all of their equipment though and drove back down the hill. MOD-6 instructed the 1ˢᵗ PLT PL to tell him the minute he saw the fighters immerging from their hide outs. Sure enough, about an hour later just as dusk was creeping in, the ACM fighters were starting back up the hill to see if we had left anything for them. The convoy was almost back to the FOB as the 1ˢᵗ PLT PL called over the net to let MOD-6 know of the enemy activity, then to the surprise of all of us MOD-6 had Willey Pete fired on all previous positions, with that insuring no matter where the ACM hid they could not escape the assassin that was going to be filling the air. "Well...I guess we won't be checking that place out again for at least three days." SFC Adams said as we heard the first round impacting. East coast reigns supreme bitches!

---

71 **PL**—Platoon Leader, the Lieutenant in charge of a Platoon

CHAPTER TWELVE
AUGUST: MALEKSHAY COP

THE LAST WEEK OF July was spent preparing for the big mission in August. Every company in our battalion (except Legion) would play some role in mission dubbed Eagle Arrow, which was broken down into a number of parts. First, the Scouts, a mortar team, and a few elements of Alpha Co. would insert a day prior to the mission starting at the end of Route Ram, so they could overlook into Pakistan and seal off that ACM supply route. They would be the farthest advancing element.

Next, MOD along with elements of the ANA (Afghan National Army) would push out a few hours before dawn to form a security net around the new COP. Also at this time the Air Force would bomb key targets on the border, which included ACM caves. MOD was to clear all the way to the border, and 3rd PLT would clear Route Shadow for the first time. At night we were to set up patrol bases, so the security net could remain in place.

Additionally, an Engineer battalion would push out after MOD and the ANA made their initial sweep that morning for any ACM fighters. The engineers were to construct the new COP across from hilltop 2474 and an access road that led up to the COP, which was the road we tried to squeeze-up the first time when were ambushed in July. The COP would be in the shape of a triangle more or less with three guard towers, nine shipping containers that could be used for barracks, an aid station, etc., and two earthen ramps that overlooked the sides of the Hesco barriers that could support a Humvee. These ramps were for additional fire support on the sides.

Finally, a platoon from Delta Co. would take over security at the FOB. Also, elements from Echo Co. would provide additional logistical support, bringing extra trucks, mechanics, and armorers for weapons. Anvil was even going to play a role, by God!! Upon hearing this I promptly went to check my pants for stains. They would push out a little farther left to make sure ACM fighters did not maneuver around the 1st BN[72] elements. While all of this was going on, Eagle 6 would be flying around in his on Blackhawk monitoring progress from the air, and when he wasn't in the air, he would be running the show from Bermel. He wasn't going to let 1st BN, or Task Force Eagle, run into any trouble! After it was all said and done, the mission was supposed to last twelve days. Sounds good right? Yeah, well…so did the D-Day invasion on paper.

We heard the helicopters fly over around 2300 on August 1st. That was the Scout element going to insert on the border. They would be over watching the COP build site from the mountain where they inserted for the next thirteen days…good times. As the sun started to rise Delta Co rolled into Bermel with Echo and a RCP team.[73] RCP teams are the engineers that travel in front of convoys to clear the road of IEDs. Our battalion Lt. Colonel and Command Sergeant Major (Eagle 6 and 7) were also riding along with RCP team.

Final preparations were made. We loaded the trucks up with about five days' worth of food and water. After the five day mark, elements could pull back to Bermel to re-fit (re-stock on water, MRE's, and shower) and then head back to the COP site or wherever they were stationed. It had been four months since we had gotten to Afghanistan; the time seemed to fly by. I guess when you're busy doing something different everyday it makes the time pass quickly, much better than office work! Then again, an air conditioned, sand free office did have its appeal from time to time.

MOD, Anvil, Eagle, Engineers, and the ANA were all ready for the green light at 0300 on August 2nd, 2007. Counting the ANA, as well as the Scout and Alpha elements already stationed by the border, we were a force of about 360 personnel about to cover the area that had been giving us problems since day one. We hoped that the ACM would see or hear us coming, tuck tail, and run back to their hide-outs in Pakistan. If not, the jets, helicopters, and artillery barge that was about to start would send the message.

As we exited the back gate with the ANA in front of us, I saw the first bomb light up the night, followed by another, and then another. The deep boom that continuously reverberated around the valley was more than

---

72 **BN**—Battalion, a unit size designator which is approximately 700-1,000 soldiers
73 **RCP**—Route Clearance Package, vehicles designated to clear routes of improvised explosive devices

enough to wake the Muslims, and probably some dead ones as well. I don't know about everyone else, but it filled me with a deep sense of patriotism. Kind of like our own invasion of the Malekshay area, simply saying to the ACM and their supporters, "Hey, we're here, and were staying."

Two Apaches were flying near Gonjakhel with their infrared search lights on, no doubt tracking something or someone. A few Hellfire's[74] illuminated the night from their positions. The birds banked and flew in our direction, a fiery report from the Hellfire's adding to the wake of battle that now engulfed the valley. The Apaches flew over our head, circled over the FOB, and flew towards Shkin, the Special Forces FOB about 13k from Bermel.

I noticed the convoy had stopped. This would be the first snag in our invasion of Malekshay. Someone had the bright idea to place the ANA out in front, leading the charge, the only problem with that was that the ANA did not have blackout lights[75] to drive with night vision goggles. Hell...they didn't even have night vision goggles. So basically, it was too dark for the ANA to drive without using their head lights, which would give away out position. I guess it never occurred to anyone that this was going to be a problem. So 3rd PLT took the lead, and the ANA followed a few hundred yards behind us with their head lights, which split us into two different elements.

3rd PLT made it to Route Ram just as the sun was coming up over the mountains. I was as nervous as a Jew standing in front of Hitler himself. We started creeping out of the dried river bed; I crouched low in the turret, ready to let the metal fly at the first sign of trouble. Just then two Blackhawks roared over our convoy, and a wave of relief hit my soul. It was Eagle 6, controlling the operation from the air. His pair of birds flew up Route Ram all the way to the border. It was a good feeling having all of this air support at my fingertips.

We passed Gangrekhyel and continued the 3k up to the border; this route had also not been cleared all of the way since we took over the battle space. Eagle 6 continued to circle us. It was a peaceful morning. The pine trees rustled in the morning breeze, fruit from an orchard was falling and rolling on the ground. What could have been a morning of constant battle turned out to be one of the more quiet ones we had since arriving

---

74 **Hellfire**—the AGM-114 Hellfire is an air-to-surface missile (ASM) developed primarily for anti-armor use
75 **Blackout Lights**—infrared lights built onto military equipment which can only be viewed by a night vision device

in country, despite the bombs that fell earlier, the artillery that was now pounding the border off in the distance, and the radio that was constantly chatting out grid coordinates.

The ANA had caught up to our convoy. We came to a stop in a clearing a few hundred meters from the border. The ANA rode in small pick-up trucks, which had no armor. They piled in there like bunch of Mexicans and mounted automatic weapons to the roof. Eagle 6 had spotted a few lean-tos[76] against the trees that he wanted us to check out. The ANA dismounted with our rifle squads and began to clear up to the border; SFC Adams and SGT Adams were going to check out the lean-tos.

The Adamses were walking up the steep, tree-covered hillside when two Apaches flew over to go assist 1st PLT. 1ST PLT had found rockets that were set to timers and believed that the ACM were still close by. This got Eagle 6 pretty jumpy. As the Adamses were nearing the lean-tos, Eagle 6 ordered the Black Hawk gunner to open up on the lean-tos just to make sure no one was in there. Bullets ripped past the Adamses as they leapt for cover behind the trees and scramble to get their voices over the radio.

Eagle 6 let out more bursts of machine gun fire in the Adamses direction just as SFC Adams comes over the MOD frequency in an unpleasant tone telling them to "cease fire you fuck knuckles! We're in that area Goddamn it!" The firing stopped as Eagle 6 apologized with a laugh. Meanwhile 1st PLT was deciding whether to approach the rockets and attempt to wrap them in C4 or have one of the Apaches blow them up. They chose the latter option. Who really knew how old those 107mm rockets were? One wrong move and it would have been hell to pay, kind of like dealing with strippers.

1st PLT had yet to run into contact, so they continued to move to the border, allowing enough space for the detonation that was about to occur. The Apaches began firing their cannons at the rockets…and then kept firing…and then ran out of ammunition. One Apache fired a rocket at the rockets (how about that) and missed. The second fired two rockets and missed. They both fired two a piece, finally, direct hit. The only problem was that the explosion set off the ACM rockets and they almost landed on the Engineers that were now heading out towards the COP site. One of the pilots came over the net to say they had to re-arm now…ya think?

The Adams found nothing in the lean-tos. The ANA and line squads

---

76 **Lean-to**—a lean-to is a term used to describe a roof with a single slope. The term also applies to a variety of structures that are built using a lean-to roof

had found a make-shift cabin with a good number of weapons in it; they promptly disintegrated it with an AT4[77]. All of the platoons had finished their push to the border, and none had run into contact. The clear was successful. We were now going to hold this position for 48 hours to make sure no ACM got in or out.

The engineers had started on the road to the new COP. You could hear their machinery and tools hard at work. It was still pretty warm, about 93 degrees during the day; but felt much warmer in body armor. I know the engineers hated doing all of that work with wood and such while wearing that shit. I had it pretty good though, standing in the turret all day gets warm, but I wasn't climbing up and down mountains like the line squads, at least not at the moment anyway.

That night our patrol base was invaded by wild dogs. Feral dogs ran amok in Afghanistan, always in packs and always out at night. They would howl and bark while fighting over MRE trash or other goodies that they had found. Of course SFC Adams, the philosopher that he was, had three words any time he saw the savage mutts running around, "Bitch-ass dogs." It cracked me up every time.

The first 48hrs went relatively smoothly during the Malekshay COP build. It was now time to go check out Route Shadow. We hadn't cleared the route since taking over the battle space; the closest we came was overlooking it during the first COP surveying mission. Like half of the routes in Afghanistan, it too was a dried up river bed, surrounded by tall mountains which were covered in the green pines. We drove onto Shadow by way of a connector road which linked Shadow to Ram.

As soon as we came to it, we noticed a house overlooking the route that needed to be cleared. SFC Adams's stomach also had begun to rumble, he was known for being unable to hold his bowels. As the convoy kicked its engines into 4-Low to make it up the hill, SFC Adams began to dig for his baby wipes. "Oh shit, I am going to shit!" He said as he was reaching for the platoon handset. Just as we crested the hill and were on level ground, he halted the convoy and jumped out of the Humvee to run into the trees. Ever taken a dump in body armor? It ain't easy.

Our new Lieutenant dismounted the rifle squads to clear the building. Lt. Israel had been stolen from us to take command of the scouts. Our new Lt. was a doofus, a tall, over-weight, mouth-breather who probably

---

77 **AT4**—the an 84-mm unguided, portable, single-shot recoilless smoothbore weapon built in Sweden by Saab Bofors Dynamics and is used mainly for armored vehicles

joined the Army to prove his daddy wrong. SFC Adams had dubbed him, "A knuckle-dragging oaf." He wouldn't be with us long, but for now we had to put up with him.

SFC Adams came out of the woods with a pair of boxers in hand. He didn't make it all of the way to the trees as his streaked boxers clearly proved. As he neared the Humvee, he could no doubt hear our laughter since he said, "Yeah shut the fuck up Holder." A phrase I still hear to this day from the other witnesses. I am a constant instigator. He threw the boxers to the ground after a good laugh himself and lit them on fire. This would not be the last time a convoy had to stop so he could relieve himself.

With the hut being cleared, we continued to look around the site. The ACM used various markers on the trees to make a map of different areas. Such as where to fire rockets, the angle to fire them, ambush positions, etc. These symbols were all over the trees by this hut. It was no doubt a place used for refuge for incoming/out-going ACM fighters. MOD-6 wanted us to clear the route. The Humvees would provide support from the wadi as the line squads walked to the left or right of the Humvees clearing the hill tops.

The knuckle-dragging oaf was having a hell of a time with the hills. He looked a hot mess, helmet crooked and face as red as a Hot Tamale. We found multiple rocket stands. Basically these were crude pieces of metal welded together which made an angled launch pad that sat approximately two feet off the ground. The route was smoother than most, as it was used frequently for loggers. Once we made it to hilltop 2474, the wadi took a sharp turn right and headed towards Margah COP at the far end of Anvil's battle space. As our clearance ended we were ordered to drive back to Gangrekhyel to provide security for the night. We stayed amongst the vacant houses that were abandoned after the fire fight in June. SFC Adams showed us the proper way to make Spaghetti and meat sauce with MREs. He talked to his food frequently and was always giving us tips on ours.

I awoke to the sound of bulldozers. I could see the engineers up on the hill had started one of the Hesco walls. These guys were moving quickly. The north tower had also been put up but was being disassembled due to improper construction. The access road was completely finished, which also included a rudimentary helipad. Another Engineer convoy was headed out towards the COP site. It was carrying more wood for the towers, Hesco walls, a re-supply of MREs, and water. Furthermore, flatbed trucks were carrying shipping containers which were going to be transformed into bunkers. There would be four containers for sleeping quarters, one for food storage, two for supplies, and two more for an Aid Station, plus TOC (Tactical Operations Center). The convoy was about to awaken an unseen demon that was already plaguing Iraq.

The ANA was escorting the convoy as it made the right turn towards the COP site. The convoy could be seen for miles with all of the dust they were throwing up. As the lead Nissan Hilux dipped down into an old gravel creek bed, it was shredded in half by a powerful anti-tank mine, no doubt meant for one our larger vehicles. The soldiers were thrown from the bed, and the driver and passenger were ripped apart.

The explosion shattered through the quiet morning and the radio starting asking for 100% accountability to make sure no U.S. Forces were hurt. MOD-6 also ordered 3rd PLT to head towards the IED site, but to clear the road along the way. Now the game had changed. IED's were going to be a constant threat from now until we left. The problem with these silent killers is that cannot be seen. One second you're riding along, happy-go-lucky, the next your legs are broken and brain mushed from the pressure created by such a blast.

As we arrived at the IED site, I could see the windshield wipers were still on in the heap of metal that was once a vehicle. The driver's body parts were scattered, some as far as 50ft away; while the passenger had been reduced to nothing more than water and blood. One soldier in the back had died, another was sitting up about 50 yards away from the blast, and the third passenger in the back most likely had a severe internal injury as he was crying out in Pashtun. A MEDEVAC had already been raised from Orgun-E (O.E.), our battalion headquarters. The MEDEVAC was going to land about a 1k away from our current position; this required the wounded ANA soldier to be transported.

Doc Plantiko and Doc Lollino tied the screaming soldier to a liter and then fastened him to the hood of my Humvee. He was crying out and attempted to untie the straps. The other ANA soldier was placed in the back of my Humvee with a neck brace on, but was walking…he said nothing the entire time. As we start moving the ANA soldier on the hood began to freak out. I can't imagine what was going through his mind or if his mind was even working correctly due to the blast.

SFC Adams popped purple smoke as the bird came in. The Black Hawk helicopter blew dirt everywhere with its powerful wind. The flight medics jump out and prepare the wounded soldiers to be loaded up. The dead ones were back at the site, no doubt under tarps by now. The flight medic hits the tied down soldier with something strong as it makes him go silent. I duck behind my bullet proof glass to escape the tornado that the bird produces while it lifts off, knowing that those two guys will never be the same.

The next several days passed without incident. The COP was coming along smoothly and it was now time to clear some of the trees that surrounded the hillside to make a clear line of site in case of attack. Instead of having the bulldozers knock them over, because that would have been the smart thing to do, we were going to drive up there and chop down trees on a hill, in full body armor, in 90 degree weather...with axes. Sometimes the Army amazes me.

A few Afghans had beaten us there and were complaining that this was their land. Also, that these trees belonged to them. MOD-6 asked them if they knew that the Taliban had been attacking us from this area. Of course they knew nothing about that. He then asked them if they wanted to come gather the trees for market. Naturally they did not want to do this either. The three Afghan men just wanted to be paid for the trees lost; undeniably, they were going to use the money to support the ACM. This wasn't going to happen on our watch. MOD-6 sent them away with the option to collect the trees, as they were driving away I yelled at MOD-6, "You think the Muslims will chop these trees down for us sir?" He felt that this was just a ploy to size up our numbers on the hill. About an hour later his assessment was correct as the first rocket flew over the COP, impacting on the hill next to it. The ICOM started lighting up about an attack tonight...oh yes, I was hoping to turn this beast into Helms Deep.

The sunset over the Pakistan border was like a thousand before it; the orange, blue, and pink colors turning the sky into something out of fairytale. Only the one rocket had flown over us—it had been quiet ever since. The ICOM no longer voiced threats about an attack, and the silence was a bit unnerving. The Scouts and mortar team (yes they are still on that same mountain) hadn't seen anyone come across the border, but then again they could only see one area. Darkness took us. We'd see if this half-finished fortress could withstand a jihad.

I was on duty with the LRAS[78] which is a machine that allows you to see a long distance with thermal options. I had spotted one person on the hillside directly in front of us. He didn't move for a while, as if he

---

78 **LRAS**—Long Range Advanced Scouting Surveillance System, a system that uses an infrared lenses and zooming to allow the user to view farther than the standard binoculars

could feel that we had spotted him. After watching him for an hour or so, I relinquished duty on the LRAS to jump on the MK-19. I was sitting behind the MK-19 tripod at an angle. It was set up on a corner where two walls meet; I just had a plywood board holding me up there about twelve feet in the air. I just knew the first shot out of this thing was going to break the wood and I was going to fall on top of a pile of nail laden 2x4s.

Captain McCrystal did not like the suspense, and this Muslim fuck on the hillside did not help. For all we knew he could have been a spotter for a mortar attack or possibly a sniper. MOD-6 ordered the border to be shaked and baked for good measure. That would keep them out, or if they were in, that would keep them in. We were going to clear out the border again tomorrow. An explosion echoes throughout the valley before the artillery has a chance to fire. MOD-6 puts the mission on stand-by as we try to figure out what happen.

The Lieutenant for 1st PLT came over the net. They had just hit an IED, five WIA (Wounded in Action) but none KIA (Killed in Action). One Staff Sergeant has had his arm shattered due to the fact he had it hanging out his bulletproof window. Now if you have never been in an up armored Humvee, the door itself weights about 1,000 pounds. The window is about two inches thick and slides down. The SSG had his arm out with NODS in hand trying to light up the road with his Infrared Red (IR)[79] spot light. When the truck struck the IED, up goes the window on his arm. The window shattered his right arm and it also took the soldiers a few minutes to get it back down off his arm. What an idiot! MOD-6 thinks this could be a possible command detonation, meaning someone detonated the IED by hand, as an attempt to draw forces away from the half-finished COP. He then resumes the fire mission on the border, while sending 2nd PLT on foot to help secure 1st PLT. The rest of the night was cool and quiet, after the artillery barrage of course.

On August 8th, 2007 3rd PLT got an assignment to separate from the COP mission and to help the Special Forces boys down in Shkin. This was nothing new. We had helped the Shkin guys out a few times during the day, usually providing them with support as they went into villages that had not yet been reached. This time, however, we would provide support for them while they went on a snatch and grab in some remote Afghan village. 3rd PLT returned to Bermel to refit for the day and then drive down to Shkin later, as this would be a night mission.

---

79 **IR**—Infrared, light which can only be detected through use of certain devices

FOB Shkin, was a small outpost which sat closer to the border than Bermel did. It had been in Afghanistan supposedly since the Cold War era, during which time it was used by the CIA. The Special Forces (SFOD-A) teams that were stationed there switched out often, about every 90 days or so. A new team had just gotten in. As usual, they were always pretty easy to get along with.

The last mission we accompanied the Special Forces on was an Afghanistan/Pakistan border meeting. It involved the Afghan governors of the region getting together with the Pakistani governors, sucking dicks, and then never really coming to a solution about how to secure the border. The entire Muslim world just talks, for hours they would chat about the same shit and once they figured out what was wrong, they wouldn't change anything because one governor may not get along with another. They cannot put their differences aside for the greater good; it is much the same throughout the Muslim world.

That mission was a day operation, and as I said before this would be a night mission. We dicked around until the sun went down. I put an old Humvee air filter, some plastic tubing, and an air hose in SFC Adams's seat. He hated when his stuff got moved or touched. He could always tell if someone had been sitting in his seat. Of course we blamed all of this on the medic. The medic told SFC Adams it was me that put the stuff in his seat. This set off rock-throwing in my direction. Sure it wasn't safe, but that sort of thing doesn't matter when you're in the middle of nowhere.

We started the mission around 2000 that night. The stars were out in full force. Such star light is over-shadowed in large cities or urban areas, but out here that was what we relied on for the best night vision. Along with the IR lights on our Humvees, the Special Forces (SF) had a few IR spotlights on that lit up our surrounding area. It was basically like daylight looking through your NODS. In one eye you could see everything; while out of the other you could only see the night sky. We were going to a village to grab an ACM leader. He moved around frequently, and the only intelligence that came in was the HUMINT from the Special Forces (SF) spies. A recent report stated that the ACM leader would be staying at a certain house tonight, so if we wanted to grab him, now was the time. The SF could have easily snuck in there by themselves, but they were worried that this report may be a trap to grab them instead.

Our Humvees would provide an outer cordon for security. Then the SF and our line squads would sneak into the village and grab this guy, along with anyone else who looked suspect. The actual grab was only supposed to take about five minutes, but the drive at night is what made this such a long process. We had a B-1 bomber come into our airspace for air support; he was a ways off as not to spook the ACM leader. The ACM knew to look for the any sign or sound of air support; they weren't foolish.

As we neared the village, the Special Forces team dismounted their vehicles as did our line squads. Gunners, drivers, and SFC Adams continued to move the Humvees further down the road, proceeding to make a circle around the village. No one got in or out. My Humvee was parked just outside of the north end of the village, right across a vital bridge, in case the ACM leader got wind of our noise and tried to escape by vehicle.

I heard the unmistakable sound of C4 break the night silence. The mission had commenced, with two doors being splintered and SF rushing inside to survey the mud hut's occupancy. No shots had been fired, so things seemed to be running smoothly. One of our line squads detained two ACM fighters who were rushing to save the ACM leader who was in fact in the house. The fighters dropped their weapons and were flex-cuffed. Looks like three detainees were going back with us so far. Special Forces was out in just under ten minutes with their guy as well as four more, making five total detainees for the night. The trucks were mounted, the ACM were put in the back of a flatbed Humvee, and we were off. The quick ten minute mission was now going to be followed by another three-hour drive.

We returned to Bermel the next day to refit, and then headed back to the COP build site on August 10th, 2007. A shower, fresh uniform, and hot meal are always welcome. The COP build was going smoothly. Our push to the border had been a success; no other attacks on the COP (rocket or otherwise) had been attempted. Our platoon would set up south of the COP but still in sight of it for the next two days. Other platoons, engineers, and other accompanying units would begin to draw back to FOB Bermel as their work was completed and 2nd PLT took over the COP for the first time, beginning to add in extra protection, such as sandbags or barbed-wire. This was longest mission we had done so far, twelve days total. However, we would soon discover that twelve days was nothing at all.

CHAPTER THIRTEEN
XAVIER: PART TWO

RETURNING TO THE FOB on August 12th, 2007, 3rd PLT took over Force Protection for the next three days. It was nice to be able to pull eight hours of guard duty (four during the day, four at night) and do whatever you wanted during your off time. Of course there wasn't much to do. A few of us had baseball mitts or footballs shipped to us. Sometimes the Afghanis would invite us over to whoop our asses in soccer. There was a small gym where you could get your swoll on if you were into lifting weights. A lot of us just chilled in our room to catch up on movies and television shows we had missed, courtesy of pirated DVDs. We were in Afghanistan to protect the rights of all Americans...except those in the film and television industry.

One morning we woke up to the mortar team firing illumination rounds about 2 clicks out of the FOB. They had set up next to our Humvees and were lobbing the rounds just on the out skirts of Bermel. We had intelligence that the ACM were planting land mines in hopes that we would walk over them. Our platoon mounted up quickly to go assist 1st platoon who had already walked out there. Their Platoon Leader said that the guy was putting up a fence. But this could not be. What kind of ACM fighter puts up a fence instead of placing a IED? Was he hoping to trap us? Never under estimate the weirdness of an Afghani.

Further investigation did prove there was a fence, but it was more of a net really. This local had a tape recorder playing bird sounds that he thought would attract birds to fly into a net on the ground—fucking genius. There were no birds that ran on the ground in the region, only flying ones. I don't think the first thing to do on birds daily list of activities was to fly around looking for tape recordings. Muslims, what nut jobs.

Mail came a few days after the COP mission and my there was a lot of it! All previous flights out to Bermel had been mission only, but now that the COP was finished, they had room to bring our mail. I received a long letter from my dad, also one from my brother. Both of the letters had two stories in them. It seemed Xavier had struck again. This time it was going to affect me, 7,000 miles away. It seemed Xavier's superhuman abilities were now becoming transcontinental. I wondered if Antarctica would even be safe to live in.

Let's go back in time for a minute, back to Olive Garden on May 27th, 2006. Remember that? When Xavier was talking about explosives and microwaves? Well that was also the day I graduated from Airborne School, so Xavier was pumped up to join the military. He wanted to join the Marines, but for some reason I talked him out of being a bullet-catcher and persuaded him into trying to join the Army. I never thought this would actually happen, but I guess I never taught myself not to underestimate the beast…that's enough smart ass comments, class.

Think back to Columbus, Georgia. After checking into the hotel with my uncle and aunt, Xavier decided to have himself a little fun. As night fell on Columbus, Xavier used his canny ability to take things apart and slipped into a storage facility. He did not steal anything but just liked the rush. My uncle found him sitting in the lobby at 6 a.m. without his key card, due to the fact he left it in somebody's Ford Bronco that was in climate-controlled storage. Auspiciously, he was not returning to Valdosta with us, but going to his new home in Griffin, Georgia, where his parents had moved while he was off on one of his maximum security retreats.

Since I had been deployed, Xavier decided to return to public life and try to join the military. Naturally he had not graduated high school, due to some "misadventures" nor did he have a G.E.D. Yet this was during the period of an Iraqi surge and a booming economy, so the military was hurting for bodies to fill slots. I would love to meet the recruiter that yanked Xavier's chain, telling him that they may be able to get him a waiver and that he should travel to Atlanta to visit MEPS[80].

Xavier was down for a road trip. He loaded up in the van with a few more volunteers and headed to the Atlanta. The others with him had no idea that their MEPS experience would be one of a kind! Usually a MEPS appointment is early in the morning and lasts about a day. Since all Armed

---

80 **MEPS**—Military Entrance Processing Station, a facility where a civilian gets cleared to join the military

Forces use MEPS, it can get pretty crowded. The military will put you up in hotel, and you start your processing the next morning. Xavier was placed in a room by himself thank God and curiously did not get into any mischief that night.

The following morning Xavier walked in the MEPS station and placed his personal belongings inside a locked room, just as every other person that was there did. Xavier, determining that all of these test were taking too long, decided to break into said secure room and attempt to steal people's stuff. Where he was going to keep everything I have no idea! One of the many uniformed personnel confronted him; this turned into a "bull in a china shop" kind of ordeal, with six or seven people trying to bring down this lunatic in such a small space. A doctor ran up from the back with a sedative to slam in Xavier's veins. I hope the recruiter got a refresher course on how to pick new soldiers, or maybe was even hooked up to a Thorazine drip for the rest of his days.

The military didn't want to handle Xavier. Due to the fact he was not a soldier, he could not be punished under the Uniform Code of Military Justice (UCMJ)[81]. Xavier was over eighteen years of age now, had prior offenses as we all know, and MEPS is under jurisdiction of the Federal Government, so his case came with a little extra spice. Personally I'm a fan of Texas Pete, but this shit was more like Tabasco. The judge sentenced Xavier to another mental hospital for rehabilitation, banned him from ever setting foot on federal property without an escort, and barred him from joining the military. It seemed Xavier had a one way ticket back to paradise, but also had some plans of his own. As I sat on my bunk in Afghanistan reading these two letters to my roommate and others that are listening, I was getting all kind of remarks about inbreeding and marrying first cousins. Number one, marrying your second cousins is legal but not first. Number two; there is nothing wrong with swapping spit with your sister...or brother.

Xavier arrived at his new home in Texas. He was at another maximum security facility, but this one offered a program that allows patients to work on their G.E.D. while serving their sentence, oh excuse me...while they are being reformed. The teacher did not really grab Xavier's attention, or maybe Xavier just plain didn't like her, or it could be part of a more sinister plot to escape the padded walls. In any case, Xavier seized the teacher as he walked into the classroom on his second day of class and held her at

---

81 **UCMJ**—Uniform Code of Military Justice, the laws of the United States military

pencil point. He then spun her around, knocked the wind out of her, and dropped to his knees with his hands on his head, awaiting the cuffs that were sure to come.

Xavier was placed in solitary, but he was moved to Tennessee a short time after to appease the teacher and keep her from pressing charges against the institution for not having a guard present in the classroom. Shortly after arriving in Tennessee, a lawyer visited Xavier outside of his solitary cell in the open area where patients can socialize. The lawyer, obviously not reading Rain Man's file, left him with a business card. Big mistake, since Xavier's window had bars on it this time, he was planning another, slyer escape, and this card was the missing piece he had been searching for.

Two days later after acquiring a fork from the cafeteria, Xavier picked the security device to his room with the business card and said fork and let himself out into the main room of the building. While dodging the eyes of the night watchmen, he broke the fork in the lock that would have set him free. No doubt annoyed by his failure, Xavier walked up to the startled guard and made an attempt for his keys. The security guard barely put a door in between him and the brute, escaping God knows what. A man desperate to flee a situation he hates will do anything.

Now this is where I come back into the picture. Xavier, not being happy with his failed escape attempt, decided to take a more diplomatic approach to being released. He resolved to write two letters. One to The President of the United States, George W. Bush, and the other to The Secretary of State, Condoleezza Rice. Xavier pleaded that he should be discharged from prison, for he felt he had done nothing wrong. Oh and by the way, failure to exonerate him would bring about an untimely death to the President and Mrs. Rice. Now things really got Federal!

First of all, what kind of prison allows an inmate to send letters to the President? Secondly, if you see a letter addressed to the WHITE HOUSE from a crazy person, wouldn't you at least screen it? C'mon! Secret Service intercepts both letters and rains down on Xavier's life. They started interviewing everyone in it, reaching as far back as pre-school. Black Suburban's drove up to my Aunt and Uncle's house, and requested to see Xavier's room. Astonished, they complied and were thoroughly interviewed. Secret Service confiscated Xavier's complete room, down to the mouse for his computer and then made appointments with Xavier's psychologist.

The psych's opinion was that Xavier was not mentally fit enough to get to the President, but that he may be able to get to Rice. That news didn't set the Secret Service at ease one bit, especially since they found out that Xavier had three male cousins in the Army...all in the Infantry. They started looking at all three of us. The next day I am called to Captain McCrystal's room. What a coincidence that it happened the day after I got the letter! I sat down, and he looked at me and asked me if I had a cousin named Xavier, and that's when I went through the whole story.

I have no idea if my other two cousins were ever questioned. Seeing how I was in Afghanistan, and nowhere near ole G.W., I wasn't really a threat. MOD-6 just wanted to make sure I wasn't planning something when I went on leave, so he could report back. Xavier was moved from Tennessee to Miami to await trial and undergo multiple screenings to see if he could in fact make good on his threat. No one can ever really be sure what The Beast is up to.

(From Left To Right) Lowell, Clark, and Archie at the Eagle's Nest

Looking out of Malekshay COP

Watching the Pakistan border being bombed from Malekshay COP. This was after one of the ACM mortar strikes.

Over watching the Taliban Hotel from OP East in Spearay. Note the main ACM supply route to the middle right.

Two Afghan kids on the way to Orgun-E

Winter at Malekshay COP

Lowell and myself stripping at Exstatia.

*Me and the future President of
Qatar. Beer from a pitcher, into
a wine glass. I liked his style.*

*The town of Vicenza, Italy. As
seen from Mount Berico*

*1/503rd jumping into Drop
Zone Juliet at Aviano Airbase*

CHAPTER FOURTEEN
SEPTEMBER: BULLDOZERS
AND BIRTHDAYS

SEPTEMBER CAME PRETTY QUICKLY it seemed. The first four months of our fifteen month tour felt like a dream, and now there were only nine remaining. Leave had started in late August, which was eighteen days total, not including travel time. God knows it took a while to get home, due to the fact we were in the middle of nowhere. I kind of felt bad for the people that had to take leave so early. Once they made their way back to Afghanistan, they were still looking at about a year left on the tour…yikes. I would be taking leave in January, something to look forward to!

The fall rains were becoming more frequent. Hail usually accompanied them. That was no fun for me, sticking out of the turret in the middle of a hailstorm. While out on a Humanitarian Aid (HA) mission on September 2nd a storm snuck up on us. Not only did it bring the usual rain and hail, but it also decided to borrow a Tornado from Kansas. The twister kept getting closer to our position, but no one seemed to grasp the urgency of the situation. The dark, swirling funnel began to suck the air passed our faces as SFC Adams and I stood there watching it move along the fields about half a mile from us. "Let's get this show on the road damn it!" SFC Adams shouted over the PLT Net. The knuckle-dragging oaf (our fearless platoon leader) finally made it back to his Humvee, I think SFC Adams threating to leave him was a good motivator.

I tried to wrap some bandages around my exposed neck to block it from the hail, but it didn't work that well. SFC Adams thought this was a riot. Of course the inside of the Humvee got wet too, since there was a big hole in the top for me to stand. SFC Adams kept asking me to bring my knees to my chest to soak up the rain, so he didn't have to feel the occasional splash. The rain was starting to hit some of his Propel drink mix. The Tornado veered left as we made our way back to the FOB, hoping to beat a flash flood. That Muslim weather was something else!

We were on the list for the next rotation at the new Malekshay COP. Before we could rip out 1st PLT, MOD-6 wanted to go take care of some spring cleaning. Now you may think I mean cleaning, as in Clorox-fucking-fresh, but this was not the case. We had reports and evidence that there was a corrupt Afghan National Police station between Bermel and Orgun-E, (where our battalion headquarters is located) in little village named Zowarekel. Well MOD-6 and Eagle-6 did not roll over for the Afghani government as some leaders did. They meant business.

Now O.E. was about a four-hour drive through the low hills, so Zowarekel was about two hours away near the Sarobi District. You may be wondering, why that would be our job and not someone else's, due to the distance away from our FOB. The Paktika Providence was vast, with fifteen districts and almost a population of 400,000. The 1st Battalion only had around 750 soldiers to run missions for the whole providence, hence the large battle spaces. Charlie Company would help other companies out and vice versa with missions, it's one team and one fight.

Before the mission, a bulldozer arrived on the back of a flatbed with a few engineers. We knew the engineers would be accompanying us on our COP rotation, but we didn't know what the bulldozer was for. No one really cared to ask I guess. MOD-6 and the rest of the command group would be going on the mission with us to Zowarekel, along with 2nd PLT, and a RCP (Route Clearance Package) escort. I turned my turret around to face the rear as we left the FOB, smelling the Muslim flat-bread cooking, and I wondered why we were taking back a bulldozer that had just arrived. Along with where I could snatch a slice of bread out of someone's hand.

The road to O.E. has many small villages on it. The children would run out to the road as our convoy passed, holding out their hands for anything we might throw at them. Some always wanted candy, others pens or pencils. Usually we would have to throw out of our turrets at them and watch them fight over it like hungry pigeons. Our convoy had to pass through countless wadis. These river beds were no good for our vehicles, but there was no other way to go. There was one big hill that led into Zowarekel, and each vehicle had to get a running start to make it up it, as 15,000lbs isn't that easy to move.

As we arrived in the village, RCP went all the way through it and stopped. The flatbed truck that carried the bulldozer pulled up along-side of a long white building. My PLT stopped to pick up rear security. SGT Adams and I were looking at the C4 that sitting in our truck when we heard the bulldozer pulling off the flatbed. We then saw Afghan National Police walking away from their building. SFC Adams came over the PLT net and said, "MOD-6 gave them two choices: Stay in there and get bulldozed, or walk away and watch your Head Quarters get bulldozed you corrupt motherfuckers!" It appeared they got the hint.

The engineer inside of the bulldozer threw that thing in rabbit mode and plunged deep into the ANP building, shattering everything in its path. We watched the destruction and laughed as MOD-6 and 7 had people take the ANP soldier's weapons and badges away from them. Corruption in the Afghan government isn't anything new. Afghanistan is the third most corrupt country in the world, ranking up there with Honduras and Syria. If it was up to me, I would yank all of our troops out of there right now, but then again, you aren't reading this book to hear about my political ideas. We'll save those for when I reach my thirty-fifth birthday.

Making it back to Bermel after our trip lovely trip to O.E., we prepared for our COP rotation. We had already completed one quick rotation, which was four days long. It was spent making sandbags and running barbed wire around the perimeter. 3rd PLT did most of the work at the Malekshay COP to make it safer from indirect and direct fire. One of the 2nd PLT soldiers even said, "We shouldn't worry about working on the COP anymore, 3rd PLT is going out there, they'll get it done." SFC Adams liked for shit to be perfect, so we were done when he said we were done.

I have to say I didn't fill many sandbags. I was still the PLT cook, so most of my time went in to preparing three meals for 30 grown men. I did the best I could with the tools I had, but you can't make everyone happy, especially at breakfast. I don't know what it is but every American thinks he is the fucking bee's knees at whipping up bacon and eggs. I mean… there are only so many things I could do with powdered eggs. I did invent one thing that was a constant hit. Being from Georgia, I fried a bunch of stuff; I noticed we had a surplus of English Muffins sitting around so I thought, "What the hell?" I spread butter on each side of the muffin, fried it for about twenty seconds, and then covered it in cinnamon and sugar. Instant fatty hit. We called them Huffins.

As we prepared to go to the COP this time, I would have to take a lot more food, due to the fact that the engineers would be accompanying us. They were going to work on some land clearance for us and one of the earthen vehicle ramps. Since the engineers were going to be there with us, our PLT would have to give up one of the four shipping containers we called bed rooms. These containers had been out fitted with wooden bunk beds along the side to sleep six soldiers. They also had tiny A/C units and a few extension cords in them. They were rugged, but they had been called home many times.

I took my grocery list to the cooks, who were always so up-tight about handing over food. Army supply and food soldiers are the worst about handing over items. I mean it's not like it belongs to them. They bent to most of my requests, and we had the trucks loaded up. Our convoy was halted due to a V.I.P. coming in to Bermel. Now who could this be? No one mentioned Eagle-6 was making a visit. Well our guess was so far off, it was none other than The Chief of Staff, 4-Star General George Pace!

Three of us from each PLT were selected to go hear him speak about operations in Afghanistan, and I was lucky enough to be one of them. We hurried to our small chow hall and sat down. Refreshments were laid out, so I guess this wasn't a total surprise. Everyone leapt to attention as the General Pace walked in. He was a tall, good-looking man, who knew what it was to command. He spoke quickly about missions and the future, took a few questions then handed out coins. His coin was shaped like the Pentagon and weighed about five pounds! He then shook our hands and was off on his private Blackhawk. No wander the government is 14 trillion in debt.

Walking back to my truck and putting my gunner's harness back on, SFC Adams said, "Can we get this show on the road now? I'm ready for some fried ribs." With that we were off, back to do another COP rotation and have the ultimate sausage party. The engineers cleared the road with the bulldozer before we made to the COP. No wonder it was such a smooth ride. RCP was elsewhere, but I guess a bulldozer does just as good at detecting IEDs. Making our way up the winding road to the COP and over the make-shift helipad, we pulled into the gate to relieve 1st PLT.

Relieving a PLT from the COP didn't usually take more than 45 minutes. Two M240's had to be changed out from the North and South tower, and another from the East tower along with a 50. Cal. The Lieutenant (Lt.) and Platoon Sergeant (PSG) of the Platoon (PLT) handing over would brief the PLT taking over and the guards would change out; meanwhile we put all of the frozen food into our make-shift freezer, which consisted of sandbags packing tightly together and bags of ice over the food. A little

American ingenuity can overcome anything, even the arid Muslim heat. It was tough times in 'The Stan', but it got the job done. We also had shelves built for our dry goods (cereal, shelf-milk, muffins) that could support an array of can goods as well. Like I said before, it wasn't The Palms, but it was better than eating MRE's day in and out.

With 1ˢᵗ PLT driving out of the gate, I began to make dinner at SFC Adams request; we would be having fried ribs, green-beans, and boxed mashed potatoes. SFC Adams also required an onion of some sort and jalapeños (when we had them) at every meal. Most of the meat was pre-cooked, so I didn't really have to worry about food poisoning, which was a blessing in that bacteria-infested place, so I just added my own zing to everything. A favorite of most of the 3ʳᵈ PLT soldiers was macaroni and cheese with hamburger in it. What the heck is American's obsession with Mac-n-Cheese?

The next day, as I was taking supplies down to cooking shack, I saw that the engineers were surveying one of our earthen emplacements. Just then the first mortar hissed over the COP landing just above the helipad, and sending a spray of dirt and metal up on the South tower. The next had dropped in range and was now of about 50m from the South tower. "Everybody take cover. They're bracketing us!" SPC Neary yelled. He was the lead Forward Observer (FO) in 3ʳᵈ PLT. The next mortar shook the earth on the other side of the COP, closer to the North tower. Somehow the ACM shifted its fire on the other side of the COP. SPC Neary called in several targets for our artillery to hit. Once again I was stuck in an indirect fire battle.

The sound of our rounds flying overhead and impacting, combined with the ACM's hissing and hitting was nothing more than terrifying, exhilarating, and who knows what else. The last ACM round hit in front of the East tower, then all was quiet on the Eastern Front. As if the attack hadn't even happened. Were they going to assault the COP now? Had our artillery gotten them or were they out of ammo? These were questions we all asked ourselves as we sat waiting in the towers and trucks. Another hour passed before SFC Adams told us to stand down. He didn't want to get snuck up on like this again, but then again, who really liked getting mortared? Obviously the Muslim mortar men had not passed Mortars 101. Their aim was questionable.

We got word on the radio two days later that the 173ʳᵈ KIA total was now up to 13. That averaged out to almost three KIAs a month. Yet, after five months of non-stop action and witnessing people dying, we had become desensitized to death. It was all around us. Each one of our shells that bounded to the border was meant to take a life, and vice versa. Every bullet or mortar round that screamed past us was meant to end the existence of someone's son, someone's brother, someone's husband, and someone's father. War is a funny thing. We were there because our country had asked us to go. They were there because someone had filled their minds with the foolish notion that the Americans and the entire Western world were hell-bent on destroying the planet. Twisted ideas in a twisted land equal a twisted outcome.

As I was setting some napkins on our crude dining table, the ground shook with incredible force and knocked me on my tail. The only thing that saved a lot of us that time was the Hesco barrier, for the mortars were hitting right beside it on the outside of the COP. One degree different on the ACM's mortar tube would have sent rounds into our ammo cache, TOC, aid station, and dining tent where I was currently getting my monkey ass (as SFC Adams had labeled it) off the ground and to cover. This time the shells didn't pause. They followed the wall all the way down to the North tower, hitting beside it as we were running down to the other end of the COP for cover under our "hardened" shipping containers.

We guessed the ACM had thought they had zeroed in our COP and tried a "fire-for-effect" on us. Good thing they were off! The sixth and final shell stopped just beside the North tower. SPC Hampton was in there and peaked his head up. His face was white has a ghost. Who could blame him? The shelling had taken us all by surprise. The .50 Cal from the East tower started firing. SSG Manuma was on it, lighting up Hill Top 2355. About 500m away and directly in front of the East tower. The mortar team messed up and had crept over the hill to see if they had inflicted any damage on our COP. Don't ever piss off a Samoan, especially if he has a huge machine gun at his disposal.

SSG Manuma fired two boxes at the hilltop as SPC Neary called in artillery strikes to wipe out any remaining ACM. We were going to get these fools, today! Who wants to worry about getting the legs blown out from under them while they are trying to make dinner, or take a nice dump? Not this guy. One 500lbs JDAM struck directly on top of Hill Top 2355 with a sweltering, deafening report. Anyone that was still trying to hide on there was now cooked to a nice, well-done crisp. No one ever saw the B-1 that was reportedly in our airspace, but he sure saw us. That's the funny thing about air support: all of a sudden shit is just blowing up!

A pale, creamy color started to surge up from the hilltops, comparable to a dense Northeastern fog and with just as much chill. WP was being dropped on the exit routes that the ACM frequented. Either way someone was going to die today. The skirmish lasted about four minutes, and then everything went back to normal. SFC Adams had the door opened to the latrine he was in. For some reason he always did that. C'mon, sergeant who really wants to see you drop a load? Paratroopers were smoking and joking, talking about the events that have just occurred. But such is the infantryman's life. One minute your adrenaline is pumping, and you're getting the earth knocked out from under you. The next you're laughing and going about daily life as if nothing has happened. I suppose only a certain few can do it.

They next few days at the COP were quiet. Either we had gotten the ACM sluts, or they were disheartened from our bombardment of the border. Either way was fine with us. 2nd PLT would be coming out to relieve us soon. We already had a mission set out for us after our recovery day. We would be escorting gravel trucks back out to the COP, so they could pour some gravel on the HLZ and the steep road leading in to the COP. The run-off from the rain was starting to eat away at the ground. Guess the engineers didn't think of that.

That was two days away. For now everyone was thinking about hot showers, talking to their loved ones, or catching up on their favorite television series. 2nd PLT rolled up and their PSG, good ole SFC Carlson, talked with SFC Adams about where the mortars had been coming from. I helped 2nd PLT's cook unload all of his food. He was actually a chef, graduated from New York's Culinary Institute of America, but it doesn't really matter with Army food. I took my trusty M240B down from the East tower and placed it on my turret. SFC Adams walked over, looked at me, and asked me if I was giving blow jobs when we got back to the FOB. "Well if the price is right. Or I could sweeten your ass with some Pringles" I replied. "You sick fuck," he said in return.

The hot water on my back felt great. It had been ten days since we had showered. Even the smell of the purifying chemicals in the water to purify it didn't bother me. The cement showers were awash in laughter and grab-assing. The guys that were uncomfortable around naked dudes were always the best ones to mess with. SPC Lagenour, SPC Swinehart and I walked back to our hut together. It wasn't a far stroll to the front door. As I said before, the FOB wasn't too large. We dropped our towels and stepped out back to smoke a "root" or cigarette. I had never really been a smoker but started after I was wounded. It probably had nothing to do with that, more of a boredom thing really. Eventually we ordered our own rolling paper and tobacco to take up even more time.

Swinehart (who had dubbed himself Snap Dragon) and I set up our Monopoly board. We stole it from FOB Salerno on the way into Bermel, and usually played once a week when we were on the FOB. SGT Adams (my driver, not to be confused with SFC Adams) also played with us, as well as Lagenour. A running tally of who had won the most games was kept on Swinehart's door; needless to say I was usually the victor. My brother, (Mr. MBA and CPA himself) had taught the game to me well growing up. It's all about being ruthless and making those fools pay when you own Boardwalk and have hotels on it!

Swinehart was moving his piece onto Free Parking when the wall shook as if someone had been thrown into it, and then it happened again; this time people's stuff was falling off the wall. "Was that incoming?" SSG Manuma yelled. No siren yelped. We usually had one sound when the rockets started to scream in. We began to walk outside cautiously, and SFC Adams came around the corner with a smirk on his scruffily face, "Did anyone shit themselves like I did?" he asked. Which, he probably did. Just as we were inquiring about the loud boom, it occurred twice more. Now that we were outside, we could feel the concussions deep in our chest. It was much like being at a rock concert and feeling the bass bounce through you.

We all hunkered down a little bit, and SFC Adams laughed. He then told us that our new howitzers had arrived to replace the 105's. It was the new 155mm, the biggest artillery piece in the Army. It felt like trading ants for elephants. The 155s have a vastly larger shell, weighing almost 100 lbs., and they can reach a hell of a lot farther. At the moment, the 82nd FA[82] was sighting them in. I sure would have hated to live by the guns practice range, which was about 8k out and at the foot of the mountains, like the citizens of Malekshay…much louder than a train at midnight. The impact of the shells would certainly have the local tribal chiefs wanting money or food for the noise violations.

Eight Muslim gravel trucks came into FOB Bermel on September 24th, which was my 21st birthday as a matter of fact. I was attempting to drink 21 "Near-Beers" or non-alcoholic German beer, but it just wasn't going to happen. Two down and their metallic taste was way too much for me to handle. But I still got my ass beat. In the infantry, on your birthday, a soldier

---

82 **FA**—Field Artillery

gets thrown on the ground and gets the shit smacked out of his stomach. This time they included shaving cream and threw carrot cake in my face. My, that made for a good picture. This is the very definition of brotherly love.

In any case, we were going to escort the gravel trucks out to the Malekshay COP, so the Muslim slaves could lay out some gravel on the road and HLZ. Also, we were going to take 2nd PLT some re-supply ice, since we were still using the sandbag freezer. Our long convoy pulled out of the back gate and headed down Route Chrysler. It took about twenty minutes to get to the COP. Although you could see it from the FOB, the terrain is what slowed us down yet again.

I was taking up rear security as usual, and the jingle trucks were placed in between our vehicles. The jingle truck drivers were horrible at driving; they would either go to slow or too fast and speed right up on you. Luckily I was in the back and did not have to deal with that rigmarole. I turned to look out onto the barren plains of Afghanistan on my right. At that point I saw a huge dust cloud out of the corner of my eye. A concussion followed that in addition to the deepest boom I have ever heard up to that point. SFC Adams let out a loud, "Fuckkkkkk!!" My heart sunk to the lowest point of my chest. I turned fully around to face the front of the convoy and saw metal and other debris falling out of the sky like a brown rain, the dust now covering our vehicles.

SFC Adams was already on the radio asking who had been hit and ordered SGT Adams to drive up to the front of the convoy, so the medic could get out and try to provide support, if anyone had survived that explosion. Thankfully, it had been a jingle truck driver who had hit the ancient Russian Anti-Tank mine. We pulled up and I looked over at SPC Hampton standing up in his turret yelling something at me. I stood up and asked him to repeat himself. "Damn, that dude flew through the roof!" he said, which made us both kind of chuckle. His body had blown through the roof and was now lying about 100m away from his mangled truck, the other drivers had begun to gather around it.

Our interpreter said that the drivers wanted blood, plus thought that the man who blew up their friend was located in a house about two football fields away. They were beginning to mob and walk towards said house when SFC Adams cocked his rifle and pointed it at them, yelling to stay where they were. I saw that, so I cocked my M240B real quick and pointed it their way. They got the message alright. We had our suspicions about the house the drivers were referring to as well, but you can't just let a lynch mob go do what they please. This wasn't no sheet wearing KKK rally.

MOD-6 and 7 drove out with another interpreter and C-Co.'s HEMTT[83] wrecker. MOD-6 was trying to calm down the drivers. Naturally this isn't so easy when there is a language barrier. Imagine a pack of wolves trying to calm down some house cats-ain't going to happen! He did his best, but finally cancelled the mission. Hell, none of us wanted to keep going either! We were lucky; two 3rd PLT vehicles had rolled over that IED, plus one jingle truck...this would be one birthday I would never forget.

---

83 **HEMTT**—Heavy Expanded Mobility Tactical Truck, a vehicle used in the military as a wrecker, mobile office, or supply carrier

Chapter Fifteen
October: Jamal

For the first week of October 2007, 3rd PLT was linked up with a PLT of Delta Co. up in Orgun-E. (O.E.) Our missions were kind of like doing some housekeeping; we'd do some mapping of the areas, take censuses of villages, and roll into places that haven't been visited in some time. Delta Company led the way. We were just there for support and to show a larger presence in the areas. One good thing about going to O.E. was the little Afghani restaurant they had on the FOB. The Muslims cooked some delicious cinnamon flatbread, as well as beef kebabs. Well worth five bucks, this was worth about 250 in Afghani.

Returning to FOB Bermel on October 5th, 2007, 3rd PLT was up for another Malekshay COP rotation, which would last supposedly for ten days. The COP had started to take indirect fire again. The ACM had changed its position multiple times, to avoid being bombed once more. Without a doubt we still threw our own artillery at them, but the ACM are like ants: There are two more to replace every one you killed. In any case we would still be rolling out, so I had to make my grocery list for the fat cooks to deny. Sluts.

The morning of the 6th was overcast and cool. No doubt there was rain in the air, and which meant some hail too. The temperatures were becoming noticeably cooler as fall began to take us. I placed my M240B in the turret and pushed the pin through the swivel, its click was a sign of a successful emplacement. It had been almost a month since 3rd PLT had completed a COP rotation. Most of us liked it. There wasn't much to do, nothing really, other than pull your guard shift, eat, sleep, and keep yourself busy with minor details like poking holes in water bottles to wash your hands, washing the pots I cooked with, sweeping out the rooms, or burning shit. You know fun stuff. To be truthful I kind of liked the smell of the feces burning, smelled like a big roast. Don't judge me; at least I wasn't using it to cook like the Muslim folk…yet.

With the Humvees all lined up, SFC Adams signaled everyone to activate their Dukes, and we were off. The familiar path we had traveled many times to the COP was now one of the most feared roads in our battle space. What terrible, earthmoving, hidden beast was out there waiting for us? If any of us hit an IED, would our deaths be quick, or would we suffer for the rest of our lives, broken lives, never to be fully restored? These were questions everyone thought to themselves at some point or another. Though we made light of many situations (as you have to on such a long tour of duty), the worries were still in the back of our minds.

We started up the first steep hill on the access road to the COP. Our trucks were placed in 4-Low so the heavy Goliaths could climb wheel by wheel. A slight rain had begun to fall. Our changeover would have to be quick if 2nd PLT wanted to make it back to the FOB before MEDEVAC status went black. If MEDEVAC could not fly, no one could move. Pulling into the COP we could already see that 2nd PLT had its trucks lined up and ready to go. They were ready to get out of this place; I guess the shelling by the ACM had been more frequent than we expected.

Everyone hopped out and replaced guns, guards, and gumption in the towers. During our time away from the COP, it had received an actual freezer! This made planning meals easier, since we didn't have to take a shit ton of ice out there with us. We also had acquired two Afghani Propane tanks to cook over. Now these weren't any Blue Rhinos, but they got the job done. Additionally, 2nd PLT actually did some work for once and built a cook shack and had ordered two flat griddles. All of these factors were going to make my job a hell of a lot easier, open flaming everything like cavemen sucked monkey testicles. But, with all the new toys people wanted to poke their heads even more in my cookery business, again, especially during breakfast.

Their cook gave me the low down about the new freezer and cookery, as SFC Adams and Carlson did a brief changeover chat, and then they were out of there. It was probably the fastest, smoothest changeover yet. Over the next ten days 3rd PLT was going to see why 2nd was in such a rush to get out of the COP and back to the FOB. With 2nd PLT's noise fading and the Afghan quiet beginning to set in, I started to prepare lunch for 3rd PLT. SFC Adams wanted bacon cheeseburgers (with jalapeno and onion of course) and fresh cut Freedom fries. Luckily I had all of the ingredients to do that, and by ingredients I mean pre-cooked bacon, burgers, and a sack of potatoes. That shit tasted good on top of a mountain though!

During our last COP rotation, 3rd PLT adopted a mascot. I had come across him while whipping up a batch of something. Now this wasn't a dog (those usually got shot) or a cat, (those too), but an onion. Our new mascot, named Jamal, rode with me in my turret everywhere I went and even accompanied me to this COP rotation. He was very resilient in this Afghan heat, and had started to grow dreads. I placed him on the rack of spices, as we figured this is where he would feel most comfortable. I even drew a face on him, like Wilson from *Cast Away*. There is no way I would punt him though like Tom Hanks…that dick.

As I was talking to a one of our scouts (yes three of them got off their asses and accompanied us on this excursion), we heard a very distinct, deep boom off in the distance. SSG Daniel ran over and cut the generators off. Then another deep boom, but this time it hit right beside the north tower. "Incoming!" SSG Daniel yelled as we all went for cover. SFC Adams and SPC Neary ran up to the East tower to try and acquire a POO (Point of Origin) site. Other soldiers bolted for cover in the shipping containers. Another shell landed just over the north tower, right beside our gate. I ran up to the East tower, as it was closer from the cook shack, where I ran into SFC Adams. He looked at me and said, "These aren't mortars their firing at us. Hear how they sound in the air and the impact is heavier? Listen…" Sure enough, you could hear the weapon when they fired it; it had a deeper sound to it than the previous 82mm mortar tube the ACM fired at us on our last COP rotation.

Then, when the round came in, it carried a loud whoosh with a deeper, ground shaking report. SPC Neary shouted as the last round exploded, again by the north tower, "It's a Recoilless Rifle[84] they are firing at us!" Well no wonder it sounded different. The ACM had brought out the big guns to play this time! Recoilless rifles come in many forms like most weapons, but these ACM fucks had one somewhere placed on a tri-pod and were using it like an artillery piece. Also they had a spotter somewhere with a radio talking to the gun crew. Since we couldn't see the gun team, but their rounds kept getting closer, someone would have to be giving them adjustments. To add to that, the ACM were firing 105mm shells at us. Now that explains the difference in impact noise.

---

84 **Recoilless Rifle**—a lightweight, portable, crew-served 105 mm weapon intended primarily as an anti-tank weapon

The rounds stopped, only the parrot crows (the name we came up with for a type of black and white crow that had a greenish tint in the light) cawed out. It was a quick four-round test, but the ACM were deadly close to our north tower; a few more shots like that, and they would no doubt have a direct hit on it. I walked down to the piss tubes by the North tower and SPC Swinehart hurled the door to the north tower open, walked out calmly and looked down at me, "Holder…I didn't sign up for this shit." I laughed so hard I missed the piss tube, "I don't think anyone signed up for this" I said in return. I was walking back up to the cook shack to get the pork chops ready for dinner when SFC Adams called all of the Squad Leaders into the dining tent.

I had to bring them some olives with seasoning on them as well as sun tea, being the slave boy I was. I accidently left my palm leaves back at the FOB. "It was nearly 1400 when the first round impacted. Tomorrow at about 1330, we'll cut all the generators off, place gunners in the trucks on the Hesco ramps, and have the scouts on top of the east tower. I want everyone looking for smoke, dust, or anything that shows signs of a POO sight. Let's nail these Muslim cocksuckers!" SFC Adams said.

Sure enough, at around 1415 the next day (just as I put some pork and beans on to slowly simmer) the first round flew directly over the COP and hit the HLZ. Everyone who wasn't in a tower or truck took cover. SPC Neary got on the horn and chatted back and forth with Bermel's FDC (Fire Direction Control). I was in the south tower with SPC Maddalone and SSG Daniel, and we saw the next round had dropped about 100m, meaning the next one was going to be right on us. SSG Daniel said, "Get low!" With a blast I will never forget, the third ACM round hit about 5m from the South tower. The round pelted the tower with shrapnel and debris and the only thing that saved us from being mutilated were a few sandbags. "God damn that shits so fucking close!" Maddalone yelled. "God the fourth one is going to hit us!" I said back. The three of us felt we were seconds away from death. I'm not sure what went through Maddalone and SSG Daniel minds, but once again, I found myself asking Jesus to forgive me of all wrong doings. Then I told him I would see him soon.

With a loud whoosh the fourth round impacted about 30m from us, this time a little further up. It seemed the ACM were trying to sight on the east tower. SPC Herne came over the radio and said, "Men are running up the hill with radios in their hands by Gangrekhyel." SFC Adams ran down the tower as the fifth round hit on the other side of the COP, no further than 15m from the base of the east tower. "That was my favorite tree you dicks!" one of the scouts yelled. SFC Adams climbed up on top of the Humvee to see what SPC Herne was seeing.

"Light those fuckers up Herne. They're carrying A-fucking-K's for Christ sake!" SPC Herne turned the hillside into cheddar cheese with the MK-19 as the sixth ACM round slammed into nearly the same spot as the last one had. SPC Neary had given grid coordinates to the FDC back at Bermel so they could start sending counter fire our way. I heard the first 155 Howitzer fire, then the second. SPC Herne had stopped firing; the 155 sweep would do the cleanup. Two 155s can drop around fifteen rounds on an entire grid square in about three minutes, there was no escaping.

All of these sounds of war blended together in a type of dark symphony. After hearing the different noises for so long, we could tell the difference in the types of artillery, if it was out going or incoming, and the different impacts. You could name all the voices on the radio, even if you just knew them by their call-sign. It all blended together, and the crescendo was when the deadly blast from an artillery shell or a jet's bomb lit up the sky and ended the lives of our enemy. The two 155 rounds impacting on the mountain awoke me from this thought. They were followed by a deafening thirteen more.

The recoilless rounds ceased after the grid sweep. Most likely the ACM crew ran back to the border. I know I wouldn't want to be on the receiving end of a 155 barrage. We sat in the towers about another hour, just to make sure the ACM didn't try anything. I walked back to the cook shack and realized I had burned the pork and beans. Damn it!

After getting hit for two days in a row, who would have thought the third day would be any different? The ACM were right on time. It was almost 1400 on the dot when they did a fire for effect on us. Luckily all four rounds that impacted were in front of the east tower, but they sure scared the shit out of everyone in it. "Those fucks know they are getting close. It's a wonder they haven't made it inside the COP yet." SFC Adams said as I was chopping him some onion. "How much you want to bet they make it in tomorrow?" I said, "What the fuck is wrong with you, Holder?" SFC Adams replied. I didn't have an answer for him.

The ACM gave us a break for the next two days, but we still manned our post from 1330 until about 1500 just to make sure they weren't trying to pull a fast one. It was our 6th day at the COP, only four more to go until we were relieved. A dark and overcast 7th day came and almost went without a hitch. SFC Adams was about to say stand down when the first ACM round flew right into the middle of the COP and almost took out the mortar section, blowing shrapnel up into the east tower and in SPC Neary's back plate, defacing everything in the dining tent. "They have us fucking zeroed, everyone take cover!!" SFC Adams yelled.

Despite an ACM 105mm round landing 5m from the mortar team, they still got on the tube and fired our own 120mm shells back toward the ACM or at every grid SPC Neary called out. We did not have their exact location. The second ACM round came in and hit right beside the left Humvee ramp, blowing out the tires, spider webbing the windshield and windows, and throwing shrapnel into the engine. The 155's from the FOB fired four rounds onto Hill 2993, as SPC Swinehart, SGT Rodney, and I ran to grab more mortars from the ammo point. We ran right past the first ACM impact point, "God I hope a round doesn't hit the ammo point while were in it." I said.

The third ACM round impacted just outside the wall beside the east tower. We all leapt to the ground for cover, then got our "monkey" asses up and grabbed the mortar crates. As we were stepping down into the mortar pit, a B-1 flew into our battle space. I heard SFC Adams yell "Oh fuck yeah!" from the east tower. The B-1 pilot didn't waste any time; he dropped ordinance (bombs) on the side of hill 2993, as well as the border. The hillsides were awash in flames.

We all let out cheers and exchanged high fives. We hoped that between the B-1, 155s and our own 120mm mortars, we had gotten the slimy cocksuckers! The smoke had begun to rise from the border, and the ACM rounds had stopped. Everyone started to come out and check the damage to the COP, and I went to check on the cook shack as it had received a fair amount of shrapnel. "Oh God they killed Jamal!" I shouted and called for the medic. He ran over and checked out the wounded onion. A nickel-sized piece of shrapnel had ripped through Jamal; the medic said he needed to be MEDEVACED; we didn't think he would make it through the night.

The Humvee that had been hit was fucked. Three tires were blown, the engine turned over but didn't sound right, and the passenger side windows looked like someone took a tire iron to them. The HEMTT was going to have to come out with 1st PLT when they came to switch out with us and pick this broken beast up. I walked over to where the first ACM round had impacted. I could stick my arm in the hole all the way up to my shoulder. That's almost three feet. If these rounds go that far in the rock solid Afghan ground, then there is no way our "hardened" shipping containers were going to stop them! Seeing as they were just sheet metal and a few sand bags.

1st PLT arrived on October 15th to take over the COP...praise the Lord! It had been quiet since the previous shellacking, but we weren't taking any chances. The HEMTT hooked up to the truck as fast as it could, and we switched everything out with 1st PLT. SFC Adams was ready to get out of here, "The rockets that the FOB takes daily is nothing compared to this. Good luck guys." he said as we were getting in our Humvees to start the trip back to the FOB. I jumped in my turret with what remained of Jamal, and hummed taps as I placed him in the ammo can I kept my water in. I also thanked God that we all were making it out of the COP alive.

As soon as I laid my head down in my bed, SFC Adams busted in the door to our hut and said, "Get your gear on and get the trucks ready, were driving to O.E. to do a BDA[85]. The whole building let out extremely colorful language as he turned around and walked out laughing. The Air Force had bombed about fifteen guys in the hills near Sarobi, (a district by our battalion headquarters) and we were going to go check out what damage they had done. Apparently Delta Co. was tied up elsewhere. That's how it went through most of our tour; MOD was always picking up the slack of other companies.

We all dragged our tired bodies outside and did as directed, no one was saying much. It was going to be a long, dark drive to Sarobi, which would take about four hours. SFC Adams gave me two Stackers to take; he lived on those things. They did help for a few hours. MOD-6 and 7 were going to be accompanying us as well, and they weren't any happier than we were. We rolled out of the gate and through the town of Bermel on the way to Sarobi. Bermel was dark and quiet—no busy street vendors, or wood dealers, just stray dogs roaming the streets.

I'm not sure how many times I fell asleep standing up in my turret, but the bumps of the road would always wake me up. It was beginning to get colder now; all the gunners were wrapped up in neck gators and smoke jackets. I finally sat down on the netted swing that was for gunners to rest on and looked out into the night with my night vision. The stars never ceased to amaze me. You could see so many, and the sky was so clear. No smog or street lights had ever touched this land. It was pristine, except when we were bombing the shit out of it.

The sky began to turn a light blue and purple as the sun began to rise. We were nearly to the BDA sight, but I was freezing my ass off. "You good

---

85 **BDA**—Battle Damage Assessment, the exploration of a battle field after the battle is complete for documents, intelligence, and wounded soldiers

up there cock-holder?" SFC Adams said. "Roger that, just freezing my tail off." I replied. Our convoy drove through the town of Sarobi, made a left towards the hills and stopped to make sure we were going to the right spot. A few villagers were walking around, getting their shops ready. It looked like a scene right out of the Bible. No Starbucks here. Which sucked because I was sleepy, cold, and a venti Americano would have gone down smooth.

A few dogs were running around near us. "Bitch ass dogs." SFC Adams said as he got back in the Humvee. This sent me into hysterical laughter. "What the fuck is wrong with you man? Are you fucking stupid?" SFC Adams said. This brought the whole truck into laughter. We had to be there, so we were always pretty good at making the best of the situation. No one really ever broke down the whole deployment. It takes strong character to make it fifteen months seeing, sleeping, eating, and showering and so on with the same people. I have to say, Charlie Company had some of the best men in the whole Army.

Our convoy made it to the base of the hills. SFC Adams wanted to drive right up the hill, but I wasn't sure if his bowels could take it. He told SGT Adams to take lead to navigate up the hill. The other trucks would follow us. I pulled the pin the held my M240B in place and cocked it. There was no telling what was waiting for us up in these hills, "Keep a look out Holder and shoot anything that moves." SFC Adams said as our truck rolled upward. We winded or way in and out of the pine trees, making it to a ridge that forced us to halt our advance. Everyone dismounted and continued on foot to the BDA sight. SGT Adams and I stayed with our truck, as did all of the other drivers and gunners.

SPC Lagenour walked up on the first ACM fighter. His eyes were still open, but death had glazed them over. Security was set up around the BDA sight. Bodies were everywhere, fifteen total. The scene inspired silence until one of the bodies spoke. One fighter was still alive, but he was badly injured. His right leg was broken and was showing some bone. 1SG Collins fired a warning shot at him as he was trying to back away. The interpreter walked over to him, moved all of his possession, and made sure he wasn't hiding anything that could injure someone.

While the prisoner was being questioned, 3rd PLT was gathering all of the gear that the ACM had brought with them. These guys were here to stay for the winter and were well supplied with expensive gear and sleeping bags. We found the first PKM machine guns with scopes on them, plus there were a slew of batteries, anti-tank mines, grenades, armor-piercing

AK rounds, and canteens. These guys were coming to fight. There's no telling how many lives we saved by killing them and capturing their equipment.

After securing all of the ACM gear and the prisoner for MEDEVAC, 3rd PLT made its way to a snap HLZ, so the prisoner could be flown out. It turns out he admitted to being an ex-Turkish Field Artillery Officer and being trained by Iran. He was also the first prisoner captured in our province since the beginning of Operation Enduring Freedom. He most likely is still being held in one of the United States "detention centers" or could possibly be banging 70 virgins, either way he isn't in Paktika province any longer.

After the BDA, Eagle 6 wanted MOD to check out some other areas due to the fact Delta was still tied up. We drove around for a while; everyone was pissed that we couldn't go back to Bermel. SFC Adams threated to run into the next village naked. Then we got the order to make a patrol base and stay the night out on this God-forsaken hill. I jumped out of the gunners hatch after being in there for seventeen hours and stretched my legs. It was great to walk around a little. SFC Carlson and 2nd PLT joined us, with a trailer of blankets, water and MRE's but fucked up on one of the hills and flipped a Humvee.

"Sweet Jesus, what the fuck is wrong with the world, Holder?" SFC Adams asked me when the news about the flipped truck came across the radio. I couldn't help but laugh; the shit that came out of his mouth sometimes was what kept our truck sane. No one was injured in the rollover, thank the Lord, but it was still a mess to get a HEMTT out there and turn the truck back over. At least I got the Spaghetti MRE out of the whole ordeal. Throw some melted "cheese" and hot sauce in there, and you got a four-course meal!

Finally, after another day of wandering the Afghan countryside, we returned to Bermel. Mail had come while we were on Eagle 6's escapade, and I had been delivered a box of boiled peanuts from my family. Most people turned their nose up at the Southern treat, but not SFC Adams. He would ask me every time mail came if I had been blessed with any. I hit the hay early that night, only to be awoken by SPC Snyder, my roommate, jerking it in his bunk beneath me…c'mon! I should have jumped down and pulled him out of our room by his Johnson.

CHAPTER SIXTEEN
NOVEMBER: A TRIP EAST

OCTOBER WAS USHERED OUT by a rotation at the Margah COP, which was Anvil's COP. Other than an unsuccessful IED attack by the ACM on the way there, it was pretty uneventful. People were beginning to get tired of each other. We had been with each other for six whole months now, and it was beginning to show. I have to say though that 3ʳᵈ PLT really never had any fights other than minor disputes, and no fist were ever thrown to my knowledge.

On the way back to the FOB from Margah, our truck began to smoke a little. This surprised us due to the fact that we were the only truck in the PLT not to have any problems. SFC Adams made sure we were always performing maintenance on it, because he liked doing shit like that. Upon returning to the FOB, we are informed by the head mechanic that our truck needed a whole new engine! Naturally SFC Adams blamed SGT Adams and me for the whole debacle, but the real cause was an ACM bullet hole under the Humvee that had caused an oil leak, which had gotten bigger over time.

Now, the old engine was almost bone dry, so it had to be dis-assembled, and a new one hoisted in. Luckily, the mechanics had spare engines for the trucks. We started that night and finished three days later. SFC Adams was constantly harassing us during the whole process; he liked doing routine maintenance on the truck the whole time we were in Afghanistan but didn't turn one wrench on this task. I had never worked on many vehicles, so replacing an up-armored Humvee's huge diesel engine was something new to me!

Just as we were rolling the Humvee out of the mechanics bay, MOD-7 came out and informed me that I would be taking a four-day pass to

Qatar. The country of Qatar is where the military's Operation Freedom Rest is located. Which is a compound specifically designed to give soldiers downtown. Wow, my life just got so much better! The next day I was on a Chinook helicopter heading back to Salerno, leaving the hatred of my jealous comrades. I was only in Salerno a day, and then boarded a C-130 on my way to Bagram.

Bagram had it all; it was like an Infantry soldier's wet dream. Whereas we only had the shitty Army cooks at Bermel, Bagram had Pizza Hut, Burger King, Subway, Korean food, BBQ, and Green Beans Coffee Co. Plus an array of massive Dining Facilities, which had breakfast to order, Baskin Robbins, salad bars, pasta bars, and baked potato bars. To top all of that off, there was a Dairy Queen right by our tent. Screw flying to Qatar. Just let me stay here for four days, my life was good!

While in Bagram I ran into good ole Archie from Legion Co. It seemed he was on a pass as well, one that Bruder was supposed to take but had to go on a mission. He was going to be pissed when he discovered he was missing this adventure. Archie and I boarded a cramped C-130 and tried to get some sleep during the four-hour ride. The USAF had us up all night; they were constantly changing the flight times. Arriving at the base at Qatar, we were bused to the side of the USAF base that the four-day passes took place, Camp Freedom Rest.

Naturally, neither Archie nor I had any civilian clothes, so we hit up the PX when we were released. There was an assortment of activities a soldier could do at the camp. For example, jet ski, shop at malls off post, swim at the pool, hit the beach for the day, and most importantly…drink beer. Each of us was allowed two beers a night or two glasses of wine. There was also a Chili's and a few local places to eat on the camp. This was going to be a great four days!

Archie and I signed up for the mall trip on the second day. Leaving the base unescorted and with no weapons was something I had never done in a Muslim country. Were these Air Force brats' nuts? Although, after about five miles, you could tell you weren't in Afghanistan any longer. Qatar is right on the Arabian Sea and has a nice breeze throughout the whole country. It's sandy, much like the beaches on the Gulf of Mexico, and had palm trees everywhere. Also, its citizens weren't trying to kill us, which was the icing on the cake.

The town we were in looked like any other beach town in America, with the exception of the skyscrapers. Some of the people dressed in the old world Muslim attire, but most of them were outfitted like we are in the west. Archie and I could not believe our eyes! Were we in the Middle East still, or had they tricked us and flown us to California? The mall was very impressive. It was three-stories and had all the shops you would find in the States, not to mention McDonalds! One thing that doesn't change is the taste of home, and anywhere you go in the world the golden arches is it. I surprised they didn't serve some regional delicacy like Austria did, maybe fried desert rat nuggets?

After indulging ourselves on Big Macs, Archie and I tried to locate this bar everyone kept talking about. Of course you weren't supposed to drink off base, but there were rumors of a bar somewhere near the mall. After asking around, we found a cab driver who knew the way. We had four hours left to go on our pass, perfect. Little did we know that bar was in the most luxurious hotel in the whole city.

The hotel was built in the form of a pyramid, which had a golden tint to it. Pulling up to the front, the concierge opened the door for us, Archie and I looked at each other, mouths wide open. Walking in we were met with multiple fountains, which entered into vast lobby. Four auto play pianos were playing the same song, but in different pitches. It sounded heavenly. Diamond chandeliers hung high from the ceiling, and the smell of sweet spices calmed your mind like a sunset after a troubling day.

We explored a while before asking where the bar was. Our direction was turned toward the elevator as the bar was downstairs. The bar was very lavish as well, reassembling that of one I visited in Manhattan, NY. Colored fountains fell between the different shelves of beverages as neon lights under the floor gave the bartenders space a quiet glow. The bar itself was made of a fine marble, and the chairs were a deep mahogany.

Sitting down, Archie ordered Crown Royal on the rocks, I had to get a Southern Comfort and lime with a splash of Coke-a-Cola. After the first pull of our beverages, we looked at each other and laughed. Who would have ever thought that we would be sitting at a bar in Qatar together? We talked about good times in Vicenza, Lowell, and about how Clark was doing. Clark had just had his legged removed and was now in rehabilitation in Texas. We even made Bruder and the rest of Bravo Company a movie on my camera, just to rub it in.

Just as we were about to leave, we were joined by none other than the owner of the hotel! A tall, powerful-looking man, who didn't even have to speak before his pitcher of Heineken was placed before him with a wine glass to accompany it. We talked with him, and he explained how he loved Western culture, and about how the Middle East was so immeasurably different. Yeah no shit, comparing Qatar to Afghanistan was like comparing the Sun to the Moon. He bought us a pitcher of Heineken as well and went on to talk about his political agenda that he planned to pursue. He then spoke about how he built this hotel, and when we asked him what the cheapest room was a night, he replied, "3,000 U.S. dollars" Now that is money I wish I had! It appears not all Muslims countries need a few light slams every now and then.

Since our time was up, we thanked the man and he responded by picking up our whole tab. Then we quickly made our way back through the hotel to get a cab. Archie was tossing out Qatari currency like it was going out of style, tipping every Abdul, Omar, and Hussein. Which was fine with me, I didn't pay for a thing that night except for my Big Mac. We arrived back to post and still got to drink our two beers, needless to say we did not need them. After not having an adult beverage for seven months, and then drinking like a fish, you get quite inebriated. Needless to say we went to bed satisfied.

The next day was spent around the camp. Archie and I entertained ourselves with miniature golf, bowling, the pool, and purchasing items to send home to our families from the local vendors. There wasn't another mall trip to get drunk on, so Archie and I decided to split a bottle of Nyquil and have our drinks on top of that. The Nyquil shots were our preemptive strike to cold and flu season, regardless of it still being 90 degrees in Qatar. Archie had won a pool tournament, but the prize was some type of PlayStation racecar wheel. "What the fuck am I supposed to do with this on top of a mountain?" He let them keep the hook up and went for the Nyquil, which put him to sleep. Consequently, I got his beers and my own, so I was feeling pretty good. I sat down next to these Department of Defense guys, and they let me have one of theirs. I placed it beside my chair, and we talked for a while about operations in Iraq, what they could tell me anyway. I bent down to pick up my beer and tossed back the last of it. Then, it hit me…some douche back had been spitting his dip in a beer can. The dip spit splashed the back of my throat with a burning sensation and thick murky feel; but it was too late, my throat was already open, and it went down. The guys saw my face and started laughing. I placed the can down calmly and said, "Bless my soul, I just drank dip spit." My calmness really got them rolling. I quickly washed the horrible feeling down with the rest of what was left of my actual beer. My body began to get hot, and my mouth began to water. I don't think the combination of Nyquil, beer, and dip spit would sit well with anyone. I kept it down though, at least for forty-five minutes, and then up came a day's worth of business we won't discuss.

Archie and I boarded a plane back to Bagram, and before I knew it, I was in a guard tower at Bermel. My PLT was currently on a mission in O.E., so I had the barracks building to myself. It was now November 12th, and the weather was taking a turn for the cold side. Afghanistan is scorching hot in the summer and hypothermic cold in the winter. Obviously this was a sign from God that the Muslims were not living right, since they were cursed with fire and ice. I did an LCLA[86] supply drop with Anvil. A LCLA was essentially when a contractor, such as Black Water, kicked supplies out to us with parachutes on them. The Black Water pilots would fly their small planes right above the ground, trying to get the supplies as close as possible. The next day they were going to our COP to resupply it, but luckily I wasn't on that mission.

Waking up early to pull Tactical Operation Center (TOC) guard, I talked with Anvil 6's gunner, SGT Hike. We had spoken before, but we shot the shit for a good hour before they rolled out on the COP mission. Then I walked over to the tower I was going to man. As their convoy turned onto the COP access road, I heard the loudest explosion I had ever heard, it sounded as if I was by the blast itself. The TOC came over the radio and stated that Anvil was in contact, but I heard no secondary explosions or gunfire.

After about thirty minutes, MEDEVAC from Salerno flew in over the mountains to where Anvil was located. SGT Hike's Humvee rolled over a pressure cooker filled with fifty pounds of explosives. His 15,000pd Humvee did a front flip and landed upside down. The driver's door blew off and the driver was ejected; however, Anvil's Captain, CPT Boris, SGT Hike, and their interpreter were all three caught inside the now burning Humvee. SGT Hike was stuck in the upside-down turret, due to the gunner's harness, and CPT Boris could not get his seat belt off, nor door open.

The ammunition for the M240B began to explode. The interpreter was killed by stray bullets bouncing around the flame engulfed Humvee. SGT Hike was pinned to the ground and could not get free; CPT Boris was trying with all that he was to get out of the oven as he heard SGT Hike starting to yell from the flames beginning to take him. The ammo

---

86 **LCLA**—Low Cost, Low Altitude Drop, a resupply that utilizes the parachute system to drop supplies to troops in forward positions

was now cooking off like popcorn and a stray bullet slammed into CPT Boris, hindering him more. There was nothing they could do. Between the flames and bullets, the inside of that Humvee had become a battlefield of its own.

The driver was MEDEVACED to Salerno. CPT Boris, SGT Hike, and the interpreter burned alive. They were the first KIAs for Bermel; now every company in the brigade had KIA's, a number that was currently at thirty-five. The IED strike on Anvil was going to change the way we fought. Soon a Route Clearance Package (RCP) would be required to escort all convoys, and anti-IED patrols would become a regular thing. The access road to the COP would be moved, and auto-extinguisher systems would be installed in every Humvee, but right then it was time to say goodbye to our friends.

It took almost three days to recover the bodies of our fallen comrades. Anvil kept security on the sight until 3rd PLT and RCP could get back from Organ-E, pick me up, and then head out to the COP access road with Mortuary Affairs for disassembly to be performed on the charred Humvee, freeing the bodies of the men inside. A memorial took place a day later, Eagle 6 (our battalion commander) came to speak, the twenty-one gun salute was performed, and Taps was sounded as the ramp to the Chinook closed and the bodies of the men were flown home. Needless to say it was a very moving experience. It reminded me that one minute you could be talking to your friends, having a cup of coffee and the next your life could be changed forever; or perhaps taken. Life is a fragile thing.

However, life went on. You couldn't let the death of friends get in the way of the mission at hand. Swinehart and I were pulling guard duty on Thanksgiving night as we watched the COP come under assault. 1st PLT was out there. The tracers were flying from and towards to COP. I got on the radio to make sure the TOC knew 1st PLT was under attack, due to the fact that the night shift isn't always so spry. Then the horizon lit up like the Fourth of July as the bombs from unseen aircraft rocked the world of the ACM. The tracers stopped flying towards the COP; it appeared the ACM were in retreat as the bombs were now landing closer to the border.

Our 155 Howitzers began to fire, which scared the shit out of me! The tower closest to the guns always felt as if it were going to disintegrate when the guns performed a fire mission. The attack was a quick one, and a bold move on the ACM's part. Unlike Anvil's Margah COP, which was in a bowl, our COP had the high ground in all directions, but the ACM were bound to try such a stupid move at some point. Apparently the ACM leader in charge of the attack came across the ICOM and ordered the attackers to stop their retreat and assault the COP once again. We could hear their every order, as we had bought ICOMs and were on their frequency. The leader in charge of the assault force begged the ACM head honcho not to send them back. Then again, who likes getting the balls bombed off them? Needless to say, they assault force did not return that night.

The next afternoon we bordered Blackhawk helicopters flew the thirty second flight to the COP to conduct a BDA (Battle Damage Assessment). We were going to clear the bombed route to as close as the border as we could get. The scouts were inserted last night on the border to check ACM activity. We would link up with them and clear a little farther north on the way back. It had been a while since we had all performed a dismounted mission, and we were sucking air. The ground and trees were still on fire in many places, burnt Muslim crispy critters could be seen every once in a while. Although most had been dragged off by now.

MOD-6 and 7, 3rd PLT, and the scouts linked up near the border. The scouts had blasted an ACM fighter with their .50 Cal Barrett and had found a good amount of paperwork on him, plus MOD-7 had found a few suspect locals that we were going to detain. Charlie Company turned around to head back to the COP for the night. MOD-6 wanted to keep walking all the way to FOB, but that would be a total of about twenty kilometers, including what we had just trekked. MOD-7 talked him out of it, since he we already had Blackhawks coming to get us tomorrow morning.

I laid down on a cot that night, lit a cigarette, and looked up at the clear night sky. As usual the millions of stars were there to be stewards of the night. I watched the smoke drift up and away. The weather was getting cold now; soon old man winter would be here to stay. I couldn't help but think of all the soldiers who had fought in Afghanistan before me, and how many of them lay on their back looking at the very stars that glowed above us now. I took a final drag off of the cowboy killer and let sleep take me.

Two days later, November 28th, 3rd PLT took over the COP once again. This time some Special Forces boys had tagged along with us to conduct counter IED operations in the nearby villages of Gangrekhyel, Gamid Gol, and Malekshay. They also brought their friend Mable, an energetic Chocolate Labrador, who had been trained to sniff out explosives. It was a welcome change to have a pet out there and some new faces to talk to. The last PLT dog we tried to keep got its head blown off by Eagle 7's shotgun because he was worried about disease. You could hear a pin drop after that incident, when the echo of the 12 Gauge died down that is. He must have been a cat person.

On November 29th we were going to conduct the first mission out of the COP and into the village of Gangrekhyel. Our new Lieutenant, Lt. Deep, had just arrived from Italy and was ready to get into the fight. He was the first West Point graduate we had come through Charlie Company, and was already a good fit in 3rd PLT. Accompanying Special Forces would be my gun team of course, 1st and 3rd squad, the medic and Lt. Deep. Since we could no longer enter the houses of Afghanis without probable cause, the basic idea here was to just walk through a village and let Mable do her thing. If she caught a scent of something, then action could be taken.

We got all of our gear ready. The Operation Order and brief were given, and then we began to walk out of the COP down the access road. I looked back and flicked Arruda off as he was flicking his tongue out at me from the tower. The weather was cold now, and the sky was an overcast winter gray. I adjusted the M240B on my shoulders and felt the first snow flake hit my neck, looked up and realized it was coming down everywhere. We all chuckled as we thought about the many things we could be doing other than this, sucked it up, and drove on; not realizing this would be the first of many cold missions conducted within the next month.

Chapter Seventeen
December: Snow and Stench

THE OVERCAST SKY HAD yet to give way to warm sunlight. The wind swept mountain summits all around us would send a chill down our backs if we made the slightest glance toward their frozen faces. Our supposed ten day stay at the COP was almost up, but there was going to be no respite from this frozen wilderness. RCP could not get to Bermel—the snow had stopped all movement. MEDEVAC was black, which meant no one was going anywhere until this winter front decided to leave us.

My gun team had participated in a few more missions with Special Forces. We found nothing in our explorations. The Special Forces (SF) boys were beginning to miss their warm huts at FOB Shkin, and no one could blame them. We had little space heaters in our containers, but that was about it. Nothing could keep out the Afghan cold; it was as stubborn as the natives of the land it now froze. Also, no one could keep SF from doing what they wanted to do; MEDEVAC black notwithstanding. On December 10th, we heard a few four-wheelers in the distance, moving towards our door-step.

It was the rest of the SF team. They had driven from Shkin on four-wheelers, which had M240s mounted on them, to come pick up the guys with us, plus Mable. Four-wheelers were a good idea in the snow; easier to maneuver and light enough not to set off any frozen IEDs. We all shook hands with the team, and they were on their way. I have to say it was a tad bit quieter without Mable running around, playing fetch with her beloved tennis ball.

SFC Adams asked me what food we needed, if and when an LCLA could get to us. Swinehart and I made a list. Although we still had a good amount of food out here, but that to would soon change. Swinehart loved to fuck with SFC Adams. Swinehart wrote the list as I called out what food supplies we could use to keep everyone happy. There wasn't any entertainment atop this icy peak, so dinner time was about the apex. Swinehart scribed the list and took it to the boss. SFC Adams sent it over the net to go ahead and get our order in, since we all knew we weren't going anywhere.

I saw Swinehart come running out of the TOC, laughing his Ohio ass off. "Holder, what the fuck is Caucasian milk!?" SFC Adams yelled, laughing just as hard as he said it. I didn't know what he was talking about, but it appears, Swinehart replaced white milk with Caucasian milk. This didn't sound too good over the net due to the fact SFC Adams was our Equal Opportunity advisor, and he was giving the order to a black guy. Oh, the little things in life.

I'm not sure if MOD-6 knew we were dying of boredom, or if he actually needed us to recover a silly little camera, but either way we were gearing up to walk over the snow-covered mountains to hunt for a camera. MEDEVAC had gone to amber status, which technically means you can move but aren't really supposed to. Basically, don't count on anyone coming to save you if you're in trouble. Lt. Deep would lead us about 3k away to try and recover a Scorpion Camera System. The Scorpions are much like basic trail cameras hunters use for deer; they take a picture when something walks in front of them.

Why MOD-6 wanted it back all of a sudden in mid-winter I have no idea. In any case, I found myself walking down the steep embankment towards Gangrekhyel, trying my best not to bust my ass on this damn snow. We moved through the cold, foggy valley, and up another mountainside. Arruda's gun team was tasked with positioning at the summit, (lucky fucks), while I was going to stay with Lt. Deep and continue down this tundra. Everyone was sucking air. Not only were we around 9,700 feet now, but that cold, prickly sensation you get in your throat from cold air did not help respiration. Luckily, we came to the spot where the proposed camera was laying. The problem was the camera was camouflaged and not meant to be found, and, none of us had helped emplace it.

SFC Adams got a call on the net MEDEVAC was now black. Since we were already out here, we were to continue the mission. He took his rifle and rode it like a horse, his usual sign for "this is bullshit." Despite its familiarity, it always got a laugh from us. Lt. Deep had finally found the camera. It was completely smashed. Obviously, the ACM had found it before us. As we were preparing to return to base, everyone was taken by surprise to see two Afghan women, walking with two donkeys and covered in blue and purple garments, headed up with frozen riverbed. The funny thing was they were walking away from the villages and up towards Pakistan. We should have just followed them. No doubt they would have led us to the ACM Winter Retreat 2007! After letting the well-clad ladies pass, 3rd PLT began to return to base (RTB).

Over the river and through the woods, to Grandma's we all wished we could have gone. Unfortunately it was back to our small containers, which now smelled ripe since we had not showered in fifteen days. Our PLT had only packed enough for ten days, so our socks, shirts, and uniforms were dirty and soiled with sweat. No doubt we looked rough. Adding to that, people were beginning to run out of their favorite tobacco product, and tempers were getting short. Hampton would go as far as to find previously smoked cigarettes and try to rekindle their flame. The constant routine of sleeping, eating, and pulling guard duty was turning into a monotonous monster.

As if God heard our bitching, he lifted the snowy blanket and out came a bright, golden sun. Its warm light glistened off the snowy peaks, and the blue sky was the clearest I had ever seen. MEDEVAC went green, which meant RCP would soon be on its way to Bermel from OE. We were told that 3rd PLT was going to get replaced by 2nd PLT, which hoisted all of our spirits. Two days later it was so…almost. As 2nd PLT rolled into the gate and RCP turned around to head back to Bermel, Eagle 6 informed MOD-6 that they had HUMINT, which stated a 100-man team was preparing to attack and over run the Malekshay COP. We were now staying. Oh the sighs that could be heard, as well as an array of colorful language. Hey let's have a smoke!

That night we all were up, manning the towers, Humvee gunning positions, and walls. MOD-6 came across the radio and said, "Men hold that COP and give them hell. It's been a privilege fighting with you." We waited…waited…and waited. The attack never came. You see Afghans' are solar powered, so if it is 10 degrees outside and snowing, then they aren't going to leave their warm caves just to get the shit blown out of them. Thanks Eagle 6, we then hid 60 men in a 30 man outpost, sleeping conditions got really tight. Hopefully there would be no pole to hole.

RCP tried to come get 3rd PLT the next day, but as soon as the first truck made the turn for the COP access road, a powerful explosion rocked the quiet valley. Everyone survived the blast, but that meant 3rd PLT was going to be stuck at the COP a little while longer, now with twice as many people. We doubled up in the containers. Men we forced to sleep on the floor, and the smell was overwhelming at times, especially when we took off our boots! Mice were also beginning to become a problem. One or two would run across us every night, and to my surprise one even ran across my face. I should have caught that furry fucker and served it to SFC Adams.

Not only did 2nd PLT bring more U.S. soldiers, but they also brought a few Afghans with them. The ANA guys were driving a fuel truck out here to re-supply the COP with, so they too were now stuck. Luckily, they had their own little shack to sleep and breed in. Breed? Oh that's correct. For those of you that don't know, homosexual activity is not just accepted in Afghan culture but actually promoted. Women are for reproduction, men are for fun. Every Thursday, which we dubbed "Man-Love Thursday," men of all ages, shapes, and sizes, were going to have the ass examined by various probes. Some sickos would even go as far as cutting out the eyes and tongues of little boys and using them as sex slaves, but that's a different kind of book.

Getting back to civilized thoughts, for most of the time at the COP, I either had guard with Morris or Hampton. Hampton was always saying something entertaining or trying to shoot something. He would try and explain Pastafarianism (a new religion that believes in a plate of pasta in space) to me, or talk about drunken sorority girls he had deflowered and punched in the kidney for an awesome orgasm. He did get to blast a "bitch ass dog" while it was sniffing around our burn pit, but he missed a gray fox that kept running across the road. I took a picture with the burnt, dead dog—my Christmas picture. Too bad I couldn't send it to the family.

SPC Morris and I would play with the Muslim mice while on guard. We'd lay our peanut butter on the guard tower and await the first mouse to poke its head out. Of course you had to be still, but I think they eventually became accustomed to us, even expecting our food. They would fight over whatever morsel we'd place before them, then attempt to drag it down their mice holes. That was the most entertainment I had witnessed for about a month. I did manage to get one with my pocket knife. Christmas picture number two.

On December 22nd, an 82nd Colonel flew in with some of his orderlies, and a Christmas dinner. After he spoke to us, this ridiculous female Captain made us sing a Christmas song or two, but then we got to enjoy a great Christmas dinner with all of the fixings. We saved the leftovers naturally, now that the COP was running low on food. It was great to eat someone else's cooking.

As the Colonel left, RCP was attempting to leave Bermel again to come collect 3rd PLT. We watched their movement on the BFT,[87] which is a high tech GPS. They made it further than the first time, but alas, an explosion echoed throughout the valley once more. This time there were a few broken bones, but all of the RCP engineers survived. Hey better luck next time!

The sun vanished the next day and once more the snow began to fall. MEDEVAC was no doubt black, but there was some talk of anti-IED missions that would take place out of the COP. The mortar team began to fire illumination rounds every night over the road from Bermel to the COP, attempting to deter the IED team, who were currently 2 for 2. The "lum" rounds (pronounced loom) would light up the night about once an hour, only to have cold darkness swallow them up about ten seconds later.

On Christmas Eve, I was officially removed as PLT cook. Swinehart and I were preparing to fry something up, and I was checking to see if the grease was hot enough. I didn't have any water to drop in it or a thermometer, so I just spit a little in the hot pot, which of course burned up as soon as it touched the hot grease. SSG Manuma did not approve of this. It wasn't the fact that we were dirty, that the pots were dirty, or that the food was nearly spoiled that got him upset. But a little spit, that vaporized as soon as it hit the grease, he just couldn't handle; and thought was unsanitary. I was forced to step down. At least it got the nag patrol off my back at breakfast.

As my Christmas present, on Christmas day, I was forced to clean up the burn pit. SFC Adams wanted all of the scrap metal out of there, since it wouldn't burn and only took up space. So I toiled through heaps of burnt trash, shit, and dog, clearing out the metal as best as I could. This is when I was officially tired of Afghanistan and ready to go on leave, which was now less than a month away. I have to say, I will never forget that Christmas day.

The day after Christmas the weather cleared up, and some of the snow began to melt. It melted around the COP just enough that SFC Adams decided he now wanted a hole in the side of the mountain to place all of the metal cans and such in. SPC Neary and I were going to be on the digging team. What kind of fucking idiot attempts to dig through rock hard earth

---

87 **BFT**—Blue Force Tracker, a Global Positioning System used by the United States military

and wants a pit that is six feet deep by six feet wide? Well that would be Neary and me. A guard team was placed over the Hesco to make sure no ACM got us, but it felt more like a chain gang guard. At least I could spit without Manuma getting his panties in a wad!

Neary and I joked as much as possible. We would take turns swinging the pick and shoveling the dirt out. We exchanged stories about girls, booze, and drugs, all the while hoping we would run across a massive diamond. If that happened, the plan was to go AWOL to Islamabad, Pakistan and use our passports to get out of there, and sell the diamond to the highest bidder. Shit, neither one of us knew the way to Islamabad, but it sounded good for venting purposes.

December 28th marked 30 days that no one in 3rd PLT had showered. I'm sure not even Jesus would accept us into his kingdom, smelling as foul as we did. Our socks were as stiff as boards, and the armpits of our tan t-shirts would give the odor of landfills a run for their money. Also, our food was becoming quite scarce. The sun had once again disappeared, and with it the possibility of getting re-supplied. SFC Adams asked me to take an inventory of what we had to feed all 60 of us, "Yeah, we pretty much only have soup left." I told him after my account of our items. If anyone could live off soup and water, we could.

Our New Year's Eve present from MOD-6 was to go on an anti-IED mission. We were to watch over the COP access road that night. RCP was going to attempt to come get 3rd PLT once more tomorrow if the weather permitted. The night sky was starting to clear up, and with the vanishing of the clouds, went what little warmth they had trapped. The temperature plummeted to -4 degrees just as 3rd PLT was beginning to start its mission.

As I walked out from behind the protective walls of our tiny outpost and exited the gate, the cold wind took me by surprise. We were instructed to wear cold weather layers, but they did not stop the cut of the merciless wind, and they made you sweat more only improving our fantastic body aroma. The icy ground was a constant hindrance, especially for the mortar team carrying the 60mm tube. They would slide down the slippery slopes every 20ft or so. Any ACM that was out tonight would hear us coming through the snow a mile away.

My gun team emplaced overlooking the very spot where Captain Boris was killed. It was kind of eerie. We were next to a naked tree, which provided no cover from the vengeful wind. The very second we stopped moving, the coldest cold I had ever felt in my life overtook my body. I could forget about drinking any water since that froze about 2k ago, just as my sweat was beginning to do now. I whipped out a sleeping bag, and placed it around me the best I could. *I thought there was no way in a frozen hell that any smart IED team would be out in this weather, so who were the dumb ones?* Happy New Year!

We sat in that same spot for almost five hours. The New Year came and went and then Lt. Deep decided it was time to RTB thank God! Half of the PLT, including SFC Adams, were asleep anyway. There was no way I could sleep in such bone-cold conditions. We packed up, and I felt the ice against my frozen t-shirt as we began to move. At least now I could warm up. Of course we never take the same route twice, so we walked around the whole country of Afghanistan to get back to the COP. At least some folks from 2nd PLT were smart enough to have some hot soup waiting on us when we returned. I wonder if they spit in it?

On January 1st, 2008 RCP finally made it to the Malekshay COP. I swear I saw a few people drop tears as we would finally be able to shower, sleep in our own beds, get hot chow, and most importantly be able to talk with loved ones, who no doubt thought we were all dead! January 1st marked 34 days that no one from 3rd PLT had showered, and by God I could not wait to feel the hot water! RCP brought re-supply for 2nd PLT who would have to spend a few more weeks at the COP. We loaded up and began to drive back to Bermel. I turned my turret to face the rear as 3rd PLT pulled out of the COP for the final time, and of course I flicked off the guards in the towers.

Chapter Eighteen
January: The Trip Home

THE HOT WATER ON my back was like something I had never felt! I raised my head up under the raining, warm water and laughed. All of 3rd PLT was in the shower room at Bermel having a ball! We smelled like sewage walking in and roses walking out. Well, chlorinated roses that is. I walked over the sink to brush my teeth and give my face a well-deserved shave, when Hampton asked to borrow my toothpaste. "Yeah no problem man... wait...oh well." Hampton didn't like to listen to anyone, and had just dived into my toiletry back, grabbing the first tube he spied. That first tube happened to be filled with Preparation H. You know, not only does it feel gratifying on the hole, but it also works for chaffing. Hampton didn't even bother to look at the yellow goo on his toothbrush; he just wet it and shoved the whole thing in his mouth. His face after a few strokes was priceless. "Dude, what the fuck is that shit?" He said, barely touching his mouth together as he spoke. I could barely get the words out due to my laughter. I stumbled out into the snow and gravel howling, attempting to make it back to the warm barracks before Hampton, so I could spread the news.

The next few days, well, the next twelve rather, were spent on the FOB. Another winter storm had moved in, causing MEDEVAC to remain at black. The sky was a dark gray, accompanied by a frosty wind and snowflakes the size of a baseballs. At least the winter brought down time from the ceaseless rockets that usually fell on the FOB. I know I haven't commented much about the FOB being hit by rockets, but to do that would be an entirely separate book. It was an everyday occurrence from our second day on the ground until around the time we took over the COP in late November. Getting rocketed was much like getting coffee in the morning; it was just part of the routine. I know that sounds strange, that someone could get use to someone trying to kill them, or the explosions every morning, but you can't let things of that nature bring you down, especially in a war zone. That's what we were there for right, to play war? Besides, it's not the ACM that bother you after seven months of war—its seeing the same people day in and day out that starts to wear on a person. Weekends off from work could be God's gift to man, but there were no weekends off in Afghanistan.

We pulled guard duty while stuck on the FOB, hit the gym, or found other ways to amuse ourselves. One of the guys, Soto, claimed he had once been a Calvin Klein model, so we made him walk up and down our hall way, with Techno music on in the background…in his underwear. I know some of you reading this may find 30 full grown men watching another man strut around in his boxers to be one of the most homosexual things you have ever heard, but you have to do something to ease the tension. Laughing at yourself or someone else always helps.

I for one would leave messages on people's cameras. Usually it would be Snyder's, as he always would get pissed. "Holder, you fuck!" could be heard throughout the bee-hut, and everyone knew what had happened. Usually the videos would be of me touching myself in sexually suggestive manners and asking the camera if it wanted to do dirty things to my titties, every inch of them. You know things of that nature. Or Arruda and I would throw flour into the faces of sleeping people, which usually made the sleeper a little pissed. Anytime you get a bunch of soldiers together, with nothing to do, antics of all shapes and sizes will no doubt ensue.

Our hypersensitivity to war was also at its peak. At night people would shout out random things about a mission or call incoming. Sometimes people would try to climb over the walls in their sleep, yelling that the ACM were close. Imagine waking up in a dark building in the middle of a warzone, with someone yelling that the ACM had broken in and were now at your very doorstep. After a while you got use to it, just like everything else. Nothing beat SFC Adam's sleep-eating and sleep-dipping. The man would dip in his sleep and spit in a bottle, or reach down and eat cookies. It was too funny. This wasn't just an Afghanistan thing though. Back home he said he would wake up with crumbs all over him and have no recollection of a mid-night cookie raid. They say you're not supposed to wake sleep walkers, what about sleep eaters?

On January 13th 2008, the storm subsided just enough for two Chinooks to appear on the horizon. They brought mail, but more importantly they were taking me out! Taking that first step home was such a great feeling. I didn't care how long it took me to get there; I just knew I would no longer be on FOB Bermel, in the middle of fucking nowhere Afghanistan! Eight months was a long time to be in that place, a good month off was just what I needed. Everyone was beginning to get burned out, and we still had six more months to go.

Neary and I stepped into Salerno with a few more of MOD guys. Salerno wasn't snowed in like Bermel, in fact there were only remnants of snow, and it was also warmer, which suited us just fine. We hung out there a couple of days and feasted in their amazing chow hall. The food gets better as you move towards the States and gets suckier as you head back towards your FOB. KBR, the food contractor, knew how to do it right—omelets the size of a plate! No one cared about gaining a little weight while on leave; you'd lose as soon as you walked up that first mountain.

I left Salerno before Neary. He wanted to wait a little longer, due to the fact Bagram was backed up with folks trying to get out on leave. Shoot, I was ready to get there. It was one step closer home and they had a BBQ tent! I flew in on a small Black Water aircraft and thought I was nearly going to die as we skidded a tad on our landing. Bagram was a now a loud, frozen tundra. The immense mountains surrounding it were enclosed in snow. You could constantly see the wind blowing the fresh powder off of them and onto the busy base. I got in just in time, because the next day ice overtook the runway, and non-essential flights were grounded.

Two days later, I was sitting on my cot reading some junk I bought, and in walks SFC Adams. "Oh God...they let you out?" I said as I saw his grin widen. "What's up fucker?" he replied, as he dropped his bag on the cot next to mine. "Holder, this just ain't going to work, watch my shit." I then surveyed SFC Adams tromp around the entire tent, which was a huge circus tent, and pick up various items people had left, including a reading lamp, a lantern, a mattress, a book shelf, rug, and a stool. He then proceeded to make himself a little home away from home, laid down, turned on the reading light, sighed a sigh of relief, and then progressed to jump up and say, "Okay fuckstick, let's go to that BBQ tent!"

The BBQ tent turned out to be one of his better ideas. Some black KBR folks were working there, imagine that, and they knew how to make it right! I was even surprised to find good ole Southern sweet tea, along with Brunswick stew. SFC Adams and I should have bought stock in the place, as much as we ate there. He also gave me a lesson in Korean food. Turns out someone let the crafty Koreans in to set up a little restaurant. It seems no matter where you go in the military; there will always be a Burger King, and some gooks trying to sell you something deep fried.

SFC Adams and I got out of Bagram on the same bird. It was a jammed pack C-17 bound for Kuwait. As we got on board and sat down, I turned to look at SFC Adams, who had already put his poncho liner around his head, and said, "We're finally getting out of here!" He looks at me with that same grin as always and replies with the five words I still hear from folks today, "Shut the fuck up Holder." I couldn't help but laugh. We had spent eight days attempting to leave 'The Stan,' and it seemed it was finally happening. I was just looking forward to getting some McDonald's in Kuwait!

I never really cared for going through Kuwait. The sand gets in everything and is a bitch to walk on. Imagine your entire country being made of powdered, ocean like sand. Sure it sounds like a day at the beach, but believe me, it's much more annoying than your average pollen season. Luckily, we didn't stay too long. Next thing I knew, I was boarding one of World Airways outdated planes and looking forward to some tasty plane food. I love plane food, regardless if the only choices are chicken or pasta.

This was it! A quick stop in Shannon, Ireland and an eighteen hour flight were the only things standing in between Georgia and myself. It had almost been a year since I was home, and I couldn't wait to see my family, friends, and drink a cold brew. You realize, especially when you have spent the last eight months in the year 2. B.C., how much of our daily lives we no longer find as a blessing. Things like driving on a nice sunny day with friends or even just sitting down in a local restaurant. Well I was about to have eighteen days of that, and I was going to soak it in!

The Delta Connection flight descended through the clouds and made a bank to the right. I could see the Georgia pines, which were getting closer by the second. My mind drifted back to airborne school for a moment. It always does when I am flying over the trees at a low altitude. I was so excited I could barely stand it! In just a few moments I would get to see the town I grew up in, family and friends, and also have a tasty fried pork chop dinner!

The plane glided down and the engines roared into reverse. A feeling of relief and safety washed over me. For the first time in nine months, I wouldn't have to leer at everyone with uncertainty or carry a machine gun that was half the size of me just to make sure I made it back to my bed alive. Rockets and air raid sirens wouldn't be the first and last thing I heard as the day started and ended. The shower water wouldn't be chlorinated, the temperature wouldn't be -2 degrees, and most importantly, the food wouldn't be prepared by someone who didn't give a damn! Yes! I was home, bitches!

I stepped off the plane and walked into the terminal with a huge grin on my face. I expected to see my parents and sister, but all I found were my grandparents, sitting there and not fighting for once. Of course my parents would be late, always are! I talked with my grandparents. My grandfather was a bombardier in the Pacific during World War Two, so he liked making comparisons to the way the military was and the way it is now. My grandmother just liked talking about the Braves. Low and behold my parents walk in, and my dad, Tim, lifted me off the ground! "Put me down crazy!" I said, and my mother, Sharon, hugged me and cried tears of joy. I quickly ushered everyone out, as we were beginning to make a scene right out of a Lifetime movie.

I talked with my sister, Abbey, and as usual I teased her about touching children. She's a teacher, and gets pretty offended when I tell people she touches kids for a living. It's about a twenty minute drive from the airport to my house, and the whole way my dad played twenty questions with me. He likes details about everything, while my mom and I just want the gist. I accidentally dropped a few curse words, but it's hard to rope the language in after not having to watch it for nine months. Everyone was excited to have me back, and it was great to be home.

Just as I walked into the back door, the front door opened and Jay and my other best friend Hunter walked in. Those two never missed a chance to partake in Tim's cooking, which was probably the reason they were their anyway. They could give a damn about me! It was great being in a nice, warm house instead of a concrete wood building or tent in the middle of a bustling base. The quiet was relaxing, yet it was a little unnerving at the same time! We talked and ate, while I caught up on all of the hometown news and actually got to wear something that didn't have the Army's logo on it. It was great.

The next day I went and rented a white Chevy Tahoe. I sold my jeep when I moved to Italy, but this Tahoe would do just fine for eighteen days. Of course I hadn't drunk hardly anything in nine months, so hitting up a happy hour was one of the top priorities. Hunter and I met up at 4p.m. on the dot at the best local watering hole, Charley O'Corleys. Jay showed up at about 4:30, and our night got a little better when he made the comment that trivia and $10 wings and beer was being played down the street at Flip-Flops, another bar.

We moved our trio down there and proceeded to eat, drink, and be merry. Due to the fact that I had not drunk in so long, my alcohol tolerance had plummeted, much like 21st Century stocks. Six beers in, I felt like I had drank a whole handle of liquor. We made plans to take a road trip up to Athens, Georgia, and then we walked to Hunter's house, which was only a block away at the time. As soon as I sat down, Hunter lit up some ganja and passed it to me. Now I'm not really a marijuana smoker, but I'd try every now and then.

I'm not really skilled in smoker's education, so I had no idea that taking a huge hit from a gravity bong would send me into deep space nine. Next thing I knew I came to and I was standing in the middle of the room, staring at the wall. Everyone was sitting down laughing at me, but their voices seemed so distant. Was I having an out-of-body experience? Luckily, I knew you can't overdose on weed, so that calmed me from freaking out like I have seen some people do. However, I did try to call 911.

With everyone being in school and working, I had to do my best to keep myself entertained. I hung out with my parents as much as I could. One day I did an article for the local newspaper, The Valdosta Daily Times, but usually if I had nothing to do, I would grab a bottle of Captain Morgan's Private Stock and break into Jay's house. Where I would proceed to drink more than I should have alone in the afternoon, then wait for what the night may or may not hold. I only had a limited amount of time, so staying buzzed was a priority.

It was January 31st, 2008 when Hunter, Jay, and I headed out for Athens. We were going to stay with my friend Ben and see some of my other high school friends, and probably make some new ones. I have always liked road trips, alone or with friends. The trip to Athens takes about four hours; two are on interstate, and the other two are on country roads. About halfway through, we stopped to pick up some adult beverages. Naturally we had to sample a few before actually getting to Athens. I really enjoyed seeing the countryside and farmland that Georgia has to offer, especially since I didn't know if this would be my last time.

Arriving at Ben's house, we dropped our stuff and chatted while sampling some wine. Ben had arranged a dinner at a local Mexican establishment with my friend Amanda and some of her friends. Before we could do that though, we had to stop by Hunter's friend's house and pick up another passenger. You may know him as Kevin. Kevin would be joining us tomorrow night at my friend Cutler's Keg Party, while tonight would just be Margaritas and hot women. Or so we thought.

Leaving the Mexican place, my trio moved to my friend Ben G's house who was also a friend from high school. We were going to drink a few bruskies before heading downtown where the bar scene is in Athens. Hunter, Ben G, plus Jay surprisingly went downstairs to hit on some bud, but I steered clear of this due to my last run in. Jonathan, another high school comrade, arrived from Atlanta while the others were getting their high on. Jonathan's personality is much like mine but not as over the edge.

We made our way downtown around 10p.m. Now if you have never been to downtown Athens, you're missing out whether you're a drinker or not. All of the buildings are still standing from the 1800s and have been converted into shops, bars, restaurants, and anything else that your heart desired. Plus, the University of Georgia main campus is seated right smack dab in the middle of downtown, which is advantageous during football season. Being that it was almost February, there was a little nip in the air. Jay briskly found a portable space heater at Sideways Bar and made it his spot.

The bars were packed, but we expected this. We decided that it would be best to stay on the roof of this particular tavern, because fighting through the crowds was not a priority. We congregated around the heaters, drinking and laughing. It was good to be out with some of my best friends and to see some females that were actually tens in the U.S., not just deployment tens. You see, once you have been in the desert, or any extended deployment, the most heinous female would look good to you. Alcohol couldn't be used as an excuse then!

I decided I needed a fresh drink. I noticed one sitting on the bar, chilled, clear, and just waiting to be sipped. Unquestionably I didn't want it, who knows what was in that drink, could have been spiked for all I know. So I gave it to Hunter. As I return from getting my own drink, I snatched the beverage from Hunter, who had already drunk at least half of the glass. "Man that drink was just chilling at the bar, don't drink anymore of that." I said, as Hunter showed his disgust that I would give him a Roofie-calada that was obviously meant for eighteen-year-old girls. I wasn't trying to date rape Hunter though.

Regrettably, the drink was indeed spiked. Within minutes Hunter had lost all composure. Now it could have been the fact that we had been drinking for practically nine hours you might say, but Hunter and I have been known to drink for fifteen hours easy and still be good to hook. This was a side of Hunter I had never seen. I made an executive decision that it was time to vacate the premises. Hunter could barely walk now, and was being absurdly loud, and hanging on Amanda just to keep his balance. His words were slurred as he tried to buy a sausage from a street vendor. The vendor handed him a bun instead and said, "Sober up boy."

As I was walking into Ben G's house, Hunter darted pass me, ran into the kitchen table, bounced off of that, and hit the wall to his right. Then he turned and ran straight into me, his head connecting with mine. Hunter was out for the count; meanwhile, my lips were busted and bleeding. I guess I couldn't be too angry though. After all, I did give him the tainted drink. Ben loaded us all up in the Tahoe and made a swing by Checkers for a late night run. God, greasy food at two in the morning is a horrible idea, but it's good for the soul.

The next day, we recovered until about noon and then started the process over. A lunch downtown of gyros and seasoned French fries was just the ticket to nourish our alcohol-drown bodies. Walking up the hills of Athens helped too—sweat it out, sister! Tonight we were going to my friend Mikey's birthday party. It was promised to have beer-pong, keg beer, liquor, females, and of course good company. Oh did I mention Kevin would be joining us? But first, we had to get up with Cutler.

Cutler had lived with Hunter in Valdosta for Hunter's first year of college at Valdosta State University. After I kicked in his bedroom door (I'm an international door kicker) off the frame, Cutler decided it was time to transfer schools. Not that UGA was any less of a party school. In any case, he was hosting the party, and I had no idea how to get there. His directions were subpar as usual, but we finally made it. The time was about 6p.m., and the first line had just been taken. This would be my last night out while I was in Georgia, so it was going down in flames!

Walking up to the party, Jay decided to urinate on this poor bush. As I tread up to the one-story white house, I am hit by the stench of cigarettes and spilled Natural Light beer. Cutler and Mikey greet me, as we take in the festivities. Hunter and Jay are pretty good with people they do not know, so I never had to worry about them. Hell I didn't really know anyone at the party either, but everyone liked to give me their opinion about the war once they found out I was in the Army. I had to break the news to people that many times that we were indeed still in Afghanistan.

Hunter and I walked back to the Tahoe to converse with Kevin. He made my nose run a little. Returning, Jay said he noticed it a little bit, but he had yet to pick up on what was going on. Jay never could be tempted to talk with Kevin, no matter how hard I peer-pressured him. The party was going smooth, until I had to take a massive dump. Whenever I changed countries or locations, my body would stop up, and I would go three or four days without a bowel movement. It was now time.

Sneaking into the small bathroom that every girl in the place was using, I did the dirty deed. The cigarettes and blow had loosened my bowels up considerably. God bless America, it reeked. I then walked out like nothing happened and closed the door to the bathroom. I scarcely got outside before some girl walked in and about had a fit. What I thought would be a brief bitch session turned into a witch hunt for the bathroom bandit. I quickly grabbed Hunter and Jay, then we marched to the Tahoe. We had to let smoke clear before making an appearance again. The one thing I like about drunken folks is that they forget very quickly.

Walking back up to the party, Cutler had decided it was time to go downtown since the keg had been floated. Cutler was in no shape to be in public. When Cutler gets wasted, he brings his arms up and his hands to his chest, much like a T-Rex. This is the result of having two broken arms at once when he was younger. Obviously the state dependent learning had kicked in, and Cutler was going to be a T-Rex the rest of the night. We should have locked him in the closet for the antics he was about to pull.

We hit a few bars and saw some old friends. Cutler decided at Sand Bar that he could double fist beer, yet he dropped one, spilling glass everywhere. Even though Hunter and I were jacked, we weren't drunk, so we were kind of chaperones. That's the good thing about Kevin, he'll extend your party life by a good many hours. Your body will be drunk, but your mind won't. Since Cutler had started dropping drinks we all briskly moved out of Sand Bar and moved back to the top of Sideways.

Cutler and Hunter knew the owner of Sideways, so most of the drinks we half off. As last call came, Cutler decided to snag a full bottle of Patron Silver. Jay had a hankering for pizza, and the best late night pizza place in Athens, Little Italy, was only two blocks away. Cutler thought it was farther than that, and in the opposite direction, so he was going to take one way, and we were going to take the other. Hunter was going to meet us at Little Italy. Cutler, Jay and I walked out and stood at the intersection. The night life was bustling. Laughs, yells, and the smell of street vendor food were all around.

Cutler reached out to press the crosswalk button and out came the bottle of Patron, shattering on the pavement! Jay looked at me in disbelief, as he did not know Cutler had stolen it. "Cutler, where the hell did you get that!?" Jay exclaimed. Cutler turned in his nonchalant manner and said,

"I guess I picked it up somewhere. Now Little Italy is this way bitches, if I get there first yall owe me a pizza." Since you could almost see Little Italy in the opposite direction, Jay and I quickly agreed to the bet. Leaving the shattered Patron bottle, Cutler wandered off into the night. Jay and I moseyed in the correct direction.

Jay and I strolled into the busy pizzeria. The smell was delightfully overpowering. I sent Jay to snatch us up a booth before the establishment became overcrowded and I ordered us a few slices. Just as I sat down, Hunter came in and went into restroom. Who comes in right behind him after twenty minutes of roaming the streets? Cutler, of course. In all of his drunken glory, he walks past Jay and me as he tells us to go fuck ourselves. He then slings open the restroom door and throws up in the sink, scaring the shit out of Hunter. Luckily it was Hunter in there and not some drunken college girl.

Upon returning from talking with the sink, Cutler still proceeded to order a large pizza, even though he wouldn't eat any of it. We all exited the pizzeria as we discussed the mile we had to walk back to the Tahoe. The cold winter air hit our tired bodies, and all of a sudden this wasn't fun anymore. Hunter led the way as Cutler started falling behind. Jay repeatedly said he was going to take Cutler's pizza. As Cutler made a drunk dial, sat down, and then laid down in a flower bed, Jay made one last attempt, "What about the pizza!?"

"Jay, Cutler is probably going to sleep in that flower bed, so he is going to need the pie for warmth, let's keeps moving." I responded. Finally, we made it back to the Tahoe. Hunter elected that he was sober enough to get us back to Ben's house across the county. Riding home we discussed the craziness that had happened that night and all laughed about it. It had been a great weekend, one for the history books, and now it was time to start sobering up for the inevitable trip back to Afghanistan that was coming. This was my last night out in Georgia for ten months, and what a night it had been.

I spent the night before I left for Afghanistan with my family. My brother, Forrest had come down from Atlanta to see me off. We watched the Super Bowl and laughed at the commercials. These eighteen days had flown by too quickly, and I was now dreading the long trip back as well as six more months in that hellhole. I wasn't sure if I would make it back or not. Our death total in the 173rd had now reached thirty-two soldiers' and twice that many wounded. Would I be next? Sleep did not come easy that night.

Hunter and his family met me at the airport. Jay and my dad's friend Jimmy had also come. My grandmother was there and was already a crying mess. We took a few pictures, and I said my good-byes to Hunter and Jay. Hunter was drinking whiskey and coffee. His mother hugged me and cried, and then they left. Everyone knew what awaited me on the other side of the world. Death had scathed me one time, hopefully there wouldn't be another.

As the intercom called out my flight, I started giving out last hugs. My mother was crying, and then I moved onto my dad who was holding up pretty good, but when I turned and saw my brother crying, I couldn't hold it back any longer. We hugged as the security and ticket lady told me to take my time. I hugged my grandmother one last time and walked through the scanner. I walked into the terminal and waved one last wave and then boarded the plane. As it soared into to sky, I looked down at the terminal and saw my dad and mom waving into the sky and smiled. It had been a remarkable trip home.

CHAPTER NINETEEN
FEBRUARY/MARCH:
MARGAH

I TOOK THE BLANKET off my head and looked down at the arid tundra. I could hear other soldiers moving around, one of them crunching his ice. A flight attendant was moving with grace down the aisle, correcting tray tables and seatbelts. I look over at SFC Adams, who was already looking back at me, and said, "Well here we go. It's back to 'The Stan' and then back to Italy." He looked out the window for a second before sighing and replying, "You know I don't even care about this mission anymore. Most people probably don't after spending ten months here already, and we have five more to go. Jesus, fuck this."

I shared the same feeling. No one cared about the mission in Afghanistan. The men of the 173rd were missing births, deaths, marriages, and first birthdays. They were getting divorced by unfaithful wives, and washing their young years for what? For the self-centered, terrorist cell-forming, boy raping, people of Afghanistan? What people fail to see is that the citizens of Afghanistan don't give a damn. There are villages with no outside communication, and that's how they want it to stay. They make the rules and run their own town. Why would they want an outsiders coming in and taxing what meager wages they already make? No, they wanted things to stay the way they were. I mean sure, they loved Americans and other ISAF nations building roads, bridges, schools, and farms for them. Who wouldn't want a free, brand new bridge? These thoughts had to be suppressed though, for there were still five months to go.

The paratroopers were ready for coming spring, which promised an increase of ACM attacks, and get the hell back to Italy, where we could at least look at the women! SFC Adams and I were in Ali Al Salem for a day and then on a plane bound for Bagram. Bagram was still freezing; my nipples were proof of that! As I was checking in at the flight desk to get a seat to Salerno, someone called me by my first name. I turned around, and there stood an old family friend from Valdosta. Lt. Col. John Eunice was handing me one of his coins as we both smiled, and he asked, "What are you doing here!?" We talked for a second, and then he was off to Kandahar. I would be getting a plane an hour later.

It was now Valentine's Day, and I barely made it into the tent in Salerno to lay down before SFC Adams had found us a ride back to Bermel. God I was not ready to be back. I was tired from flying across the world. I missing my friends and family, and overall just not really thrilled about living in that football field-sized FOB any longer. We got on the bird, which had to make many a stop before Bermel and lifted off the cold earth. Luckily, as we were flying into Bermel, I could see most of the snow had melted. Hopefully there wouldn't be anymore.

For the next four days we would be doing Human Terrain Mapping, which is basically just taking a census of the villages in our area of operation (AO)[88]. We would walk or drive into the villages, ask to see the elder, then ask him how many Muslim sluts he had living with him. He'd give us an estimate; we would then give him some rice or beans, and then we'd be on our merry way to the next village. That idea would probably work great in America too. Although, no one here would want rice or beans—it would have to be football tickets or something of that nature to get folks to fill out the census.

On February 20th, SFC Adams decided that he no longer liked that layout of our barracks. He wanted to gut the entire insides, which included the plywood walls, doors, bunk bed, and all of our stuff, just so we could rebuild it again. This mindless process also included making one desk and at least one shelf for every room. He met resistance to say the least. Everyone was happy with his room, shelves, etc. Plus, it was Afghanistan. It's not like we could reconstruct the Hilton out of our warped plywood walls. But, it got done; after all he did outrank us.

A day later I was sitting in the medic station with a three-inch, rusty, Muslim nail hanging out of my foot, bleeding like a woman during child birth! I couldn't feel my toes, but at least I could move them. Our surgeon, dubbed the Bermel Butcher, hadn't thought to keep any tetanus shots on

---

88 **AO**—Area of Operation, the area in which an unit is responsible for

hand. I had to get MEDEVACED…again. The bird came in, and I hopped on. This time though I didn't get shot up with drugs to my disappointment. I thought we would be going to O.E. really quick; however to my surprise, we were headed to Salerno. I didn't mind that one bit!

I got out of the bird and hobbled into the hospital, which was now a real building, no longer a pile of shipping containers as it was when I was wounded. They immediately shot me up with a few drugs to kill any crazy Muslim infection and then took some x-rays. Luckily the nail had missed the bone, and my feeling would probably come back in about two weeks. A pretty mannish woman walked into the room, flushed my foot with a solution, and then stitched it up. I would have to stay off of it for three days, which was fine considering that there wasn't a flight to Bermel for the next five at least.

The next five turned into fourteen days total. Due to mission priorities and the weather, I was stuck. Again, I didn't mind because I was still getting paid to take this little hiatus. I made it back to Bermel on March 10th just in time to take part in Counter-IED Operations. This consisted of walking out six or seven kilometers and setting up an ambush, much like on that freezing night in December. Thank God it was a little warmer.

3rd PLT walked out to this hill that wasn't attached to the mountain range, but was smack dab in the middle of the valley, and hiked up it to get a good picture of everything. Naturally every night we went out was eventless. Usually I would sit there in the dark listening to Snyder bitch about the cold or something like that. He would always moan like a slut as we moved up and down the mountains. One night I fell and went down the mountain, luckily not getting my head smashed by a rock. SSG Manuma came down and pulled me up. SFC Adams came up to Snyder and said, "You see that? Holder falls head first down the fucking mountain and doesn't say a word. You walk one foot and moan like a whore. Shut the fuck up and use noise discipline." I couldn't help but laugh.

On March 15th I was talking to Maddalone while he was up in the guard tower by our barracks. I took a drag off a smoke, looked up at the vast blue sky, and then was on my ass, rocked by explosion. "What the fuck was that!?" I yelled up to the tower. I looked around and seeing that I had obviously not been hit by a rocket, nor did I hear one. Maddalone looked down and said, "Dude they just blew up the ANA gate!"

"Who blew it up?" I said, starting to walk off in a hurry to go help. "I don't know man, it's just gone!" Maddalone said as I was now running towards the gate with medics carrying their aid bags. As I ran through the

ANA compound, around the Hesco corner and to the gate, all I saw was a situation of mass confusion. It didn't help that no one spoke Pashtun. Bodies were everywhere, body parts were everywhere. I looked up and saw a dead woman's head and torso looking down on me up from one of the ANA towers. A man was just outside of the gate, trying to crawl toward us using only his arms and crying out in pain. The scene was chaos. I attempted to pick up an ANA soldier and place him on a stretcher, but to my dismay his head came off when I lifted him up from behind the arms. I couldn't help but throw his limp body down as his head rolled towards me. I leapt back through the smoke and moved on to the next live person, who could be helped.

Everyone who could walk was directed to our small aid station, and those that had to be carried were supported with stretchers or in our arms. The screams of the wounded continued to echo off the FOB walls. MEDEVAC birds had been notified of a mass casualty event and were on the way as medics started a triage section by our aid station. It had been a lone suicide bomber that caused this act of destruction. He didn't even hit the Americans but his own Afghan people instead. He wounded twenty of them and killed twelve. I will never understand how a person can be capable of such senseless death.

On March 21st 1st Battalion kicked off another COP building mission. This time we were going to construct a mammoth COP at Margah to replace the run-down one that was currently being occupied. The new one would be built atop a nearby hill which overlooked the town and was virtually impossible to be overrun. Also, as before, everyone was playing a role in the building of it, but the mission wasn't going to start with the same flare as the last one. No, there would be no bombing and artillery campaign, nothing to make your dick hard. This time we were just kind of going to stroll out there and start construction.

MOD was going to be pulling outer security the entire time. Since Margah was in the valley and not in the mountains like our COP, little hiking would be necessary. We would be driving around some in the day and then set up a tight perimeter at night. As I said before, there really wasn't any danger of the ACM sneaking up on construction due to the terrain, and there were about 300 paratroopers with the might of the American military at their fingers to ward of any ACM fighters that were feeling Froggy. Much like last time, construction was supposed to take fifteen days on the COP; however, we would also be building a madrassa (school) in Margah to replace the one that the ACM had recently blown up. It was a hearts and minds mission to show that we were committed to the citizens of Margah.

With construction of both the COP and madrassa taking place at once, we had to be extra careful that one of the ANA or ANP personnel providing extra security were not part of the ACM, who might sabotage the Madrassa operation. The ACM wants the people of Afghanistan to stay illiterate and uneducated. So they can interpret the Koran to the illiterate and silent majority in whatever way suits their purpose. It was a wise tactic to keep the sheep silently chewing their grass. Either way, the madrassa was going to open this time; Eagle 6 was making sure of that!

RCP started the mission, clearing up the wadi road to Margah. They were followed by a Delta PLT and Alpha PLT for security, and then came the engineers. MOD would be taking the road across the valley once RCP cleared all the way to Margah, then turned and cleared our route. While we were waiting a few hours for RCP to make it back to Bermel, 3rd PLT was tasked with a quick LCLA drop. The FOB needed to restock on Class V (ammunition) due to the fact that the other PLTs supporting us came like thieves in the night and robbed our ammo point; the filthy rogues.

We drove out the still tattered ANA gate about a 1k away from the FOB to set up the usual DZ. Our re-supply drop zones were nothing more than our Humvees for security and a trailer to carry the supplies. Being that I was SFC Adam's gunner, it was my job to look for the aircraft and listen to the radio, along with SPC Martin, one of our Forward Observers. We had also switched drivers. SGT Adams was moved to Alpha Company, so our new driver was also our new medic, Doc Lolino. Lolino was a guy about 5'6, with dark Italian-looking features, and covered in tattoos. His whole right arm was done up like Spider Man's outfit with the red and blue to match. I'm still not sure if he felt that he actually was Peter Parker. Either way he fit in better with the 3-5 truck crew than Doc Plantiko did, who was now in 1st PLT.

SFC Adams got out of the truck and said, "Make sure ya'll two listen for the FOB or plane. I don't want to walk back here and find you two fags tickling each other's assholes." Of course I couldn't help but laugh at this comment. It was SFC Adam's observations or rants about food, Propel Fitness water, or anything else he considered indispensable to talk about that kept me sane for fifteen months. Standing up in a turret all day every day can get very monotonous without some form of entertainment!

Before SFC Adams could walk away, we got a call over the net from the pilot. "MOD 3-5, this is Moose 2-3, approximately three minutes until drop." SFC Adams responded and looked around for the small Black Water plane as we all did as well. Usually they would be flying about 50ft off of the ground like kamikaze idiots. This time though, they were nowhere to be found. "Holder, what the fuck is that?" SFC Adams asked. I turned and looked toward the sky in the direction of his gaze, hardly making out the shape of a plane.

"I think that's a C-17." I replied. SFC Adams turned to Martin and me, "So much for a 'Low-Altitude" drop.' The C-17 was about a mile up, soaring in our direction. At this rate our hassle free re-supply was about to get scattered into the wind. Just as the jet's loud engines loomed overhead, silencing our conversations, the parachutes started opening above us... well some of them. "Move the trucks!" SFC Adams shouted as a few of the pallet's parachutes cigarette rolled[89], plunging the live ordinance towards the brown earth. Even if the pallet didn't explode upon impact, it would still kill the gunner of the vehicle if one was struck and possibly everyone else inside. All of the vehicles had backed up just far enough as the pallet slammed into the ground, accelerating crates, cans, and wood shards at life-ending speeds. Luckily, there was no explosion, only a pain in the ass mess to clean up; God bless the Air Force.

We returned to the FOB just as RCP was pulling in. It was now time to push out and pull security. This time, there would be no mountains to clear, no new roads to explore, and no doofus Lieutenant to make us laugh. This time we were just going to sit and wait for anything crazy to happen. MOD-6 and 7 lead the way with 1st PLT to the verge of the mountains in Margah. We would be about three miles behind them. The scouts had found an old fighting position that had great observation of the valley and surrounding hills. We would occupy the hill and circle the vehicles up for security on all sides, much like a wagon train back in the day of the Oregon Trail.

Now unless you're in prison reading this book or have some type of sitting fetish, I doubt many of you have sat in the same location for five days. This is the exact reason I do not go into much detail about everything we did. For one reason this book would have to be a five part series. Another is most of the time we sat around gawking at each other's asses, waiting for something to happen. It's wasn't like World War Two, or even Vietnam, where you're constantly pushing out to engage the enemy. No, three-fourths of the time was spent following false leads, doing HA

---

89 **Cigarette Roll**—when a parachute deploys from the bag but does not open.

missions, and providing security. That's why soldiers get complacent… boredom, the number one killer.

While sitting in this location, I was facing a Muslim household. I'm sure they didn't really appreciate us playing war in their backyard, but I was entertained a little watching them. I would give them names, and observe them go about their daily task. However, I almost shot up their house one night due SFC Adams freaking out in a dream. It was about 0400 in the morning, and I had just taken over the last guard shift in the turret, starting my day of standing, and crazy Adams started having a night terror shouting, "They're in front of us! Shoot em! Hey shoot them!!" Of course he woke everyone around our vehicle up, and we all cocked our weapons, preparing to unload in this poor family's living room. Luckily, he kicked the dashboard and woke himself up. We were still trying to figure out what was going on. Lollino had already called to other trucks on the radio. SFC Adams looked around, and Martin asked him where they were. "Where's who?" he said, obviously as confused as us.

"Were you dreaming or are there really people about to kill us?" I said down into the cab. "I guess I was dreaming," SFC Adams responded, as he started to chuckle to himself. Meanwhile I had to check my drawers to make sure I hadn't relapsed into shitting myself. On the morning of the fifth day, we received news that an Alpha Co. soldier had been killed up in Spearay by a sniper. Snipers were becoming more prevalent in the mountainous region, especially father up North where 2nd Battalion was stationed. With four months to go, that brought our KIA total to 38 paratroopers. Spring was here now, which was the beginning of the fighting season in Afghanistan. The ACM had been thawed out from winter's frost. They were ready to play. Undoubtedly there would be even more memorial services to attend in this wasteland. Since the 173rd Airborne Brigade was so small, everyone knew someone that had been killed or maybe even all of them. But you couldn't let it get to you; we still had a mission to finish; and by God we all wanted to make it back to honor their memory.

On that same day, the ACM graced us with its presence. Remember how I said we had been sitting in the same spot for five days? Well that should be plenty of time for the dumbest ACM fighter to get our round-about location and drop some effective ordinance on us. Well the guys that day must have been fresh spring trainees, because all that did was stir the hornets' nest. I was sitting in my turret, minding my own business, when the mountain beside us started blowing up. Of course we all turned that way with our guns, and Hampton even started opening up on it with the .50 Cal, but that fool didn't see anyone since the mountain was across the river and about 1k away. Hampton never missed an opportunity to waste ammo.

SFC Adams came over the radio to tell Hampton to cease fire. MOD-7 then came over the net and said, "Their backkkk." Eagle-6 came over the radio and said, "I want that mountain leveled and a gun sweep on the entire area." No sooner had he spoken a 1000lb JDAM, which was dropped danger close to our position; turn that mountain side into a sweltering incinerator. I had never seen such fire power up close. Now that will give you a hard on!

After the 155s from Bermel finished their sweep of the area, Capt. McCrystal decided it was time to change positions. I waved to my friendly Muslim family across the street as they gave me blank stares and then turned the turret around to face the rear of the convoy. We would be driving over to the halfway finished COP to pull security for the night and then open the madrassa in the morning. The Governor of Paktika Province would be flying in to participate in the ceremony, plus supposedly 500 people were attending; tight security was going to be needed.

That night SFC Adams showed us the proper way to make spaghetti from one of the dehydrated cold weather MREs. I know dehydrated noodles and sauce doesn't sound that good, but buddy let me tell you: if you add some hot sauce to it and throw it on some shelf life bread, there isn't anything better, not in Afghanistan anyway! Along with the cooking lesson, SFC Adams also commandeered my boiled peanuts. Frequently he would also yell out, "Martin, water!" Which in Adams's terms meant, "SPC Martin, would you please hand me a water?" It always cracked me up. To repay SFC Adams for his ways, Martin and I would speak in flamboyant dialogue together. We would speak with lisp and rub each other. Often around the time SFC Adams was ready for the "ground sleepers" to vacate the truck, so he could stretch out.

As we lay behind the truck, in our green sleeping bags, SFC Adams would shout out homophobic profanities, which always made us laugh. We weren't that worried about being attacked in the valley. You could see or hear someone coming from a long way off. Everyone would take turns on watch, which was done by switching out shifts inside of turrets. Three shifts of four hours was usually the norm. I always took the last shift since I had been standing in the turret all day any way.

It was still rather cool as the sun's rays started turning the sky blue and purple. It was always so clear in the morning. Industry, cars, and other 20th century creations have yet to touch Afghanistan. Smog and pollution were unheard of. The trucks were loaded up, and 3rd PLT met the rest of the company around the almost-finished COP for the opening of the madrassa. MOD-6 discussed each PLTs role in the security for the day, and then we all went to our positions. We would be providing outer security, while 2nd PLT and 1st PLT provided security around the madrassa itself. This included checking all of the civilians for anything that could be used as a weapon, keeping them in certain locations, and making sure no one was posing as ANA or ANP personnel. Sounds like the airport doesn't it?

I saw some ANA soldiers walking with a goat, so I assumed they had been put on hors d'oeuvres detail. I also expected they were going to walk to the small ANP station at the old Margah COP to butcher it. Boy was I wrong. One of the soldiers brandished a dull, rusty knife and just went to cutting on this poor goat's neck in the middle of the road! The goat struggled and let out ear-piercing bleaks, but it wasn't enough to stop the Afghan, who looked up and smiled after he sliced the goat's throat. I kind of waved and smiled a nauseous smile. "Did you fucking see that Holder?" SFC Adams asked in a disbelieving tone.

The crowds started to gather for the commemorative opening of the madrassa. Individuals were showing up from as far away as Shkin, which was about 20k from the madrassa. There is no telling what time in the morning they started their journey. A number of Afghans drove motorcycles, and the richer ones had old 1980's model cars. Every once in a while you would see a new Toyota Hilux. These had to be checked especially well, a vehicle- born IED (VBIED)[90] in a crowded setting such as this would be a catastrophe.

Just around 10:15 a.m. a pair of Blackhawks circled the madrassa and COP site. It was the Governor of Paktika. No doubt he felt like a badass. The birds landed just outside our perimeter, and he was picked up by MOD-6 and 7. The show had begun and there was no room for error. We had rebuilt this school after the ACM blew it up to show we were committed. If a security breach was allowed with all of these troops around, what would that say about the Americans? To the Afghans we were the most powerful force in the world. Perfection was needed.

Capt. McCrystal spoke to the crowd briefly, which of course had to be translated by an interpreter. Then the Governor said something in his

---

90 **VBIED**—Vehicle Born Improvised Explosive Device, an explosive device built into a vehicle to enhance its destructive properties

Muslim tongue, and that was it! I was pretty surprised how quick the ceremony went. I was expecting at it to be at least an hour. Some of the crowd walked through the school, others celebrated, and then they all moved to a designated spot to eat the slaughtered goat which was now cooked and seated on a pile of rice and beans. I just got some flatbread out of it, sticking my hands where the dirty Afghans had been was just something I was not down for. Most of them had not seen a bath in a river in quite some time!

Later that day we were to move our position, but that order was cancelled. Eagle 6 had been watching what he thought was the ACM emplacing IEDs on one of our routes. To make sure he was right, he had RCP clear the route, which resulted in a soldier breaking his legs when his truck hit the IED. Not really the approach I would have taken, but I guess it got the job done. Our new orders were to move back to the FOB, 3rd PLT only, and conduct another series of anti-IED missions at night. None of us were really exhilarated about rambling around all night, but hot showers and our own beds sounded great!

Returning to the FOB, we filled our Humvees up with fuel…well, we watched the Muslim worker bees fill them up. Ah, the joy of slaves. Then we staged them in front of our barracks as we did after every mission. Martin would walk around slightly leaned back, moving his arms up and down like Sasquatch. This always cracked me up. Maintenance was done on the trucks, such as blowing out the air filter, tightening bolts that could have come lose, plus filling up fluid. The terrain for Afghanistan was a dirty diseased slut that loved fucking our vehicles up, but with proper service, they would glide smoothly through her; condoms in hand of course.

SSG Manuma received some bad news from home as we were finishing up with the trucks. His new born son was severely sick, and he would be on the next bird out of Bermel, not to return. Weapons squad helped him pack up his belongings in anticipation for the Chinooks that were coming to drop off mail in addition to supplies and then take him with them. He had been our leader for almost two years now. He had trained, led us in combat, and developed each squad member to be a better soldier. Now in the last quarter of the game, he was being taken out. Of course we were all content, as was he, that he got to get home; this was his fourth deployment after all. But none of us wanted to lose the big Samoan.

The Chinooks landed in a windy, brown cloud. The personnel remaining in Bermel disembarked, and then the mail plus other goodies were unloaded by fork lift or man power. The PLT all shook SSG Manuma's hand, wished for booze in their refrigerators when they returned to Vicenza, and I had to give a goodbye to him in the most homosexual voice I could muster. Manuma climbed on the chopper, and shot a final bird our way with a grin. His leaving reminded each of us that this campaign would be drawing to a close soon. There were about four months left and one more critical mission; after that it was a wrap! The Chinooks showered us with a gust of dirt as we took the mail into the FOB, opened it like it t'was Christmas morn, and got ready for the night's mission.

Chapter Twenty
April/May: Spearay

THE ENTIRE MONTH OF April was spent on counter IED night missions and guard duty at the FOB. The other PLTs were tasked out, leaving us as the only MOD PLT in Bermel. SFC Carlson's 2nd PLT had been sent to the Bandar Checkpoint to help out Delta Co. and 1st PLT was manning our COP. It was basically like a month off other than the aimless strolls we took at night, which never produced anything of interest. Jumpy, hypersensitive paratroopers that are cooped up for too long begin getting into mischief, and with no entertainment other than what our minds could create, the mischief begins to get creative...and violent.

Most of the soldiers in the PLT had ordered Air Soft guns. These guns fired the little plastic BBs at an alarming rate of speed. Now of course no one got the little pistol or rifle you see in Wal-Mart. Oh no, leave it to infantry soldiers to buy the exact replicas of the weapons we were using. I'm talking about M-4s, M-14s, and there were even a few automatic M249s in the mix. Since we weren't in a position to go participate in the war at the moment, we'd make our own. With eye protection on, the paratroopers of 3rd PLT invaded each other's barracks like it was Normandy. The sound of BBs bouncing all over the place and yelps of people being hit echoed throughout the FOB.

I was pretty jumpy after being hit back last June, so I didn't really join in on the invasions. I would lie as flat as I could on my top bunk and cover my body with blankets, which was to protect from the constant ricochet of flying debris. Those suckers stung! Fresh welts could be seen in the shower. Those that were captured by the opposing team could easily be identified by the eight or nine welts on their backs. If captured, you were forced to stand facing the door, pull up your shirt, and get shot in the back from about three feet away. Not my idea of a good time.

If you thought Air Soft wars sound like a good time, then you would love getting shocked by Tasers. One of our gear heads, Fikar, loved ordering things. He would order custom-made shotgun scabbards, scopes, and projectors. Eventually he snagged a Taser. Once again I only watched as the idiots of 3rd PLT shocked each other, sometimes on their balls. God I hope those that got it on the sack weren't planning on having children anytime soon! At one point Martin was the loser of a bet. He either had to get Tased on the ear, or run one full lap around the FOB naked. Wisely he took the lap. With only sunglasses on, this Bangor, native sprinted through the gravel, catching the eye of every homosexual Muslim on the FOB and probably some Americans as well.

These antics just didn't go on during the day. If we weren't on mission at night, folks would put on their black Spears Gear, which is a silky newer version of Long Johns, and skulk over to Anvil's side of the FOB. They would wait in the shadows until unsuspecting Calvary Scouts walked by, then proceed to grab them, or jump out and scare the hell out of them. This game climaxed when all of 3rd PLT dressed in black and grabbed up MOD's Executive Officer, 1st Lt. Richmond, and tied him upside down to the flag pole. It was his birthday, so a present was due! We pulled down his shirt and slapped his stomach with shaving cream-laden hands, leaving a fresh red hand print every time.

Also, during this month a church was built on the FOB by the Muslims. How about that, Muslims building a Christian church? A very un-infantry type of soldier came to the FOB around the time the church was finished to allow us to record a message on camera so he could send it to our families. It was a good idea on paper, but of course the paratroopers of 3rd PLT can turn anything upside down. This time it was my turn. The camera man was speechless when I was through.

I'm capable of producing many different voices. This time I employed my black preacher voice to give a sermon in our new church by God! With all of 3rd PLT gathered, I shouted about giving money to my church, which I deemed Whiteside Baptist. Then I ranted about devil Jews, homosexual Muslims, President Obama, and Hilary Clinton I then got some people to testify and then told the camera guy that I wanted to take him to bed when I was through preaching. It lasted for about five minutes and was no doubt the most unreligious sermon of all-time, but it set everyone at ease and provided good entertainment!

Luckily the month-long mission in Spearay was almost in our grasp. We were all getting restless just sitting around on the FOB and doing the meaningless counter-IED missions. The final proof of this boredom was when Hampton killed a dog with bolt cutters while he was on guard duty. He just walked up to this unsuspecting pooch and bashed it over the head. Poor thing never saw it coming. When word of that reached SFC Adams while we were at chow, he had to ask Hampton if he was crazy or something. His little outburst caused the command to believe we were all starting to lose our minds, which may not have been too far from the truth.

Spearay COP was located at the Northern corner of Alpha Company's Area of Operation, barely in the Kwost Province. Spearay is also known as Warzistan, which might ring a bell if you have ever heard about the U.S. bombing it with our unmanned drones. Charlie Company was to occupy the COP as well as the Outpost (OP)[91] East, which sat 100m from the border of Pakistan. OP East was the front line. We were to deter ACM fighters from crossing the heavily used supply route, as well as expand the COP's defenses, which meant adding Hesco walls, filling sandbags, and once again chopping trees by axe on the side of a mountain.

Spearay COP was not tactically planned when it was built. Actually it wasn't built, more like occupied. The COP was inside of an old Afghan home. It had a courtyard, which was now the mortar pit, and then several rooms that were used to house the platoons, and function as an aid station and TOC. There was no running water and electricity was sporadic at best. There were no showers, sinks, or toilets. All that would have to be built. To top that all off, the COP was surrounded by towering mountains. If the ACM wanted to, they could easily muster a force and overrun the hastily fabricated base.

The mission started May 1st, 2008 and was to be MOD's final big mission of the deployment. This breathed new life into us. There was talk of us going home before the fifteen month mark, which also got us all excited. We were going to be airlifted into Spearay by Chinooks, which meant you could only take what you could carry. Infantry soldiers are masters at packing comforts. Some would trade a pair of socks for a DVD player; others would give up a t-shirt or two for that extra carton of smokes. All of us usually had a stool tied to our backs, we didn't want to sit in the dirt unless absolutely necessary.

---

91 **OP**—Outpost, a non-fortified position that can be taken down or evacuated easily usually closer to the front line than the Combat Outpost

Along with our bags, we were also going to load an ATV Gator on one of the Chinooks. It would be used to transport sandbags and such. SFC Adams cleverly drove it on the bird, so he could drive it up the hill to the COP when we finally got boots on the ground. Charlie Company had a reporter attached to it as well for this mission. John D. McHugh, from the *British Guardian*, would be imbedded with us. He had just returned to country after being shot in the stomach while imbedded with troops up in northern Afghanistan. Fully recovered, this redheaded Irishman was ready for combat.

The Chinooks glided down onto our HLZ, tossing the sand and rock in every direction. After the incoming cargo was offloaded, it was our turn to get on board. This was it. We were getting ready to occupy an area known for its snipers, hour long fire fights, and indirect fire attacks. Now if that doesn't get your blood pumping, nothing will! The birds flew low to the earth with their ramps down. I always liked flying over new villages and land I hadn't seen. Though most of it looked like the same, brown, gray, and sporadic vegetation, it was always better seeing it from the sky. The view from my turret was never so fulfilling.

The birds touched down on the Spearay HLZ and I ran off before everyone else with my gun team to provide security. MOD exited the birds quickly, as our vacant seats were filled with Alpha Company soldiers that were ready to return to their FOB and get a shower. MOD had 71 soldiers coming to occupy the COP as well as OP East, which included MOD-6, 7, 3rd PLT, a mortar team, as well as 2nd PLT. We also had one of the first Afghani doctors tag along with us to interpret and provide guidance on the local populace. As the paratroopers of MOD began the hike up the hill to the COP, SFC Adams drove over to my gun position, looked up at me grinning like a jackal and said, "Bet you wouldn't mind a ride would you Holder?"

"Well as a matter of fact that would be grand," I replied. "Well fucking sucks for you fagget!" SFC Adams responded as he drove off howling in laughter! Cocksucker. Entering the COP I was met with a smiling and familiar face, which was non-other than Captain Israel. "Holder! Boy sounds like you're gonna be hiking up that mountain with me in a few minutes," Captain Israel said. "I may have to let you attend that excursion on your lonesome sir," I responded, as I was huffing and puffing from hiking up the hill to the COP. He slapped me on the back and walked over to talk with the other 3rd PLT soldiers. I found a spot where I could drop my bags. The chamber in which we were staying required you to bend over to get in but was a huge room. It was also considerably cooler than that outside air, which was due to the layers of mud that made up the ingredients to this structure. There were also three windows to provide fresh air but could also be used as machine gun positions if the need arose.

I was briefly informed that I indeed would be ascending to OP East with my gun team. We would be a part of the first group of soldiers that were going to occupy the mountain top. Since the mission here was going to be thirty days, we would send two different teams to man the OP for fifteen days at a time. I didn't really mind living atop of a mountain. Sleeping in the dirt was sleeping in the dirt; the only thing that changed was the location. I packed a poncho and liner, a light weight sleeping bag I had ordered which had a built in bug net. As well as ammo, three t-shirts, three pair of socks, and a little hygiene kit. Only three shirts and three pair of socks for fifteen days? Yeah it was rough living, and we all did our best to stay clean, as well as keep the smell down. But what are you going to do? This was Afghanistan, not Buckingham Palace.

With my gun team ready to go, as well as the other soldiers, we began to follow Captain Israel up the beaten path to OP East. MOD-6 and 7 would be going as well to take a look at the OP, but would not be staying. John was also tagging along to take some photos. Walking out of the COP and then to the right, we went downhill one little, but that was about it. The rest of the way was going to be a meandering uphill battle with the gravity monster. The gravity monster was a term we used when someone was having difficulty breathing while climbing a mountain; which was practically all of us! This climb was going to go from around 10,000ft, which was the altitude of Spearay COP, to around 12,899ft which was the tallest peak around; the peak OP East currently sat on.

About ten minutes into this trek, I immediately regretted coming to Spearay. It was near 85 degrees, which would be a nice day if you had shorts and flip-flops on to stroll around with. Walking up mountains with a M240B, a full assault pack, and body armor in 85 degree weather is a different story! Also, we were hauling a MK-19 up the mountain. The soldier's with pieces to that mammoth gun in their packs were sucking air hard. Frequent halts were needed. Captain Israel was bounding up the mountain like a Billy Goat, but then again he was only carrying his rifle and water.

One thing I have to say is the hike up to OP East was scenic. The highlands were covered in trees, and there were old towers dating back to the time of Xerxes. Some of the rock formations were breath taking. It would be a great country to hike in during the summer, and snow ski during the winter; if it wasn't filled with mad Muslims. John was constantly taking photos of the landscape and of the paratroopers walking up the hillside. "God yall need to get some mules," He said just as we began the final steep ascent to the OP itself.

The final hill leading to OP East was barren. All of the trees had been blown down with Detonating cord, which provided a boundless field of fire so the ACM could not sneak up on us. Snyder was in front of me for the whole trek but I finally had to pass him. He was carrying more weight that I was, but I wanted to get this climb over with! I made it to the little Hesco perimeter wall and up into the OP then had to drop to a knee. My uniform and helmet were soaked in sweat. Captain Israel tossed me a bottle of water and motioned for me to look down the mountain to watch the other paratroopers battle the hillside. I redirected my gaze down the hill while trying to catch my breath.

The view was amazing. Directly to the front of the OP was the border of Pakistan. It was a hill dubbed target red, which was a pre-determined target for artillery. You could see the Pakistan checkpoints in the river valley to the right, and a palace off in the distance. To the left of OP East was the main supply line in and out of Pakistan. There were also a few vacant houses about two kilometers away lying just off the route in a little bowl. We named them the Taliban Hotel. You could see everything from the OP; it was literally on top of the world. The COP looked small from this altitude, as did the farms in the valley.

OP East wasn't much, as I'm sure you can imagine. There was a small tower facing the hill we had just walked up. Beside the tower was a sort of patio made of sandbags. It was used by the scout snipers as a place to lay, to look upon the Taliban Hotel; as well as get a decent shot of the supply route if needed. At the far end of OP East was another small tower. It over looked the river valley and the Pakistan checkpoint. The south side of the OP was a cliff face that dropped about fifty feet. Barbed wire surrounded the few parts of the OP that could be accessed by foot, as well as Claymore mines.

There were no sleeping quarters, but merely three foot Hesco squares lined up to get cover behind in case the ACM attempted to assault the OP. Old, tattered parachutes provided limited overhead cover from the elements. Food and water were dropped in by helicopter, as well as ammunition. The interpreters had their own sandbag and Hesco area where they could get cover in case of an attack. There was also a two man team of intelligence officers that were living in OP East. They had been on top of the mountain for two months, boy did they look rough. They had a few tarps and Hesco that made up their home.

MOD completed the hand over with Alpha Company and I took first guard shift in the East tower, which was the tower facing the Taliban Hotel. I watched the paratroopers that were headed back to the COP descend from OP East, and then I turned my attention to the check point on the Pakistan border. We had a spotting scope so I attempted to get a good look at guards on duty. Directly in front of the Pakistani check point sat an ANP check point. Bribes were known to flow through both check points, more frequently than any drugs or ACM fighters.

The next day we built a fighting position and installed the MK-19 facing target reds. The fighting position was made of mostly sandbags, and we dug about three feet down to provide better cover. Doc Lollino had dug a slit trench, which was basically a trench in the earth where we could piss and take dumps in. Personally I found it quite hard to straddle a trench when the time came, but it was the most sanitary answer in conditions such as these. We tried to rearrange some of the parachutes to provide better cover from the rain that was sure to come. A few improvements to the rustic OP were never a bad thing.

If you weren't on guard, there wasn't much to do. I had brought a few books, others were into Sudoku; but we all tried to pass the time with some kind of activity. Hours upon hours were passed cutting down each other's moms, talking about political views, past missions, or trying to convince this home-schooled, redheaded religious fanatic named Floyd that he was indeed gay. SSG Daniel and I would attempt to get Floyd to admit to the possibly that he could in fact be homosexual until he would go red in the face and stop talking to us altogether. Some may call it bullying; we called it passing the time.

The following day we ventured over the border into Pakistan. My gun team, along with 2nd squad, moved up target reds to check out the hilltop. We were also going to set up trip flares in case the ACM tried to hike up there and get a good machine gun position facing OP East. Any flare that was tripped would be met with a wall of metal, and then have 155 artillery rounds dropped upon it. On the Pakistan side of reds you could see more of the town and palace that lie out in the distance. The land also dropped considerably in elevation. The Pakistan side was more flat farmland, whereas the Afghan side was purely mountainous.

Heading down target reds, after the flares had been set it, we circled the OP. SSG Daniel wanted to see if there was any possibility of the ACM sneaking up behind the OP. No way was that going to happen. The terrain surrounding the OP was treacherous. It took us nearly three hours to complete our journey around the hill top, due to the fact we had to go down the mountain and then back up because of the cliff face. Luckily we made it back through the wire just in time. Rain had started to fall, and it was followed by hail. Our parachutes took a beating, but held up well during the storm.

That night we sat around the TACSAT[92] radio and listened to Eagle 6 discourse roughly the preliminary re-deployment plans for the 1/503rd. It was getting closer, everyone could feel it. That day marked one year that the 1/503rd had been in Afghanistan, only three more months to go. God willing we all would be stepping off a plane soon to see our wives, family, friends, or just crack a beer! Eagle 6 said our Operation Enduring Freedom campaign was the most successful war campaign in history, I don't know if agreed with that, but the radio did break up the wearisomeness of messing with Floyd.

The next few days passed effortlessly. We would do four hours of guard during the day, and then four at night. The most exciting hour during the day was burning the MRE trash, and throwing the spent radio batteries in the fire. They would melt with a flash, providing a gunshot like boom. After that hour was up, boredom's grasp would slowly clench down on your soul, sucking the life out of you! Well it wasn't that bad…but close.

On Mother's Day however I was able to call my mom. The intelligence team had a satellite phone they let us use. I'll never forget her surprised voice when I told her I was calling from on top of a mountain in the middle of nowhere. That was the first call I had made since I had returned from leave. We talked for about five minutes about this and that, and then my time was up. It was back to the East guard tower, just in time to hear the ICOM radio pick up chatter about a possible attack.

Darkness took our valley. I couldn't see my hand in front of my face until I put my night vision on. By now everyone could do everything in the dark that they could in the light, but seeing was a plus. The ANA COP a few miles away on another steep hilltop, lit up with tracer fire. The assault had started. We were going to deter an attack on our position before one could begin. Snyder and I took the poncho off the MK-19 and prepared

---

92 **TACSAT**- Tactical Satellite Radio

to fire about ten rounds on target reds. The paratroopers in the COP had already started hitting a few targets where the ACM could set up fighting positions, with 120mm mortars, MK-19 rounds, and the .50 Cal. Snyder fired his rounds, just then machine gun fire shot into the sky on the other side of target reds. Oh, the ACM were there, but now they were getting spooked since we were turning the hillsides into spheres of fire. I heard the artillery fire from FOB Tillman; it was about ten seconds until time on target, then the ground shook with implausible might. The only way to hear each other during this anticipatory strike was to yell, even though Snyder was one foot from me.

The artillery was flying so close overhead it sounded like a freight train. The new FDC at Tillman was getting awful close to our position. The 82nd had redeployed recently and they handed over the FDC to the 101st Screaming Eagles. They either didn't know we were on the OP, or had the wrong grid given to them all together. The rounds were falling like rain, and getting closer to our position. I could just see them adjusting fire on target red, which was closer than danger close, and missing the target. Then, the last round hit, and once again it was a quite night; as if nothing had happened.

The radio blared out, asking for a SITREP[93]. The ANA COP was also dark now, and other than the few shots fired on the other side of target reds, there was no ACM incursion. We all manned our positions for another hour before standing down. Once again the ACM had been deterred, but who could blame them? I know I sure wouldn't storm an uphill position, with all hell breaking lose around me!

As the sun crested over the mountains that next morning, I could see our replacements trudging up the hillside. Our time was up at OP East. Most of us wanted to stay, due to the fact that chopping trees and filling sand bags awaited us down at the COP. SFC Adams and Lt. Deep were leading this mission and boy, it was a pleasure seeing Adams suck air! I knew better not to say something to him when he was just getting into the wire, but Snyder didn't. "Hey SFC Adams, looks like you were having a hard time coming up that little ole hill!" Adams responded, gasping in between words, "Yeah…Snyder…how about you…elevate…your legs…on that sandbag wall…and don't recover…until I say so." Snyder got down with a laugh and propped up his legs, now his arms were holding up his body, and he wasn't laughing anymore!

---

93 **SITREP**—Situation Report, a report given that outlines a certain circumstance

The change over went smoothly. I would be leaving my M240B up at the OP so my walk down would be scenic. Or at least I thought so until SFC Adams put a broken chain saw on my back. I didn't mind. It was no heavier than anything else I was use to carrying. Our group exited the OP and headed down the hill. Lt. Deep wanted to walk over and check out the Taliban Hotel, and the route the ACM used. On the way across my rucksack strap broke, there went the chainsaw down the hill.

Recovering the chainsaw, and enduring verbal abuse from SFC Adams, we went through the Taliban Hotel. It was built much like the buildings at the COP. A few tables sat in one room, with a few AK rounds sitting on top, as well a copy of the Koran. Other than that nothing of interest was to be found. No doubt the rebels that had occupied this structure had moved on once the OP had been built. Our group rambled down the hill and back into the COP. Going down the mountain was much more pleasurable than going up!

Walking in, we dropped our gear in our designated sleeping spot. The mortar team sergeant, SGT Erickson, had taken up the job of cooking. Now he was the target for SFC Adams and when Adams just didn't quite agree with certain ingredients, God bless Erickson. Erickson had cooked us a roast and some potatoes, which sure beat an MRE. After lunch I took a bird bath, which consisted of bottled water and a bar of soap. You really just hit the main parts that you could without getting fully undressed. Getting your feet was a definite, then your legs, arms, hands, hair, face, and armpits. It felt great, as did laying on a cot and not the ground.

The next day we began construction on the new guard tower. We were going to have to extend the wall with new Hesco, and then build the tower out of sandbags. Where were the engineers when you need them? A lot of work had already been completed while we were up on the OP but there was always more that could be done. Due to Snyder's remark to SFC Adams up at the OP, my gun team would be filling sandbags. I hated filling sandbags.

The Hesco team atop of the hill was unfolding the Hesco for the new wall while my gun and I were filling sandbags at the bottom for the tower. Luckily we had a small Bobcat frontend loader to haul dirt from the bottom of the hill to the top to fill the Hesco. The wall went up quick. Now sandbags were just needed and thank the Lord we had filled enough by the time they were necessary, or SFC Adams would have been down there harping until it was done. After we filled the bobcat up with sandbags time and time again, the tower was finally complete. Now we could see down the trail to the OP better.

The next two days were spent pulling guard. We were waiting on a shipment of chainsaws to come in for the trees that still needed to be cut down. The axes we getting dull, but if the chainsaws never came we would be hacking like lumberjacks once again. The days and nights had been quite, minus one failed rocket attempt by the ACM. Our display of fire power had deterred any attack on both positions. The attacks were taking place back in Bermel. Without daddy around, the kids will no doubt begin to act up. Rocket attacks had stepped up on the FOB and Malekshay COP, as well as the IED findings. Soon we would be back to give the children a spanking, but for now we had to try and talk some sense into the people of Warzistan.

Captain McCrystal held a meeting with the local leaders attempting to sway their allegiance to our side. But the problem with the Warzi tribes was that they had family both in Afghanistan and in Pakistan and the family in Pakistan were ACM. Plus, the Warzi tribes considered their land to be and independent country, so that didn't help with trying to rally them for the support of an Afghan government. We were fighting a losing battle with these people, much like trying to pull a mule that had made up his mind he wasn't budging. But the talks continued. After all, that's what we were sent there to do.

Four days later the chainsaws arrived. Low and behold only two out of ten worked and then those two failed as well. God bless the USA! No wonder we outsource everything. We were back fighting the hills with axes and fire. John was walking around with his camera capturing material for *The Guardian* newspaper. Most of his work from his time with us can still be found online at his website. He made the comment, "It's not every day you see men in armor hacking at trees on the side of a hill in 90 degree weather." I guess that's true. I was all for paying the Muslims to do it.

But at the time you don't think of what you're doing as abnormal or hard work, it just needed to be done and when something needed to be done, we had to do it ourselves. There was no heavy machinery to move the earth; it was down to your own two hands. I never dreamed I'd be hacking away at trees with a dull axe, in full gear, with the risk of getting shot at. Then doing a horse's job and pulling the trees down the hill so they could be burned. But when it came down to it, you just got to go with the flow. The men of Charlie Company did that pretty well.

Just as the last fire was being lit, SPC Strobell lit himself on fire! After lighting wood on fire all day, and getting a little JP-8[94] on his clothes each time he poured some out, the man finally lit up like a Christmas tree. In his haste to put the fire out on his body and hands, he kicked the JP-8 can over, which then caught fire as well. No one was really concerned about Afghanistan burning, but Strobell needed to be put out. Soto pulled his emergency release tab on this body armor, and then put his hands down in the soil. Strobell's hands and parts of his arms were crispy, a MEDEVAC was surely needed. I voted we finish cooking the rest of him and have ourselves as feast. I wasn't a real big Strobell fan.

The medics took Strobell to our make shift aid station to wrap his burns and give him some pain killers. Since we were so close to re-deploying, Strobell would not be returning to Afghanistan. 1SG Collins briefed him on the process of getting back to Italy once he had healed, but I think Strobell was so high on pain killers he didn't catch most of it. As the MEDEVAC touched down, John had his camera rolling. The purple smoke of the smoke grenade smelled like eggs, and the wind from the bird was like a hurricane. Strobell climbed on, and once again a Sky Soldier had been taken out of the fight.

On May 30th, 2008 Alpha Company retook control of Spearay COP. We completed all that was asked of us and more on COP construction. Plus, other than Strobell's mishap, hadn't lost anybody in combat. With news swirling of being replaced around June 20th by the 101st, everyone was excited to be going back to our home, good ole FOB Bermel. Once again it had been thirty days since any of us had showered and the promise of hot water, talking to loved ones and our own beds was enough to even make SFC Adams smile. The Chinook lifted its heavy body off the ground, turned in place to face Bermel, and we were off. Another month down!

---

94 **JP-8**—Jet Propellant Number eight, a fuel used by the United States military

CHAPTER TWENTY ONE
JUNE: THE LONG, HARD
ROAD, OUT OF HELL

IT WAS JUNE 2ND, 2008 and it had been a year to the day since Lowell had died. I still couldn't believe that he had been the first one killed. I couldn't believe we weren't going to have some more crazy times together when we got back. I had heard from Clark finally. He had lost his leg from the knee down and was now in Texas at a rehabilitation center. The fool was even in *People* magazine posing with President George Bush! He was recovering well. As for the other folks in Legion, we were all making plans for trips we should take when we got back; each of us were ready to get out of this hell hole.

On June 5th we got the news that we would indeed by leaving early! The 101st were already starting to trickle in and in the next few weeks our replacements would be here! This changed everything. We started to inventory all of our equipment and pack it up for shipment back to Italy. Just when we thought we would get away with just doing a few missions around the FOB to show our presences, Eagle 6 wanted MOD to support Delta Company in Zerok. All of our hearts sank. It was too late in the game to be going on crazy missions like that. Zerok was a COP much like Spearay, but was constantly being assaulted and mortared by the ACM. Between the Bandar checkpoint and Zerok, Delta Company was having a hell of time. We were all starting to have a hell of time now that spring was here. With a battle space the size of Delaware, and only 700 paratroopers to occupy it, man power was getting thin as well as everyone's patients.

We were re-deploying sooner than later now, so we had to complete out first round of psych evaluations before heading off to Zerok for the last hoorah. Also a few of us were going to meet with a psychologist up in Orgun-E before the mission. I know a lot of folks didn't like talking to a shrink, but I didn't mind. I have always liked psychology, why not play patient for a while? What I wasn't expecting from our little chat was to be placed on Zoloft! Heck a lot of us were placed on some type of anti-anxiety/depression medicine. Maybe were we a little crazy, but what normal person volunteers to jump out of perfectly good airplanes? Between the Zoloft and the malaria pills, your dreams become very vivid!

On June 10th MOD left for O.E. one more time. It was a great feeling to know that other than the drive back to Bermel from O.E., this was the second to the last time we would have to drive this four hour stretch of death. Also, we had to be back in Bermel by June 25th due to our fly date to leave country was June 27th. That was also very motivational for everyone. The end was in sight. Shoot, we didn't care if we got stuck in Salerno or Bagram on the way back, just as long as we weren't on this FOB on minute longer!

Once we got to O.E., I was informed that I would not be participating in the Zerok mission. The battalion intelligence team needed people to fill spots and help train the new 101st soldiers trickling in. I have to say I was disappointed, but it was a safe bet that I would be making it back to Bermel in one piece! It was also a nice change of pace. I had been standing in that turret for 400 days now; someone else could take my spot.

Staying in O.E. was almost like a vacation. It was much larger than Bermel, and had a nicer gym, better dining facility, a little Muslim restaurant, and I even got my own room! The thing I liked most though was seeing how war was run from behind the scenes. War is like any other business really, other than the customer's fire back! It takes transportation, communication, human resources, money, equipment, planning, and an array of people to deliver the United States war machine product. Let me tell ya, were the best at it!

The TOC in O.E. was filled with screens displaying different maps, information, live feed from planes, and also there were tons people bustling around to make sure our product was delivered as ordered and on time. I can't imagine what the huge TOC's, say in the Pentagon, look like. I thought I would get to work in there, but alas; I would be in a smaller, less profound office. I would be staring at regular laptops and working with a guy who I swear was a German spy, as well as this other weirdo who would always close his eyes and grin at you. I could not believe these people were running the battalion intelligence team.

Life at O.E. was pretty dry. This was my first time living the "fobbit" life style. I would have gone bonkers if I had to work in office for the entire deployment. I thought being on an Intel team meant I would get to go out, gather the Intel, talk to shady characters and so forth. No, I was mistaken. We sat in that office and looked at different mIRC[95] chats, which the military uses to talk over the internet instead of calling every single base every time there is an update. The mIRC is constantly being updated with weather, enemy/friendly activity, and if someone is taking rockets, mortars, or any other type of enemy fire. Communication has come a long way since Private Snuffy had to carry a wire in between trenches in World War One.

As I was looking at MOD's mIRC chat window, the window popped that they were taking rocket fire at Zerok. The rockets were impacting near the ANA and the ETT[96] positions. ETT's are usually a team of four which can be American or any coalition force that mentors the ANA, ANP, or other Afghan forces. They go everywhere with them, which included venturing into battle with those mad men. The rockets, turned to mortars, and the mortars turned their eye to the hill top 3rd PLT was currently occupying.

The first mortar flew over 3rd PLT's position only to directly hit the compound the ETT team was residing in. The ACM then put another mortar on that position before adjusting fire. The damage had been done. The front wall of the compound was gone, and the blast mangled the ETT team as well as the ANA commanders in the mud structure. A nearby medic was first on the gruesome scene and before he took a step towards the wounded in action he told the TOC to call for MEDEVAC.

The ANA commander had been killed. The first ETT team member the medic came to was missing his left leg, and a few ribs were poking through his skin. Another ETT team member had all of his front teeth blown out of his mouth, and his testicles were severely damaged, as they hung about two feet from his body. His arms were shattered, and he had no idea where he was, only that he was excruciating pain. The last two ETT members were blown out of the building and were killed in action.

---

95 **mIRC**—Microsoft Internet Relay Chat, an online chatting system the military uses in its virtually battle command

96 **ETT**—Embedded Training Team, a team of four to six personnel that trains and guides foreign military forces

The mortar team adjusted their fire on the hilltop 3rd PLT was on. SSG Daniel saw the destruction that the screaming shells caused to the ETT building and he knew these were not untrained locals on the mortar tube. He had the gun teams pack up in a hurry, but it was not quick enough. The first mortar slammed into the bottom of the hill and SSG Daniel yelled out, "Grab the gear you got packed and let's make a run for it! Check your sensitive items real quick and move the fuck out to the COP!"

The next shell detonated on the hillside above the hilltop 3rd PLT was on, showering them with dirt and debris. With that they were out of there. Redeployment was way too close to waste any more time. Grabbing what they could, the adrenaline pumped paratroopers ran down the hill towards the COP. The vacant position erupted into flames as two mortars struck it. Zerok COP was surrounded by mountains, which didn't provide any relief from the shelling, but it did have better cover.

This accurate fire on MOD promoted Eagle 6 to unleash the artillery and Air Force on the mountains of Zerok. MOD was supposed to leave the COP that day, and their replacements were already there. These shells proved they were going to have to fight their way out of Zerok, and it was a long, three mile road, out of hell. Eagle 6 had the artillery perform sweeping zones, as the USAF hit individual targets of interest. Nothing could have made it out of that barrage alive. The artillery stopped just as the MEDEVAC for the ETT's was coming in. With the lull in ACM activity, MOD began to pack up their trucks to return back to O.E.

When there is a mass-casualty event, the aid station will ask for blood or help from the EMT's that were trained back in Vicenza. Back at O.E., I ran to the HLZ to help with the WIA. The ETT with the shattered arms was conscious but drowsy from pain medication, and the ETT with the ribs exposed was conscious but staring off into nowhere. I lift the left side of the four-man liter and attempted to cover the ETT with the shattered arms as best as I could from the rotor wash. What I thought was extra bandages on his chest was actually his testicles that had gotten injured. The flight medic told us to watch them and be careful not to injure them anymore as we transported the injured soldier into the emergency room.

As both ETT's were getting prepped for surgery, I got some blood drawn, and then headed back to the Intel office. I got in just in time to read Eagle 6 was hitting a few more targets ahead of MOD as they started to move out of Zerok with RCP in the lead. Now that the bombing was over the long convoy started to move the back way out of Zerok, a route that had not been used in three months. Not the way I would have picked, but I guess it would have to do.

The trucks drove slow, slow enough for ANA soldiers to walk the same pace a little above the trucks on the hillsides; which was to deter any close ambushes. This idea did not have the desired effect. The first RPG buzzed past SGT Matlock's truck and into the hillside. Then the AK, PKM, and sniper fire opened up from all sides on the sluggish moving convoy. Soldiers inside of the new MRAP[97] vehicles and old Humvees alike started to prepare ammo for the gunners and CLS[98] bags for the wounded.

SPC Hampton turned his .50 Cal onto the ridge and began to throw as much lead as he could towards the enemy. Between the incoming rounds and out-going rounds you couldn't hear a thing. SPC Neary was talking with the FDC back in to O.E. to coordinate a new set of fire missions as all of the ANA collapsed back onto the trucks for added protection. There was no better cover for them, they either had to stand and fight or make a run for it back to Zerok. As Hampton changed ammo cans out and began to fire once more, his gun jammed. He attempted to pull the charging handle backwards, as bullet bounced off of the MRAPs roof. He cleared the weapon only to have it malfunction once again. The head space and timing was off, now he would be forced to use his M4.

Hampton turned to see an RPG headed for SGT Matlock's truck. It hit the top of the turret and the gunner, SPC Blizzard, disappeared inside of the truck. Another RPG, this time an armor-piercing RPG hit the back of the MRAP. It went through the spare gas cans, through the outer MRAP hull, through the cabin, and back out the other side of the MRAP; barely missing SGT Peachy and not exploding on the inside. The APRPG detonated just as it came out of the MRAP, which shield the dazed paratroopers from the blast.

The convoy stopped as SGT Matlock's MRAP was engulfed in flames. SGT Peachy could hardly hear himself think has he struggled to gain his wits and get out of the burning vehicle. SGT Matlock attempted to open his door but the blast jammed it. Peachy cut the seat belt off him and felt his right arm throbbing with pain. He moved over through the smoke to see if Blizzard was still alive.

---

97 **MRAP**—Mine Resistance Ambush Protected, a vehicle designed with a V-shaped hull to defer blast and ambush from breaching the armor

98 **CLS**—Combat Life Savers Course, a course designed to teach combat soldiers how to treat trauma as scene on the battle field, as well as life treating injuries, and give intravenous fluid

SFC Adam's Humvee started to drive around the convoy so Doc Lollino could get to the wounded. They didn't get far before the ACM brought up a Soviet heavy machine gun named a Degtyaryov-Shpagin Large-Caliber or DShK. The DShK's shells are twice the size of our .50 Cal and the sound of it firing was unmistakable. The ACM team turned the mammoth weapon towards the convoy and began to fire. The bullets were walking up the open ground toward convoy and the last one went through a MRAPs tire as the ACM's position was vaporized by the Hellfire missile of a Predator drone overhead. That Predator saved a lot of paratroopers.

SFC Adam's Humvee reached the downed MRAP just as the driver for it, SPC Soto, got the driver's side door open. Blizzard had come to but was now coughing from smoke inhalation. The MRAP was fully involved and time was not on the paratroopers' side. The crawl space to get out of the driver's side door was not an easy one to get to from the back, especially with all of our gear on. SGT Matlock turned from the passenger side seat to help pull Blizzard out of his gunner's harness which was caught on the ammo cans. SGT Peachy cut it from the other side to free him.

SFC Adam's gunner, SPC Bragg, provided what cover he could as Doc Lollino, SFC Adams, and SPC Martin jumped out to help the paratroopers exit the burning MRAP. The ACM near the scene directed all fire on the MRAP and Humvee. A hand full of ANA soldiers ran up the hillside to provide cover fire. The MRAP that was now behind SFC Adam's Humvee made room inside for the WIA as the wind shield splintered from a sniper round.

SFC Adams grabbed Soto and they made a CCP (Casualty Collection Point) behind his Humvee. It didn't provide much cover, but some was better than none. Finally SGT Peachy exited the MRAP. All of the paratroopers were out now, and Doc Lollino had SPC Martin call up the MEDEVAC. Doc Lollino and SGT Peachy knelt down beside the Humvee to inspect Peachey's arm quickly. The shrapnel was deep and the blood was oozing out. SPC Bragg called out that an RPG was in the air and Doc Lollino covered Peachy as it hit, and flung searing metal into Doc Lollino right shoulder.

The ground began to shake from the artillery that SPC Neary had directed in. Yells of joy could be heard throughout the fire fight. Fire raining down from the sky is always a welcome sight. Also, two A-10 Thunderbolts had checked on the battle space. The tide of battle was now in our favor. The ACM still continued to harass SFC Adams position as the artillery had not hit every ambush point. SFC Adams got the WIA into the MRAP behind his Humvee and began to move again. A MEDEVAC bird was en route to the safest location. The A-10s also made sure the area was secure, spraying 30mm cannon fire on to the HLZ. The rest of the convoy regrouped as the ACM began to break contact. The battle lasted for about two hours and was approximately two miles long. The tattered MRAP was going to have to be drug back to O.E., since we could not leave it. That would take a while.

I got to the aid station just in time to see SGT Peachy be put to sleep for surgery. The doctors also intubated him so his lungs could get proper oxygenation due to smoke damage. SGT Matlock, Blizzard, and Soto also had to have shrapnel removed. They too had smoke inhalation damage and kept coughing as we were talking. SGT Matlock even got caught smoking a cigarette by one of the doctors. You weren't telling that Texas boy what to do! SGT Peachy came out of surgery talking nonsense. He had shrapnel removed from his right arm and neck. All he could talk about was getting his loofa from Bermel because he wanted to exfoliate. He also wanted to grow a long beard and get fat. All of his medication induced craziness started to disappear when I told him that the shrapnel had damaged his tattoos.

All of them were to be flown to Bagram for smoke inhalation treatment. SGT Peachy was still half way unconscious so he would stay on the litter. As the Black Hawk started its rotors we carried Peachy out. I stepped up on to the bird and placed my side of the liter down, shook hands with Peachy and told him that we'd be drinking back in Vicenza soon. As their bird bound for Bagram lifted into the air I thanked God that MOD still had not lost a paratrooper to death, prayed for the families that had lost someone, and thanked him again that I had made it through this battle of heart, soul, and mind.

CHAPTER TWENTY TWO
JULY: HOMECOMING

MOD MADE IT BACK to Bermel on June 24th, 2008. The first wave of paratroopers would be leaving in four days. In that four days we had to train up our 101st replacements, pack and inventory the remaining equipment, and then switch the COP out one more time. No one cared though. You could have said we were storming the Pakistan border and it wouldn't have mattered. Our time had come, we were out of there!

All of us were selling electronics to the new 101st guys, and would laugh when they would jump a mile into the air as rockets landed close to the FOB. Everyone was making plans about the first thing they were going to do once they got back to Vicenza. Alcohol was usually included. We finally knew it was real when our trucks were handed over to the 101st. God that was a great feeling. Arruda, Maddalone, Snyder, and I ate our last meal in Bermel together. We talked about everything that had happened over the past fourteen months. One thing we sure would not miss was the roast beef that was constantly served. To this day I still refuse to eat roast beef. We laughed about the crazy times in the barracks, being stuck in Malekshay, and talked about friends we had lost. All of it kind of seemed like a dream. Had we really done all of this? Time had gone so quickly.

On the eve of our departure I stood looking at the star-filled sky. I smoked a cigarette with SPC Myers, who was one of the mortar men. As we were talking the Malekshay COP got attacked. The new 101st guys were going to get hardened real quick it seemed. There was nothing we could do except watch the tracers fly towards the COP and away from it. Apaches were off in the distance flinging ordinance on ACM positions, and then the sky lit up. No doubt it was some sort of guided missile launched from a fighter jet. Both of just stood in the quiet. We smoked and watched this fire work show, which stopped as quickly as it had started.

June 28th was here! Everyone was anxious to be on their way. Friends, family, and booze awaited us back in Vicenza; there was not a sad soul in the bunch. We made our way to the HLZ one last time with our bags and weapons. So many times we had unloaded birds or driven across the HLZ to go out the back gate, and this was the last time each of us would stand on it. It was a surreal feeling. The birds touched down and sprayed hot air in our smiling faces. We placed our bags in the middle of the Chinooks, strapped ourselves in, and cheered as the behemoth flying machines lifted off and turned towards Salerno.

The way back to Italy was exactly the same way you took to Afghanistan. We went through Salerno, feasted on Dairy Queen in Bagram and then made it to Mannas, Kyrgyzstan. We all climbed aboard a World Airways Jetliner; hopefully this one wouldn't break, and sat back in our seats. Everyone was in the best mood. We would be back in Vicenza by sunset. The plane lifted off and we were on our way. All I really wanted was some airplane food!

The plane touched down with a thump in Italy at Aviano Air Base. We all cheered as the wheels hit the ground, shook hands, and played grab ass. I was first to step off of the plane and smiled as the fresh Italian air hit my face. I walked down the stairs to a wall of hands begging to be shaken. We turned our weapons into the armorers and got aboard the buses. It was weird giving your weapon to someone. It was the piece of equipment you had trusted your life to for so long. As the buses drove out of Aviano another cheer was let loose from our ecstatic lungs.

The feeling of riding back in these buses, seeing the traffic, and the vegetation seemed like a dream. Had Afghanistan even happened? Or was all of this some kind of experiment? It was amazing to know that the vehicles passing you were not attempting to blow you up, or that the next corner was not hiding an ACM ambush position. No, there were no rockets or mortars screaming in, plus no roast beef…life was good.

The buses pulled into Vicenza and then Camp Ederle and once again a cheer echoed throughout each bus. The buses pulled in front of our little parade field. Families were cheering, music was playing, and all kind of signs and streamers were flying. We all walked off the buses with huge grins and got into formation. The General said a few words, and then dismissed us from our duty of war to regain or individual lives. Families were reunited, friends hugged, and each of us shook hands one more time. It had been a hell of a ride, one that would never be forgotten.

I grabbed my gear and started to walk towards the barracks. The sun had begun to set and the trees were in full bloom. It was a peaceful feeling, one that is hard to describe. I couldn't help but take in everything and realize that I was indeed no longer in Bermel. The smell of the fresh, clean air was almost overwhelming. I opened the door to my room, and found I was still rooming with Snyder. I dropped my bags then opened the refrigerator. Snyder walked in and smiled. SSG Manuma had come through; there was one Corona for Snyder and me.

We popped the caps, clicked the bottles together and each took a long sip. I walked over to the window and glanced out at our colorful surroundings. I could hear church bells of in the distance, and song birds singing their sweet melody. The cool wind came through the open window seal as I took another long swig of the refreshing beverage. I breathed a long sigh of relief, smiled, and turned to leave a sexual welcome home message on Snyder's camera.

GLOSSARY

1SG, 1ˢᵗ SGT—First Sergeant, the highest ranking Non-Commissioned officer of a company

.50 Cal—.50 Caliber fully automatic machine gun

A-10 Thunderbolt—an American single-seat, twin-engine, straight-wing jet aircraft developed by Fairchild-Republic in the early 1970s. The A-10 was designed for a United States Air Force requirement to provide close air support for ground forces

AAR—After Action Review, the report given on the positives and negatives of a mission

AB—Ammunition Barer, soldier that carries ammunition for a M240B gun team

ACM—Anti Coalition Militia, remnants of the Taliban government, mercenaries, and local fighters that fought against ISAF forces

ADVON—Advanced Party, personnel that arrive on site of a base ahead of other members of their unit to insure everything is in working properly.

AG—Assistant Gunner, the backup gunner for a M240B gun team

AIT—Advanced Individual Training, the training soldiers go through to obtain a designated area of expertise in the armed forces.

ANA—Afghan National Army

ANP—Afghan National Police

AO—Area of Operation, the area in which an unit is responsible for

AP—Armor Piercing, a type of ammunition designed to go through heavily armored vehicles

ARPG—Armor Piercing Rocket Propelled Grenade, a type of grenade that is fired from the shoulder and is designed to go through heavily armored vehicles

AT4—the an 84-mm unguided, portable, single-shot recoilless smoothbore weapon built in Sweden by Saab Bofors Dynamics and is used mainly for armored vehicles

B-1 Bomber—The Rockwell B-1 Lancer is a four-engine variable-sweep wing strategic bomber used by the United States Air Force

BC—Battalion Commander, a Lieutenant Colonel that is placed in charge of a battalion

BDA—Battle Damage Assessment, the exploration of a battle field after the battle is complete for documents, intelligence, and wounded soldiers

BDE—Brigade, a unit size designator which is approximately 2,000 soldiers

BFT—Blue Force Tracker, a Global Positioning System used by the United States military

Black Hat—the name given to an instructor at United States Army Airborne School due to the black baseball cap which an instructor wears

Blackout Lights—infrared lights built onto military equipment which can only be viewed by a night vision device

BN—Battalion, a unit size designator which is approximately 700-1,000 soldiers

Carbenari—The State Police assigned to the different regions in Italy

CAS—Close Air Support, support given by aircraft to ground troops during a battle

CCA—Close Combat Aircraft, support given by helicopters to ground troops during a battle

CCP—Casualty Collection Point, a designated area where injured soldiers will go during a battle

Cigarette Roll—when a parachute deploys from the bag but does not open.

CLS—Combat Life Savers Course, a course designed to teach combat soldiers how to treat trauma as scene on the battle field, as well as life treating injuries, and give intravenous fluid

COB—Contingency Operating Base, a base that is larger than a forward operating base and usually has an landing strip, helicopter pad, and hospital.

COP—Combat Outpost, a position that is closer to the combat front than a Forward Operating Base and is usually fortified with towers, walls, and holds thirty to sixty troops

CREW—Counter-Radio Controlled Improvised Explosive Device Electronic Warfare, a system designed to intervene in radio controlled explosives.

CSM—Command Sergeant Major, the highest ranking Non-Commissioned Officer in a position of command

DGD—Dead Gunner Drill, a drill used to simulate the gunner of a M240B machine gun team being killed in combat and the Assistant Gunner taking over the gun

Dismount—to get out of a Humvee, or other military vehicle

DZ—Drop Zone, an area designated to drop soldiers, equipment, weapons, or supplies into by parachute

ETT—Embedded Training Team, a team of four to six personnel that trains and guides foreign military forces

FA—Field Artillery

FDC—Fire Direction Control, the center that controls and directs artillery fire as well as some aircraft

FO—Forward Observer, the soldier on the front line that communicates with the Fire Direction Control and aircraft as to where ordinance should be dropped

FOB—Forward Operating Base, a base that is smaller than a Contingency Operating Base and larger than a Combat Outpost which houses approximately 200-500 soldiers

HA—Humanitarian Assistance, assistance given to humans that in need, which may include water, food, shelter, clothing or all four basic needs

Hellfire—the AGM-114 Hellfire is an air-to-surface missile (ASM) developed primarily for anti-armor use

HEMTT—Heavy Expanded Mobility Tactical Truck, a vehicle used in the military as a wrecker, mobile office, or supply carrier

Hesco—a durable wall developed to cut down on construction time that is little more than burlap placed over wire, which is then filled with dirt

HLZ—Helicopter Landing Zone, a designated space large enough for a helicopter to land

Hollywood Jump—a jump out of an aircraft by paratroopers with no combat gear adorned

HUMINT—Human Intelligence, intelligence obtained from a human source

ICOM—a type of radio developed by the ICOM company

IED—Improvised Explosive Device, a homemade explosive device used to disrupt or destroy property, commerce, an human life

IR—Infrared, light which can only be detected through use of certain devices

ISAF—International Security Assistance Force, the multinational force in Afghanistan that is rebuilding and securing the nation

JDAM—Joint Direct Attack Munitions, is a guidance kit that converts unguided bombs, or "dumb bombs" into all-weather "smart" munitions

JP-8—Jet Propellant Number eight, a fuel used by the United States military

Jumpmaster—an expert Paratrooper qualified to teach, train, plus inspect the equipment worn by paratroopers. Jumpmasters also control Paratroopers exit out of an aircraft.

KBR—Kellogg, Browning, and Root, a contracted company the military uses

KIA—Killed In Action, when a solider is killed in combat

LCLA—Low Cost, Low Altitude Drop, a resupply that utilizes the parachute system to drop supplies to troops in forward positions

Lean-to—a lean-to is a term used to describe a roof with a single slope. The term also applies to a variety of structures that are built using a lean-to roof

LRAS—Long Range Advanced Scouting Surveillance System, a system that uses an infrared lenses and zooming to allow the user to view farther than the standard binoculars

M240B—an air-cooled, open bolt operated, fully automatic machine gun that fires a 7.62mm NATO round

MEDEVAC—Medical Evacuation, efficient movement and en route care provided by medical personnel to the wounded being evacuated from the battlefield by aircraft or ambulance

MEPS—Military Entrance Processing Station, a facility where a civilian gets cleared to join the military

MGLC—Machine Gun Leaders Course, a course designed to teach soldiers about heavy automatic weapons

mIRC—Microsoft Internet Relay Chat, an online chatting system the military uses in its virtually battle command

MK-19—Mark-19, a belt fed, fully automatic grenade launcher

Mount—to get in a Humvee or other military vehicles

MP—Military Police

MRAP—Mine Resistance Ambush Protected, a vehicle designed with a V-shaped hull to defer blast and ambush from breaching the armor

MRE—Meal Ready to Eat, a pre-packaged meal that is light weight and can be eaten without heating

MWR—Moral, Wellness, and Recreation, a facility designed for soldiers to relief stress, utilize a phone or computer, and play sports

NODS—Night Observation Device, lenses that are worn that allow the soldier to see during hours of darkness

OP—Outpost, a non-fortified position that can be taken down or evacuated easily usually closer to the front line than the Combat Outpost

PFC—Private First Class, the rank given to soldiers after at least one year in the United States Army

PL—Platoon Leader, the Lieutenant in charge of a Platoon

Platoon—a unit size designator of the armed forces which consists of approximately thirty soldiers.

PLF—Parachute Landing Fall, the proper technique of making a landing on solid ground, or water after exiting a military aircraft

POI—Point of Impact, the sight where ordinance impacts the earth or fortified position

POO—Point of Origin, the sight where ordinance is fired from

Privea—the private dance room in Italian gentlemen's clubs

PSG—Platoon Sergeant, the Non-Commissioned Officer in charge of a platoon

PV2—Private Second Class, the rank given to soldiers after at least six months in the United States Army

PX—Post Exchange, a merchandise store similar to Wal-Mart on United States Army Forts

RCP—Route Clearance Package, vehicles designated to clear routes of improvised explosive devices

Recoilless Rifle—a lightweight, portable, crew-served 105 mm weapon intended primarily as an anti-tank weapon

RPG—Rocket Propelled Grenade, a shoulder fired grenade designed to destroy vehicles and troop positions

RTB—Return To Base

Ruck March—the forced march of troops, usually in a type of formation, over an extend period of time.

SAW—Squad Automatic Weapon, the M249 machine gun which is carried by at least one soldier in each infantry squad, excluding weapons squad

SFC—Sergeant First Class, the rank that proceeds Staff Sergeant

SGT—Sergeant, the first rank of the Non-Commissioned Officer Corps

Shura—Arabic for consultation. The Quran and Muhammad encourage Muslims to decide their affairs in consultation with those who will be affected by that decision.

SITREP—Situation Report, a report given that outlines a certain circumstance

SP—Start Patrol, the starting point of tactical movement by soldiers

Specialist—a rank given to soldiers with at least eighteen months in United States Army

Squad—a unit size designator of armed forces which consist of six to eight soldiers

SSG—Staff Sergeant, the rank after Sergeant

Support by Fire—a fighting position occupied by heavier weapons to support a unit advancing on a target

TACSAT- **Tactical Satellite Radio**

TC—Truck Commander, the soldier that sits on the passenger side of a Humvee and directs it where to go

Terp—interpreter

TOC—Tactical Operations Center, a facility where combat operations can be ran

TRADOC—Training and Doctrine Command

UCMJ—Uniform Code of Military Justice, the laws of the United States military

USAF—United States Air Force

UXO—Unexploded Ordinance, projectiles or mines that have been fired but did not detonate

VBIED—Vehicle Born Improvised Explosive Device, an explosive device built into a vehicle to enhance its destructive properties

Wadi—the Arabic term referring to a dry riverbed that contains water only during times of heavy rain or simply an intermittent stream

Weapons Squad—the squad in an Infantry Platoon that usually consist of two M240B gun teams

WIA—Wounded In Action, when a soldier is wounded during combat operations

WP/Willy Pete—White Phosphorus, a chemical used in artillery shells to displace oxygen

Zulu—Greenwich Mean Time